A Novel SECRET

Other Books by Anna Durand

Brit vs. Scot (A Hot Brits/Hot Scots/Au Naturel Crossover)
The American Wives Club (A Hot Brits/Hot Scots/Au Naturel Crossover)
Banished in the Highlands (A Hot Scots Prequel)
Dangerous in a Kilt (Hot Scots, Book One)
Wicked in a Kilt (Hot Scots, Book Two)
Scandalous in a Kilt (Hot Scots, Book Three)
The MacTaggart Brothers Trilogy (Hot Scots, Books 1-3)
Gift-Wrapped in a Kilt (Hot Scots, Book Four)
Notorious in a Kilt (Hot Scots, Book Five)
Insatiable in a Kilt (Hot Scots, Book Six)
Lethal in a Kilt (Hot Scots, Book Seven)
Irresistible in a Kilt (Hot Scots, Book Eight)
Devastating in a Kilt (Hot Scots, Book Nine)
Spellbound in a Kilt (Hot Scots, Book Ten)
Relentless in a Kilt (Hot Scots, Book Eleven)
Incendiary in a Kilt (Hot Scots, Book Twelve)
Wild in a Kilt (Hot Scots, Book Thirteen)
Lachlan in a Kilt (The Ballachulish Trilogy, Book One)
Aidan in a Kilt (The Ballachulish Trilogy, Book Two)
Rory in a Kilt (The Ballachulish Trilogy, Book Three)
The Dixon Brothers Trilogy (Hot Brits, Books 1-3)
One Hot Escape (Hot Brits, Book Four)
One Hot Rumor (Hot Brits, Book Five)
One Hot Christmas (Hot Brits, Book Six)
One Hot Scandal (Hot Brits, Book Seven)
One Hot Deal (Hot Brits, Book Eight)
One Hot Favor (Hot Brits, Book Nine)
Natural Obsession (Au Naturel Nights, Book One)
Natural Passion (Au Naturel Trilogy, Book One)
Natural Impulse (Au Naturel Trilogy, Book Two)
Natural Satisfaction (Au Naturel Trilogy, Book Three)
Fired Up (standalone romance)
Echo Power (Echo Power Trilogy, Book One)
Echo Dominion (Echo Power Trilogy, Book Two)
Echo Unbound (Echo Power Trilogy, Book Three)
The Janusite Trilogy (Undercover Elementals, Books 1-3)
Obsidian Hunger (Undercover Elementals, Book Four)
Unbidden Hunger (Undercover Elementals, Book Five)
The Thirteenth Fae (Undercover Elementals, Book Six)
Cyneric (Undercover Elementals, Book Seven)

A *Novel* SECRET

A Hot Brits / Hot Scots / Au Naturel
Crossover Book

ANNA DURAND

JACOBSVILLE BOOKS · MARIETTA, OHIO

A NOVEL SECRET
Copyright © 2023 by Lisa A. Shiel
All rights reserved.

ISBN: 978-1-958144-20-6 (paperback)
ISBN: 978-1-958144-21-3 (ebook)
ISBN: 978-1-958144-22-0 (audiobook)

Manufactured in the United States.

Jacobsville Books
www.JacobsvilleBooks.com

Publisher's Cataloging-in-Publication Data
provided by Five Rainbows Cataloging Services

Names: Durand, Anna, author.
Title: A novel secret / Anna Durand.
Description: Marietta, OH : Jacobsville Books, 2023.
Identifiers: ISBN 978-1-958144-20-6 (paperback) | ISBN 978-1-958144-21-3 (ebook) | ISBN 978-1-958144-22-0 (audiobook)
Subjects: LCSH: Novelists--Fiction. | Secrets--Fiction. | Triangles (Interpersonal relations)--Fiction. | Americans--Fiction. | British--Fiction. | Romance fiction. | BISAC: FICTION / Romance / Romantic Comedy. | FICTION / Romance / Contemporary. | FICTION / Romance / International. | GSAFD: Love stories
Classification: LCC PS3604.U724 N68 2023 (print) | LCC PS3604.U724 (ebook) | DDC 813/.6--dc23.

Chapter One

Owen

WHEN A GUY NEEDS TO GET AWAY FROM IT ALL, HE SHOULD go to a resort or at least a beach, but that's not my style. Where am I right now? Not in my house in Yestermont, Wyoming. Nope, I took the advice of my only real friend, Munro MacTaggart, and flew to London. The grouchy Scot had told me, "You work too hard. Take a holiday. The UK isn't awful."

Yeah, Munro will never get a job at a travel agency.

So maybe he didn't actually tell me to go to London. I took his advice and ran with it, choosing a location for my trip based on the scientific method. That means I went to a maps website, shut my eyes, and randomly dropped my finger on the computer screen. *London, here I come.*

An overnight flight brought me to this country. Now it's my job to make this trip an adventure.

My first day in England hasn't exactly been scintillating. As I stroll down the sidewalk in a quaint part of the city that lacks the hustle and bustle of the most popular areas, I find myself shuffling my feet. The thrill of seeing a new place has already faded. Now, I just feel like a divorced loser who can't get laid. That's exactly what I am. I need to find something better to do than meander down a street populated by kitschy shops that seem like they don't get much traffic.

So, what am I going to do?

I stop in front of a store that sells cuckoo clocks, but that only holds my interest for a couple of minutes. Then I cross the street to check out a candy shop. Do Brits have their own kinds of sweets? They must. I wander into the shop to browse the selections and wind up eating things I've never heard of, which seems appropriate since I came to this country to escape from my dull existence back home. Apple drops taste better than they sound, but I skip the licorice. . Never liked that stuff.

After my experience at the candy shop, I continue down the sidewalk but can't find anything else that interests me. I pop another apple drop into my mouth, scanning the signs further down the street.

I stop, my attention glued to a particular storefront.

The sign announces that it's Goodburn's Literary Treasures. Now that sounds like my kind of place. I push through the door, which makes a bell ring above my head, and step into a different world, one populated with books that lie in haphazard stacks on tables or on scuffed wooden shelves along the walls. I even find what looks like an old toy box filled with children's books. I don't see anybody manning the desk at the back of the shop.

I pick up a well-worn copy of a Danielle Steel book and flip through the pages. Hey, I've read this one. Better look around for something different. Something I wouldn't normally read. Something quintessentially British. I did come to this country to have an adventure or at least an experience that isn't like every single day back home. While I wander aimlessly among the piles and shelves of books, I suddenly realize I have no clue what I'm trying to find. A book that represents British literature? That's awfully vague.

"Oh, good morning. I didn't realize anyone was here."

The sweetly sexy voice that spoke those words originated from behind me. I've been standing in front of the shop window considering whether to buy a copy of , though I've never been a big fan of kids' books. I turn to look at the woman who had spoken to me. And I freeze. The dark-haired beauty behind the counter looks gorgeous from this distance, but as I shuffle across the shop and draw closer, I realize she has beautiful eyes that shimmer with the luster of polished emeralds.

I stop at the counter and push one hand into my pants pocket, trying to seem casual and not like I want to vault over the counter to kiss her. "Good morning. This is a really cool shop."

"Thank you. Are you American?"

"Yes, I am. And you must be British." Could I have thought of a stupider thing to say? I'm out of practice when it comes to flirting.

The beautiful girl smiles and laughs. "Yes, I am British. What gave me away? It must have been . That book was written by an Englishman."

. I'm still holding that book. A grown man who's into a kids' book? Yeah, she probably thinks I'm a married guy looking for a quick hookup, or maybe a perv who gets off on illustrations of goofy bears.

I set the book on the counter. "Sorry, I forgot to put this down. I was looking for a story that's quintessentially British. That probably sounds dumb."

"Not at all. I'm happy to give you recommendations. Is this your first visit to London?"

"Yeah. I live in Wyoming, in a small town that doesn't have any good bookshops. This place is amazing."

She smiles again, and this time her cheeks dimple. "It's always wonderful to hear that. I'm Poppy Goodburn, the owner of this shop."

"Nice to meet you, Poppy. I'm Owen Metzger."

"You must be a connoisseur of rare and forgotten books. Goodburn's Literary Treasures specializes in those, though we also stock new titles."

I hunch my shoulders. "Not really a connoisseur. I stumbled onto your shop and thought I'd take a look. I do love books, but I doubt you have the kind I usually, uh, read."

Why did I hesitate when I said that? Because Poppy doesn't seem like the type of woman who reads the genre of books I focus on—or the kind I write.

"You might be surprised," Poppy says. "We stock many genres, and as I said, not all of them are old books. We also have rare editions."

"Maybe I'll do some more browsing."

"Please do. And if I can help you in any way, don't hesitate to let me know."

"Thanks, Poppy."

She starts flipping through papers, probably doing some kind of bookkeeping or whatever shop owners do.

While she does her thing, I hunt around for something that might pique my interest. So far, the only thing that fits the bill is the woman behind the counter. But I'm here in London to get the full British experience, and that means I should continue my search for a quintessentially British book, though not one aimed at kids. It should be something…intellectual.

A book catches my eye, and I pick it up. Of course I was drawn to a Nora Roberts book from twenty years ago. But I don't want Poppy to see me buying a romance novel. Still, I can't resist flipping through the pages. Oh, damn, I read this one already too. Hardly a surprise since I've read all the famous authors in that genre at one time or another. I set the book down and keep hunting.

"Still can't find anything?" Poppy calls out.

"Uh, no, I'm having trouble with that. Guess I shouldn't have set an impossible goal for myself."

Poppy comes out from behind the counter and roots around among the myriad books inside this shop. Finally, she raises one and grins. "I have just the thing for you, Owen."

"Great. What is it?"

She trots over to me and holds out the book, tipping it up so I can see the cover. " by Alfred, Lord Tennyson."

"I've never read that one." I take the book and cautiously open it, afraid I might break it or something. "How old is this edition?"

"Not as old as it might seem. This version was published in two thousand and eight, but it wasn't well taken care of."

"What's the story about?"

Poppy smiles, clearly loving that she gets the chance to explain it to me. And she opens up the book to show me the interior. "This edition has lovely illustrations, doesn't it? is a retelling of the leg-end of King Arthur and Camelot that's told in a series of narrative poems. It's really quite beautiful. I think you'll enjoy it."

"Yeah, it sounds great. I love the movie musical , but I've never read any text versions of the story."

She grins and leans in to whisper, "I love the musical too. Please don't tell anyone, though. Many of my customers are avidly devoted to books and will rant and rave about film or stage versions."

"Your secret is safe with me."

Poppy is standing so close to me, raised onto her toes with her lips an inch from my ear, that I can feel her breaths tickling my cheek. She smells good, like roses and honeysuckle, and I want to turn my head toward her so I can press my lips to hers. But that would be weird. She'd probably smack my cheek hard and yell for a cop to come arrest me.

I might be slightly paranoid. My experience a couple months ago left me a little off kilter. That tends to happen when a guy gets trapped in a cabin in the remote wilderness of Wyoming while bad guys try to break in, determined to murder his friends. But I shouldn't think about that right now. Or ever again. Forgetting isn't easy.

At least those bad guys had been totally inept. I don't have post-traumatic stress, but I wish I hadn't stayed in Wyoming when Munro and Natalie fled to Scotland. I missed the big showdown at a medieval castle.

"Are you all right, Owen?"

Poppy's question snaps me back to the present. "Yeah, sure, I'm fine. And I will definitely take that book."

"? That's wonderful. I'll ring up the purchase for you."

"Great, thanks."

At least she's not leaning in to whisper into my ear anymore. I'd been a split second away from kissing her.

I follow Poppy to the counter and watch her carefully wrap the book in brown paper, then slip it into a cute little white bag that has cute little twine handles. She hands me the bag.

"Enjoy the book, Owen. And please come back if you need more reading recommendations."

"Absolutely. Thank you for your advice, Poppy."

As I head for the door, I pass by a section of the shop I hadn't noticed before, the section that offers a display of recent romance novels. A particular cover has grabbed my attention, and I can hardly believe what I see—because my latest book is there on the shelf. What are the odds of that happening? I go to a random little bookshop in London and stumble onto my own novel.

I shake off my surprise and head for the door but hesitate on the threshold. I glance back at Poppy, but she's busy doing stuff behind the counter. With a sigh, I walk out of the shop and start off down the street again. Where am I going? No idea. But I know one thing. I want to see Poppy Goodburn again.

But how will she feel if she finds out I write steamy romance novels for a living?

Chapter Two

Poppy

FOR THE PAST HALF AN HOUR, I'VE BEEN DROPPING THINGS—PENS, papers, books, even the handset of the telephone on the counter. I've never been so clumsy before in my entire life. The problem might stem from the fact that I can't stop thinking about Owen Metzger. He seemed like a lovely man, and I'm not referring to his good looks, though he definitely is quite attractive. Owen's eyes are such a deep blue color that they remind me of lapis lazuli stones. The ancient Egyptians adored lapis and used it often in jewelry.

But Owen's eyes are far more beautiful than stones.

A thunk snaps me out of my daydreaming.

I glance around but can't see what I've dropped this time. Then I go around to the other side of the sales counter and see it. The paperweight I use to keep receipts from flying away has tumbled to the floor. I snatch it up and return to my side of the counter.

Stop thinking about Owen, you idiot, or you'll never get any work done.

I doubt I will ever see the man again, which means this flutter in my belly and my distracted state will both fade away eventually. What are the odds Owen would ever return to my shop? He's a tourist, so he will go home soon.

At last, I manage to banish thoughts of Owen and focus on opening the box of new arrivals. For my shop, "new arrival" has multiple meanings since I also receive used books in my ship-ments. It's simply that I haven't carried those titles before, which makes them new arrivals. I do carry actual new books, but a small shop like mine can't compete with the big chains. That's why I focus on hard-to-find editions.

While I'm cutting the box open, my mobile rings.

I grab it and say hello, cradling the mobile to my ear by hunching my shoulder.

"Hello, Poppy, how are you today?"

"Dominic?" I would recognize my cousin's voice if he'd only spoken the word hello.

"Yes, it's me, pet. I hope you're not working too hard again."

"Did you call strictly to imply I'm a workaholic?"

He chuckles. "I'm not implying anything. You *are* a worka-holic, so I don't need to state the obvious."

Maybe I do work too hard, but that's no one's business but my own.

"You should take a day off now and then, Poppy."

I sigh and give up on pulling books out of the box. Dominic must want something or else he wouldn't have rung me. But he will force me to chat to him before he'll get round to the thing he wants. "How are you and Chelsea settling in at your new house?"

"Very well. Now we just need to help her mum and dad find a place of their own."

Rubbing my neck, I lean my hip against the counter. "Will you all be living near the school?"

"In the village. The school is two miles away. You would know that if you'd come to visit us and let me show you Plitherington Girls' Academy."

"Why do I need to see that? I don't have any children."

"Not yet," he says in a sneaky tone. "Who knows what might happen in the future?"

Oh, bugger. I think I know what Dom wants. "No meddling in my life. Understood?"

"You had no problem with my mates meddling in my life."

"I wasn't there for most of that. Please do not try to push men in my direction because I'm simply too busy to date. I don't care about that rubbish, anyway."

He clucks his tongue. "Don't get shirty with me. My wife wor-ries about your happiness, and I care about hers. This whole scheme was not my idea, so please don't be angry when you find out."

"Find out what?" Every hair on my body has gone stiff, and gooseflesh pebbles my skin. Why? Because I know what Dominic is trying to tell me. "No, no, absolutely not."

"What are you saying no to?"

"I don't have time to become the next target of the American Wives Club. And I don't want to date. I've told you that already. My shop is the main focus of my life."

Perhaps that does sound a touch pathetic. But starting a business is hard work that requires long hours. Dating is at the bottom of my list of priorities.

Owen's face flashes in my mind. His lovely smile. Those beautiful eyes. His cheerful demeanor.

"Still there, Pops?" Dominic asks.

"Yes, of course, I'm here. Sorry. And I've asked you many times not to call me Pops. It makes me sound like an elderly man."

"Point taken. But habits are hard to break." He falls silent for a moment, then sighs. "No more talk of dating or meddling, for now. But please come to dinner at ours. Chelsea would love to see you."

"Yes, I'll come. Just tell me when."

"Tonight. Seven o'clock."

"I'll be there."

We say goodbye, and I go back to unboxing books. Maybe I do occasionally think of Owen, but that's nonsense. I spoke to the man for five minutes, ten at most, which means he should not still be in my thoughts. To distract myself from thinking about him, I decide that instead, I will mentally prepare myself for whatever meddling my cousin and his mates might dream up for me. I'm not the sort who gets easily upset. But the idea of other people poking their noses into my life for the sole purpose of pushing me into the arms of a man they selected… It makes me want to hide in the storage closet.

I finish putting out the new stock, then go home to change into casual clothes for dinner at Dominic and Chelsea's house. The drive there is relaxing and free of blaring horns or loud vehicles. The further I get away from the city, the quieter everything around me becomes. I love London, but I'd grown up in the countryside, so I feel most at home in the counties.

When I arrive at Dominic and Chelsea's house, I've barely gotten out of the car before my cousin and his wife rush out to greet me. They both give me boisterous hugs as if they haven't seen me in ages.

"It's so wonderful to see you," Chelsea tells me once she finally stops trying to hug me to death. "Come in and see how we've decorated the place."

"What took you so long?" Dominic asks. "We've been virtually begging you to come see our house, but you kept brushing us off."

"No, I didn't brush anyone off. I've been busy, that's all."

They seem to accept my statement, since they lead me into the house instead of continuing the inquisition. I adore Dom and Chelsea, but I have a feeling dinner will involve plenty of not-so-subtle comments about how I need a boyfriend. Once we've gone inside, I see Chelsea's mum and dad already sitting at the dining room table. Hugh and Avery Parrish are here too. I know Dom and Hugh have become good friends, but I can't imagine why Lord and Lady Sommerleigh would drive all the way out here on short notice. Well, maybe they had all planned this dinner party in advance but no one informed me until today.

Of course, the more likely scenario is that Dominic rang Hugh and told him how awful it is that I don't have a man in my life. Chelsea and Avery are both members of the American Wives Club, which includes all the American women I know who married British men and became friends. The club began in Scotland and spread into England, though technically, the version here is called the British Branch of the American Wives Club. It's bloody confusing—and bloody annoying.

The meal Dominic and Chelsea cooked for us is delicious. But dinner includes more than good food. It's also an excuse to interrogate me about my personal life in a polite manner, at first, but things become more overt during dessert.

Chelsea, who sits beside me, pats my hand. "We're so glad you came tonight. And we hope you won't be offended by our surprise."

My stomach seems to have dropped straight through the floor and into the center of the earth. "What surprise?"

A knock at the front door spurs Dom to jump up and hurry over there. When he pulls the door open, I can't see the visitor yet. But Dominic grins and slaps the visitor's arm. "Come in, Julian. You're just in time for drinks in the sitting room."

Dom leads the guest toward that room and waves for the rest of us to follow them. The sitting room isn't large, but it has just enough chairs for the six of us. Naturally, Dominic urges the newcomer to sit on the love seat beside me.

"This is Julian Parry," Dom says. "He teaches biology at Plitherington. Julian, meet my cousin Poppy. She owns a bookshop in Croydon."

"Brilliant," Julian says as he turns toward me. "I love books."

Dominic set me up with a coworker from his school, without my permission, without even warning me about his plan. This might be the most humiliating moment of my life. I've never been on a blind date before, and I don't know what to say to poor Julian, who seems to be doing his best. Was he blindsided as well?

"I imagine you've read a lot about biology," I say. "That sounds interesting."

No, it doesn't really. But I'm trying very hard not to embarrass myself or Julian.

He begins to tell me all about his job at Plitherington, including detailed descriptions of the textbooks he uses in his classes. He clearly loves biology, but I never wanted to know the minute details of how viruses and bacteria get into the bloodstream and cause illness. Julian doesn't give me a chance to ask questions. All I can do is nod and smile.

I shouldn't have said his job sounded interesting. It's dead boring.

Dominic is wincing. Chelsea has her teeth clamped down on her lips, while Hugh and Avery keep exchanging awkward glances. Chelsea's parents gaze out the window with pinched expressions.

When my "date" takes a moment to drink some wine, Dominic desperately tries to steer the conversation in another direction. "Poppy, I'm sure Julian would love to hear about your shop."

"Oh, yes," Chelsea agrees. "It's the cutest little bookshop in Croydon, or in the whole of London, I'd say. Why don't you tell him about it, Poppy?"

Though it's the last thing I want to do, I turn to Julian and explain. "My shop specializes in rare and used books as well as new ones, everything from Danielle Steel to Alfred, Lord Tennyson. What sort do you like to read?"

"My favorite right now is the latest edition of *A-Level Biology.*"

And he dives back into a monologue about that topic.

Bugger me. I'd assumed he would talk about the sorts of books that can be found in a shop, not in a classroom. I should have been more specific.

Once the wine runs out, Julian announces that he's too knackered to stay any longer, and he apologizes for leaving me so soon. I smile and tell him how nice it was to meet him. But in my mind, I'm screaming, "Leave, you sodding bore!" If only he could hear me, Julian wouldn't want to see me again.

He kisses my hand. "May I ring you sometime?"

"Um, well, my mobile is broken. I need to buy a new one." Yes, I am a horrible liar.

Dominic virtually shoves Julian out the door. But since he works with the bloke, Dom walks Julian to his car and waves as his coworker drives away.

Thank goodness that ordeal is over.

Chelsea, Dominic, Hugh, and Avery follow me out to my car. Each of them wears a sheepish expression. I climb into the driver's seat and roll down the window so I can speak to them.

"Don't you lot ever, ever, ever do that to me again."

Chapter Three

Owen

THE SOUND OF MY PHONE RINGING WAKES ME UP, AND I yawn and fumble to grab the device. I need to blink several times before I can read the words on the phone's screen. A groan rumbles out of me. The last person I would want to talk to is calling me, and I know if I don't answer, she will keep calling until I do. So, I push up into a sitting position, leaning against the wall since this bed doesn't have a headboard.

And I swipe to take the call. "What do you want, Naomi?"

"To talk to you, obviously."

I yawn again. "Come on, it's two in the morning."

"Two o'clock? In what country? You live in Wyoming, where it's seven in the evening."

"And that's still too damn late here. Or too early, depending on your viewpoint." I rub my eyes and grab the glass of water I'd left on the nightstand, taking a sip. "I repeat, what do you want? And don't give me that 'to talk to you' nonsense. You never call unless you want something more than a chat."

"Maybe I miss you, Owen."

"Bullshit."

She pauses, and I can hear her breaths whispering through the intercontinental line. "If it's two a.m. where you are, that must mean you're overseas."

Yeah, she's trying to wheedle my location out of me. Not sure why. Naomi divorced me years ago and swore she never wanted to see me again. But a few weeks back, she started calling me—and I started screening my calls.

Maybe I'm a coward. Some people might call me that, but not answering my ex-wife's calls can't compare to what I did back in Wyoming. Bad guys with guns and a serious grudge against Natalie laid siege to Munro's cabin, and with no cops around to help us, we banded together to get the job done. Those jerks went to prison. So no, I don't feel like a coward. Naomi has no right to contact me anymore.

"If you miss me so much," I say, "why did you divorce me in the first place? Oh, wait, I remember. You announced that my career is 'asinine' and 'juvenile,' and I should get a 'real job.' And of course, there's the real gem of your tirade—when you called me a wuss who can't get it done in the bedroom."

"Please forgive me, Owen. I was wrong to say all of that."

"So, I'm not a wuss with a stupid job anymore, huh? What about the bedroom comment?"

"I regret saying those things."

Do I trust her? No way. "We are never reconciling, Naomi. Good-bye."

I hang up, then mute my phone and try to go back to sleep. Amazingly, I do manage to catch some more z's despite my ex-wife's bizarre attempt to convince me she wants me back. I'll believe that when aliens land on my front lawn.

When I wake up in the morning, I feel pretty damn good. Why? Not only did I sleep well, despite Naomi's weird call, but I also had hot dreams about a luscious bookshop owner who speaks with a sexy British accent.

Maybe I don't want to get married again, but I could have a vacation fling with Poppy. Assuming she wants that. I've never been the fling kind of guy, but meeting Poppy has made me consider doing things I would never done before. Yesterday, she had smelled so good, looked so good, and tickled my senses with her sweet British accent. Why shouldn't I have a little fun? I've earned it.

My hotel is moderately swanky, and it offers a generous breakfast buffet. When I go downstairs to find something to eat, I see a sign promoting the "full English" breakfast. I've heard of that, but I don't know what it means. The sign on the buffet table shows me which foods I should grab if I want the full English experience. That means bacon, sausage, and baked beans as well as fried eggs, tomatoes, and mushrooms. That's only the beginning, though. It also includes buttered toast, black pudding, and something called bubble and squeak. When I ask another guy who's eating alone, at the table beside mine, he informs me that bubble and squeak is leftovers, mostly vegetables, from a Sunday lunch.

It all tastes better than I expected.

Now that I'm full and feeling good, I decide to do more sightseeing. Alone. Again. My solo vacation is starting to feel like less of a holiday and more of a pathetic excuse for a divorced man to hide from his life.

Screw that.

I hail a taxi and get dropped off right in front of the door to Poppy's bookshop.

As I approach the door, I experience a twinge of worry that maybe she won't want to see me again. If she tells me to go away, at least I'll have tried. But if I want to go out with her, for a fling before I fly home, I should probably tell her what I do for a living. Poppy owns a bookshop, and I saw romance novels in her collection, so maybe she won't call me a wuss.

Time to man up and find out.

I push through the door, which makes that bell ring above my head. Poppy is standing behind the counter, biting down on one side of her bottom lip while studying something I can't see. The tinkling bell draws her attention, making her glance up and smile.

"Owen, you're back. What a lovely surprise."

"Yeah, I'm back." I walk over there as casually as I can manage, trying not to convey the impression that I've been desperate to see her again. I have been, obviously. But I'd rather she didn't realize that. "I read some of the book you recommended. It's really good. I've heard the King Arthur legend before, but Tennyson really makes it come to life."

"Doesn't he? I love his way of describing those events. But I must admit, I prefer books that have happy endings. Life has enough trials and tribulations that I'd rather read love stories, the kind that end well. I do adore a good romance."

She loves romance? Maybe Poppy won't think my career is unmanly after all. Should I tell her about my books? Nah, it's way too soon to bring up that subject. I could test the waters, though.

I lean against the counter and pick up a brochure about a publishing conference, pretending to skim it. "Do you get a lunch break? It seems like you run this shop all by yourself. That must be exhausting."

"Every job can be that way now and then, can't it? I love my work, so that makes it easier to handle the stressful times."

Okay, I was way too vague. Time to be more direct. "I was wondering if you'd like to have lunch with me."

Her eyes widen. "Oh. I see."

I resist the impulse to scratch my cheek because I know that's a nervous thing. Seeming anxious won't help me make my case for convincing Poppy to go out with me. "Well, would you like to have lunch with me?"

Her lips gradually slide into a sweet smile. "Yes, I would love that."

On the inside, I'm fist-pumping and whooping. On the outside, I smile and say, "Great. Mind if I poke around in your shop until lunchtime? I really do love books."

"Have at it." She hesitates, glancing around as if she's worried someone might overhear, then leans toward me. "This week has been rather slow, and I'd been thinking about heading over to the publishing conference at the Olympia Grand. It's a beautiful venue, and there should be plenty of things to explore, whether you're a book lover or a bookshop owner."

"Are you asking me to go there with you?"

"We could have lunch and explore the conference."

I can't help it. I grin. "That sounds perfect."

She grins too. "It's a date, then?"

"Yeah, it's a date. When should we go?"

"Right now. Have you hired a car? We could go in mine if you haven't."

"I've been traveling by taxi. Your car would be perfect."

Poppy locks her cash register, grabs her coat and purse, and leads me out of the cutest little bookshop in the world, locking the door behind us. She switched the "open" sign to "closed" too. This might be the cutest bookshop, but its best feature is the woman behind the counter—the cutest little bookshop owner in the world.

We walk around the back of the building to where Poppy had parked her car. The lot is reserved for the owners of the shops along this section of the street. We pass by a couple of big SUVs and a few sedans. Then we reach Poppy's vehicle.

I stop and stare at it. "Is this your car?"

"Yes." She clicks her key fob to unlock the doors. "Climb in, Owen."

"Uh, I think we have a problem." I pat the roof of the car. "This is a tiny tin can on wheels. I'll be squashed like a sardine inside this thing."

"Rubbish. My father is bigger than you, and he fits in my car quite well."

He's probably just too polite to admit to his daughter that he's uncomfortable. Don't Brits have a reputation for politeness? Either way, I don't see how I'm going to fit inside this car. "Maybe we could take a bus instead. One of those double-decker models. That's quintessentially British, right? I'd be getting the full-on London experience that way."

"You don't want to ride in my car, do you?"

I scratch my cheek and wince.

She tips her head to the side, studying me. Then the cutest girl I've ever met shakes her head. "The red buses don't service this part of the city. But we could take my car most of the way there and switch to a red bus for the remainder. How does that sound?"

"Perfect. Thank you for compromising with me, Poppy."

My ex-wife would never have done that. Hurricane Naomi always got her way because she blustered until I got blown down and gave in.

Poppy and I climb into her sardine car, and somehow, I manage to squeeze myself into the passenger seat. I can see why she likes a tiny car. It's easier to maneuver around a big city. Fortunately, Poppy doesn't drive like a maniac. She obeys the traffic laws, and I get to see some more of the city on our way to the conference venue. My sexy tour guide finds a "car park" that's located right at the end of a red-bus route, so we can easily climb out and wait for the next bus to stop here. A few minutes later, I'm sitting on a bench on the open-air top of an iconic London bus with the wind whipping my face. Poppy looks so beautiful, smiling while her long hair fans out behind her.

I want to kiss her. Need to kiss her.

So, I cautiously slide an arm across the seat's back, snaking it closer and closer to her. She notices but doesn't seem to care. Instead, she wriggles a little closer to me. Our eyes meet. I lean toward her, just as she leans toward me. Her hair whips around us, lashing my face, but I don't care. Her eyes drift slowly closed while I lower my mouth toward hers and my eyes shut too. Then it happens.

I press my lips to hers.

She grasps my shirt to tug me closer, and I slip my tongue between her lips, desperate to taste her, while I can feel her taut nipples even through my shirt. She moans when I begin to explore her mouth, lazily coiling my tongue around hers and flicking it to tease the roof of her mouth. Luckily, we're alone on the top level of this bus, but even if someone else should climb up here, I wouldn't stop kissing Poppy. I wrap my arms around her and tug her close. She feels warm and soft and tastes like everything sweet and luscious in the world, like warm toffee and decadent chocolate with a hint of single-malt Scotch whisky distilled in the Highlands.

Maybe I've spent too much time with a Scot.

"Hey, mate, this is a family-friendly bus."

I peel my lips away from Poppy's and look at the British man who spoke. He's smirking, so I doubt he's genuinely offended by seeing me and Poppy making out. The guy's two friends rush up the steps too, pushing their "mate" out of the way. The trio hurries to the back of the bus.

For the rest of our scenic tour of London, Poppy and I manage to keep our lips to ourselves. We glance at each other often, though, while grinning like idiots. I feel like a teenager who just had his first make-out session with a hot girl, the one he's had a crush on for years. But I'm too damn old for that. Too damn screwed up too.

That's why this can only ever be a vacation fling.

Chapter Four

Poppy

OWEN KISSED ME. I MET HIM YESTERDAY AND HAVE BARELY spent a total of half an hour with him, yet I let him kiss me. And I don't regret it. I've never done anything like that before, not with a virtual stranger. But I've done something else that's completely out of character for me and also another first. I agreed to shut down my shop and take Owen to a publishing conference, letting him ride in my car and then climbing onto a red bus for the remainder of our journey.

Yes, I've gone insane. But it feels wonderful.

When we climb off the bus, we still need to walk a little ways to reach the Olympia Grand. I've heard about this venue, and I've driven past it many times, but I have never set foot inside the building. My first experience at the Olympia Grand will be with a man I met yesterday.

Owen clasps my hand as we enter the venue, and I don't mind that at all. He has surprisingly soft hands for a man, but I assume that simply means he doesn't do hard labor. I wonder what he does do for a living, but I can't ask him that right now. We need to speak to one of the docents who greets us as we enter the building because I have a ticket, but Owen does not. Fortunately, we're able to buy one for him. This publishing event isn't as big as the London Book Fair, so it doesn't sell out in advance.

Now that we both have tickets, we walk into the venue proper, passing right under the banner announcing this as the Indie Publishing Expo. Owen smiles and keeps holding my hand while we explore the displays and chat to each other about which books we like and which sound like utter rubbish. Since Owen isn't interested in children's books, we skip those tables. There are plenty more to choose from, so we won't run out of options anytime soon.

We've just finished browsing a display of science fiction titles when Owen glances at his watch. "Hey, it's one o'clock. We did agree to have lunch together. Still want to do that?"

"Yes, of course I do. And there are several options to choose from here inside the venue."

"Let's check those out."

We spend fifteen minutes to wandering about in search of the perfect restaurant, but it was worth the wait. We wind up eating the most delicious hamburgers I've ever tasted and drinking strawberry lemonade. I'd never tried that before, but I learn Owen loves that drink, so I try it too. I can understand why he loves it. The sweetness of the strawberries mingles with the lemonade in the most perfect way. After our meal, we return to the book expo and have even more fun because we've found a huge display of science fiction adventure novels that includes a lifesize doll of an alien that has tentacles. It looks bloody ridiculous to me, but I can't help laughing at the way Owen pretends the creature is attacking him.

Then it's time for the last display. This one features romance novels.

Owen tries to steer me away from it, but I insist that I want to explore this author's books.

"Why won't you look at these romance novels?" I ask him. "They won't jump out to bite you. And it's not as if your mates will show up to harass you about being seen in the vicinity of steamy books. You don't know anyone here in London. That's what you said."

"Yeah, that's true." He scrunches up his face. "But, ah, I'd rather not look at the romance novels. Okay? Can't we just go now?"

"I want to add more romances to my stock at the bookshop. But you can wander back to the science fiction display while I look at this one. I'll meet you there."

He relaxes a bit, though he still seems oddly anxious about the display in front of us. After a moment, he exhales a long sigh and slumps his shoulders. "No, I'll stay with you. Let's look at the romance novels."

He takes my hand as we approach the display. Though he hadn't wanted to accompany me over here, now he relaxes as soon as he sees the books spread out on the table. It almost seems as if he had been expecting something horrible to happen when he saw these books, and now that the worst hasn't come to pass, he feels free to explore the display.

As we're leaving the venue, I have to ask him a question. So, I stop us just past the doors. "Why were you upset when I suggested we should look at that selection of romance novels? You seemed almost frightened of what you might see."

"I wasn't afraid." He shoves his hands into his trouser pockets and hunches his shoulders. "It's just that, uh, I thought the author might show up and…recognize me. Her books are here, but she isn't."

"Why on earth would a British romance author recognize you? Are you a celebrity in America?"

"Not exactly."

I can't understand why he's being so cagey. Unless he's part of a mafia family. Or perhaps a fugitive on the run from the law. "Owen, why won't you tell me the truth? I thought we were becoming… mates, I suppose."

"It's kind of complicated. See, I'm not exactly poor. But I'm not exactly rich either. My career has been on the rise for the past few years, and I've been keeping it a secret from everyone I know."

"But why?"

"I'm pretending to be someone I'm not. Everyone who knows me thinks I write technical manuals for a living."

I set my hands on my hips, trying to seem determined and stern, though I've never been good at that. "I do not like playing mind games. If you honestly want to spend time with me—"

"Why should I tell you all my secrets?" He seems annoyed now, and we've begun to speak in raised voices, drawing the attention of passersby. "We just met, and I'm going home to America next week."

"Then don't tell me. I'll go back to my shop and forget about you." I glance around and realize a small crowd has gathered to watch us, as if two people having an argument is a sporting event. I lower my voice. "Please, Owen, could we get in my car to discuss this?"

"Yeah, that's probably a good idea."

But we took a bus to get here. That means we'll need to do that again or find a taxi. I seize Owen's arm and start off down the street. We get lucky and see a taxi, and the driver stops for us when I wave my arm. We say nothing to each other during the ride back to where I'd left my car, and we remain silent until we've both shut our doors. Now safely ensconced in my car, I turn toward Owen as much as I can in the cramped space.

"Should I take you back to your hotel?" I ask. "Or would you rather hail another taxi?"

"Back to my hotel. Then we can talk some more, hopefully when we've calmed down."

"That sounds reasonable."

I have no bloody idea why I care about learning Owen's reasons for behaving the way he did at the expo. So what if a romance author might have learned that he doesn't write technical manuals? It makes no sense. But I say nothing as we drive to the hotel and park in the garage. Owen keeps glancing at me sideways while we walk into the lift and still seems a bit tense as we're carried up to the tenth floor.

Then he clears his throat. "Listen, I'm really sorry about the way I acted. My career is kind of a sore spot for me, and I'd like to explain why."

"You owe me no explanations."

"But I think I do. You see, I like you, Poppy, a lot. And I'd love to spend more time with you until I go home."

"You mean as friends."

"No." He turns toward me and bends his head until his lips graze my ear. "I'm insanely attracted to you."

A sensuous warmth ripples through me, and I've begun to breathe more rapidly. "I'm very attracted to you too."

"What should we do about that?"

"Not sure. Do you have an idea?"

"Yeah, I do." He slips an arm around my waist and draws me close. "Let's have a vacation fling."

Sex with a man I met yesterday? I've never done any such thing. I'm a good girl who follows the rules and has very little fun in the process. But I can't do what Owen suggested. I might like him and want to kiss him again. And maybe I loved spending time with him today. But attraction isn't a good enough reason to do something so reckless.

What has being a good girl gotten me? Bad blind dates, useless boyfriends, a lonely apartment above my shop, and a distinct lack of anything resembling a good time.

I rotate my head toward him, and our lips brush. "Yes, I want to do that."

"Seriously?"

"Yes."

He grins, and it's the most adorable thing I've ever seen. "I'm really glad you said that. Should we kiss now?"

"Naturally."

The lift stops, and the doors slide open.

A middle-aged couple get in and start discussing what they want to order from room service. Dear heaven, I need Owen to kiss me and seduce me. But we can't do that until these annoyingly happy people go away.

Finally, the lift stops at Owen's floor. He grasps my hand to almost drag me out into the hall. The doors shut, and we are alone again. I have to jog to keep up with his walking pace, but at last, we reach the door to his room. Owen swipes his keycard and swings the door open.

He stands aside and waves toward the threshold. "Ladies first."

"Thank you."

I stroll into the room and take in the surroundings. It's not the poshest suite I've ever seen, but I wouldn't be comfortable in a decadently luxurious room. I doubt Owen would either. This is a charming and comfortable suite.

Owen shuts the door and walks up to me, pulling me into his arms. "How do you like my digs?"

"It's lovely. Whatever it is that you do for a living, you must earn a good income from it."

He winces. "Yeah, I need to tell you about that before we, you know, do what we talked about doing."

Owen is so adorably sweet when he gets embarrassed. I would like to know his secret, but only if he's ready to tell me. I agreed to a holiday fling, which means he has no obligation to confess to me.

He leads me toward a plush sofa and waves for me to sit down. Then he settles onto the cushion beside me. "Let me start by saying I haven't been with that many women. I had three long-term relationships before I met the woman I would marry. We were together for five years, but I spent a sum total of twelve years with four different women."

Are we sharing our sexual history or only our dating history? I'm not sure. So I decide to follow his lead. "I've had two long-term relationships, but nothing in the past four years."

"I appreciate you sharing that with me. But the point I'm getting to is, uh…" He stares down at the floor and grips the back of his neck. "I kept my profession a secret for a long time. Only my best friend and my ex-wife ever knew what kinds of books I actually write. And she wasn't happy about it. That's why it's hard for me to tell you the truth."

"Oh. I see." Should I ask a question? I can honestly say I'm feeling rather uncomfortable. Does he write bomb-making manuals? Manifestos for terrorists? "Just tell me what it is, Owen. Please."

Someone bangs on the door.

Owen leaps up and races over there to swing the door open. "Naomi? What the hell are you doing here?"

A tall blonde woman pushes past him, sashaying into the living room. Her brows rise. "If you're the maid, you can go now."

"I am not the maid. Who the bloody hell are you?"

Owen rushes to position himself between me and the other woman. But she pushes him out of the way.

"Who am I?" she says, hands planted on her hips. "I'm Owen's wife."

Chapter Five

Naomi

I DRUM MY FINGERS ON MY HIPS WHILE I SCRUTINIZE THE frumpy little British girl my ex-husband has invited into his hotel suite. A man like Owen would find her attractive, but I'd say she's pretty in a schoolgirl kind of way. He probably wants to do something kinky with her, like play out his principal and student fantasy. Well, no, that doesn't make sense. Owen never wanted to play sex games when we were married, and if he wouldn't do it with me, he wouldn't do it with anyone.

Owen scowls at me. "I repeat, what the hell are you doing here, Naomi?"

I roll my eyes. "Why do you think I came all the way to London? Before I answer that question, I want to know who this little girl is."

"Little girl?" The child in question says, puckering lips and straightening her spine. "I am an adult. And my name is Poppy Goodburn."

"I'm Naomi Hansen. Let's not shake hands, honey. That would be awkward since the man you're sleeping with is my husband."

"Ex-husband," Owen snarls. "Who I am or am not sleeping with is none of your damn business."

The pretty little girl jumps up. "I should leave. This is…too complicated."

She scurries toward the door, yanking it open, and rushes out.

Owen sprints after her. The door slams shuts behind him. But he clearly caught up to her because I can hear them out in the hall, arguing in a disarmingly polite way.

Do I restrain myself and stay right where I am? Of course not. I wouldn't be the evil bitch ex-wife if I did that. So I march up to the door and plaster my ear to it. Hmm, I still can't understand what they're saying. They must have gone a bit further down the hall. What should I do now? Restraint has never been my forte, but I don't care to have strangers hear me arguing with Owen and that doe-eyed child. Might as well pretend to take the high road.

I return to the living room and settle onto a high-back chair near the floor-to-ceiling windows. That gives me a gorgeous view of downtown London, and I can even see the Millennium Wheel.

The door bursts open, and Owen marches into the room.

A thrill races through me. But it quickly disintegrates. Why?

Because Poppy the doe-eyed damsel has returned too.

Owen sits in an armchair kitty-corner to me while his new lover drops onto the sofa. She bites the inside of her lip, clutching her little purse on her lap.

I sit back and cross my legs, which makes my skirt ride up just enough to ensure Owen has a fantastic view of my calves and part of my thighs. But he doesn't look at my legs. No, he keeps his focus on Poppy.

Time to stir the pot some more. "So tell me, Flower Girl, how long have you been screwing my husband?"

"Ex-husband," Owen snarls once again.

The doe-eyed child lifts her chin. "My name is Poppy, not Flower Girl."

I give her my best 'I don't give a damn about you' smile. "Yes, I know, dear. But a poppy is a type of flower. You haven't answered my question."

"Because it's none of your business."

"Ah, yes, I know what that means. You haven't fucked Owen yet."

"You haven't either. Not for years, I imagine." Poppy leans forward a touch. "How long have you been celibate?"

So, the Flower Girl has a spine after all. I might be starting to like the doe-eyed damsel, but I can't let her know that. "How did you meet Owen?"

"He came to my bookshop."

"Naturally. Owen undoubtedly seduced you with a selection of sappy garbage from his latest masterpiece."

Poppy seems mildly confused. Has Owen not told her yet what kind of books he writes? Well, it is humiliating for a strapping man to pen that sort of tripe.

Owen grips his chair's arms and glowers at me. "Shut your trap, Naomi. I have half a mind to call security to drag you out this hotel, since you aren't a guest."

"The other half of your mind is too busy fawning over a child to have the wherewithal to get rid of me. Why haven't you shoved me out the door yet, hmm? Guess you aren't as anxious for me to leave as you think."

Poppy leans back and crosses her legs. Since she's wearing pants, she can't flash Owen any leg cleavage. She now has a glint in her eyes and a slight upward slant to her lips. "Owen invited me here. You had to crash the party."

"I admire your spunk, sweetie. But Mommy and Daddy have a few things to discuss in private. Why don't you go back to your charming little shop?"

"Not unless Owen asks me to leave."

Okay, it's time to play hard ball with this girl. "Have you read any of Owen's books yet? I tried to read one way back when we were still together. I think it was called *Depths of Desire*. Isn't that an awful title?"

My ex-husband scowls at me yet again. "It was called *The Heights of Passion*."

"Big difference."

Poppy glances between me and Owen several times. "What sort of book is that?"

I chuckle. "Romance, dear little Poppy. The kind with lots and lots of sexual content that involves moaning and thrusting and 'blossoming passion.' I think he used the word 'throbbing' a hundred times in that book."

The doe-eyed damsel's eyes flare wide. She stares at Owen as her jaw slowly drops. "You write romance novels?"

He slouches in his chair and avoids looking at her. "Yeah, I do."

"Are you well known in America? I haven't seen your books listed in the catalogs of new releases I receive every month."

I laugh again. "No, you wouldn't. You see, Owen writes under a pen name."

"That's not uncommon in the publishing industry. What is your pseudonym, Owen?"

He slouches deeper into his big puffy chair. "Ah, it's, uh…"

I smirk. "Desiree Lachance."

Dear little Poppy's expression goes blank briefly, then she blinks several times while staring at Owen. "I stock your books in my store."

"Yeah, I know. I should've told you this morning, or at least when I asked you to come back to my hotel with me. I'm sorry, Poppy."

"That's what you were trying to tell me earlier."

He nods.

"It's not your fault." She swings her gaze to me. "It's her fault."

"Mine?" I say with a laugh. "I just got here, honey. Owen's the coward who couldn't tell you the truth. If I hadn't said the words out loud, he never would have, trust me. Owen is not a strong man."

A muscle ticks in his jaw. "Shut up, Naomi. It's time for you to leave." He springs out of his chair and stalks up to me. "Say good-bye. Now."

"I'm not ready to leave yet. Poppy and I haven't gotten to know each other."

"And you never will." He seizes my arm and hauls me out of my chair, dragging me over to the door. Then he yanks it open. "We were finished a long time ago. Go home and get over it, Naomi."

He shoves me out the door and slams it shut.

Does he honestly believe that will stop me? I came here for a reason—several of them, actually—and I will not fly home until I've done what I came here to do. I've stirred up the hornet's nest, at least. Those two will be stinging each other for hours and will probably split up before they ever get around to screwing. Phase one, accomplished. Tomorrow, I will move on to phase two.

The doorman hails a taxi for me, clearly unaware that I'm not a guest at this hotel. During the ride back to where I'm actually staying, I consider the serendipitous way my encounter with Owen had gone. I had no idea he would have a sweet little thang in his suite with him, but busting in on my ex and his new Flower Girl gave me an even better idea for how to get what I want.

By the time I walk into my hotel room, the adrenaline rush has begun to wear off, leaving me wiped out. I order a pizza and eat it on the bed. Well, this room doesn't have much space. Even the bathroom is tiny, and the table by the window is so wobbly that my pizza would have fallen off it. So, I lean back against the wall and eat while watching a terrible show on a TV that dates back to at least the nineteen nineties. That's right. While my ex-husband lies in the lap of luxury, I'm stuck in an old motel on the outskirts of London, barely inside the city limits.

To relax, I do my favorite yoga routine. Thanks to the smallness of this room, I can just barely find enough space for my workout, though I do feel calmer afterward.

What is Owen doing right now? Screwing his new thang? I don't want him back, though I need him to believe I do. Well, maybe I do kind of want him back. But that's not the main reason I'm here.

Owen won't learn the truth from me. Not until I get what I need.

Chapter Six

Owen

NAOMI HAS CRAPPED UP MY LIFE AGAIN. I HADN'T SEEN her for years or heard from her until this morning. It wasn't enough for her to convince a judge that I should pay alimony. No, she wants to screw up my love life too after I'd finally resurrected it. Poppy decided to go home after the fiasco in my hotel suite. So yeah, life sucks right now.

This morning, I can't decide whether I should call Poppy or fly back to America with my tail between my legs. She gave me her mobile number. And I know where her shop is. I don't want to give up on starting something with her, even if it's only for the duration of my holiday in the UK. But I wouldn't blame Poppy if she never wants to speak to me again.

Hurricane Naomi made landfall and blew away my chances with Poppy.

This morning, I trudge downstairs to the dining room and pick at my food without eating much. It figures that when I find a woman I really want to get to know better, my ex-wife would show up. How did she even know where to find me? It's not like I posted my itinerary online for the whole world to see. She must be psychic. Or psycho.

Not eating makes me feel oddly full. And after fifteen minutes of studying tourist brochures in the hotel lobby, I've had enough. Time to find out if I've lost Poppy before we've even had sex. So, I jump in a taxi and head for her shop. But, just my luck, we get stuck in a traffic jam due to construction work. I drum my fingers on my thighs, getting more anxious the longer it takes for the traffic to clear.

My phone rings.

A glance at the caller ID assures me it's not Naomi. "Howdy, Munro. Missing me already? I mean, it's been two days since we last talked."

"Haud yer wheesht, Owen. I've been ordered to give you a message. It's urgent, apparently."

"Okay. What is it?"

"If you go to Poppy Goodburn's bookshop, you will be murdered by Dominic Rigby."

This must be a practical joke. Munro MacTaggart isn't the type to pull a prank like that, but maybe one of his cousins talked him into it. And who on earth is Dominic Rigby?

"Did ye hear me, Owen?"

"Yeah, I heard you. But I've never met anyone by that name."

"Aye, but ye know Poppy Goodburn. Don't you?"

I scratch under my collar because this taxi is stuffy and I always start to itch when I'm sweaty. "Sure, I know Poppy."

"Dominic is her cousin."

"Uh-huh. Still not getting the urgency. I'm on my way to Poppy's bookshop right now, though." If the frigging traffic ever clears. I must be cursed. "Can you enlighten me, Munro?"

"No. I was to deliver the message, that's all. Now I need to find my wife and shag her. Good luck, Owen."

He hangs up on me.

I really didn't need to hear about his urgent need to "shag" his wife. Munro used to be the most tight-lipped man on earth, but ever since he met Natalie, he's gotten into oversharing.

At last, the construction jam clears enough that we can get through it. A few minutes later, I'm stepping onto the sidewalk in front of Goodburn's Literary Treasures. I can see a few people inside, two of them men. Did her cousin bring a friend to help with disposing of my corpse? Guess I'm about to find out.

I pull the door open, stepping aside so two women can exit. Then I ignore the other customers and march up to the sales counter.

Poppy's head springs up, and her eyes go wide. "Owen. I thought—I wasn't expecting—"

"Relax. I didn't bring Naomi with me. I hope she's on her way back to America, though I can't confirm that." Leaning in, I speak in a softer voice. "I don't care about her. I really need to talk to you about last night. Please."

"I'm working."

"Okay. I can wait."

She bites her lip as the cutest dimple forms between her eyebrows. But then a customer approaches the counter, and I have to move out of the way. She does seem to be busy this morning, so I browse and pick a few books I honestly would like to read. I'm not just sucking up to the girl I desperately want to fuck.

The doorbell chimes.

I instinctively glance in that direction and see a man sauntering into the shop. Something about him reminds me of Poppy. Maybe it's his dark hair. Poppy's is the same shade, though this guy has brown eyes instead of green. I can tell that when he brushes past me to reach the sales counter. Another customer has just walked away, and the new guy engages in a hushed conversation with Poppy that involves irritated facial expressions and hand gestures. Finally, she throws her hands up and stalks into the back room.

The man turns around, leaning against the counter. His attention lands on me.

Well, I am now the only other person in the shop. But Munro had warned me that Poppy's cousin wants me dead, so… Nah, this can't be him. Munro was playing a joke, that's all. I believe that for about five seconds.

That's when the dark-haired man saunters up to me. "You must be Owen, the American prat."

Maybe this is my first trip to England, but I'm pretty sure "prat" is not a cordial greeting here in London. I decide to take the high road and offer him my hand to shake. "Yeah, I'm Owen Metzger. Are you Poppy's cousin?"

He glances down at my proffered hand, and his lip curls. "Yes, I'm her cousin, Dominic Rigby. Poppy is like a sister to me, and I don't appreciate an American wanker upsetting her."

I'm one hundred percent positive "wanker" is an insult. Even I watch the occasional British TV series. "I think we've got some crossed wires here, Dominic. Why don't we sit down and straighten things out?"

"Crossed wires? Poppy turned up at mine last night very upset."

"At your what?"

"My *house*. You know absolutely nothing about England, do you?"

I'm developing a strong urge to deck this guy, but knocking out the teeth of Poppy's cousin won't help me make things right with her. So, I shove my hands into my jeans pockets and try to act casual. "Listen, I have no idea what you're talking about. Poppy seemed okay when she left my—Well, the last time I saw her."

"In your hotel suite. I know that's where she was because Poppy told Chelsea all about it, and Chelsea told me."

"Jeez, you Brits are big-time gossips. And who is Chelsea?"

Dominic slants toward me. "My wife."

"Uh-huh. I need to talk to Poppy, not you. So either move your ass on your own, please, or I'll move it for you."

"Go on and try it. An ex-cricketer can bash the brains out of an American romance novelist any day."

I think cricket is some kind of sport, but I'm not sure about that. Is it the game old people play at nursing homes? The one where players use wooden mallets and the balls roll slowly? Whatever. This "wanker" is really starting to piss me off. I've had enough, so I push past Dominic and ring the little bell on the sales counter.

"You don't listen, do you?"

Dominic can taunt me all he wants. Screw him. I ring the bell again.

A hand seizes the back of my shirt and hoists me off the floor. My feet dangle a few inches above it. Dominic growls into my ear, "Sod off, Desiree Lachance. Keep away from my cousin."

This jerk-off knows my pen name? Poppy must have mentioned it. I don't blame her for anything she might've told her cousin, not after the stunt my ex-wife pulled last night.

Dominic drops me, and I tumble to the floor—just as Poppy emerges from the back room. She gapes at me.

No, that wasn't humiliating at all.

I clamber to my feet and brush off my clothes. If that British dickwad thinks I'll give up, he doesn't know squat about Americans. I approach the counter again. "Poppy, could we please talk? Alone?"

Dominic seizes my shirt, from the front this time, and shakes me. "You're either selectively deaf or a complete bloody moron. I told you to stay away from my cousin."

"Go play with the crickets, dumdum. Oh, sorry, I meant Dom-Dom. But that's the same thing, right?"

He pulls his free hand back, fisting it, about to lay one on me.

"Stop this now, Dominic," Poppy shouts. She pounds her fist on the counter. "Let go of Owen immediately."

Dominic sets me on my feet and looks at Poppy. "Are you sure you'll be safe with this twat?"

"Yes, I am. Go home, Dom, and tell all your mates that I don't need protecting."

"I'll come back in an hour to check on you."

"No, you will not." She makes a shooing motion with her hands. "Bugger off, Dominic."

He frowns but stalks out of the shop.

I can't help grinning at Poppy. "You're one tough chick. It's hot."

"Thank you." She studies me for a moment. "What happened with Naomi?"

"Nothing. I ordered her to go away, and she went. I have no clue if she's still in London, and I don't care." I rest my elbows on the counter, which places my eyes at the level of her breasts. I swear I didn't do that on purpose. "Is your cousin always such a cutthroat?"

"No. Dom is a very sweet man. I can't imagine what got into him today." She scrunches up her face. "Well, perhaps I can imagine."

"Dominic said you told his wife about me, and she told him."

"That's right. I know I shouldn't have talked to Chelsea about what happened last night, but I was very confused and needed advice. Chelsea has become like a sister to me." Poppy sighs and closes her eyes briefly. "Chelsea asked if it was all right for her to tell Dom what we talked about. He could see I was upset when I turned up at theirs. I agreed because I assumed Dominic would react like he usually does—in a calm and rational manner."

"Oh-ho, no. He went straight for the jugular."

"But he didn't hit you. He snarled a bit, that's all."

"I know. If he'd really wanted to whale on me, he could've done it."

She rests her elbows on the counter too, and now our faces are inches apart. "After the way Dom behaved, I'll understand if you don't want to keep seeing me."

"I survived a literal siege a few months ago. I think I can handle your overprotective cousin." I clasp both her hands in mine. "Nobody is going to chase me away before we've even gotten the chance to get to know each other."

"Will you tell me about the literal siege sometime?"

"Absolutely." I lift one of her hands to kiss it. "But first, could I take you to lunch? My treat. We'll go someplace nice."

She smiles, and the sweetness of that expression makes me want to kiss her right here, right now. "I would love that, Owen. I'll close the shop again. It won't hurt my virtually invisible revenue stream."

"Uh, do you happen to know a good place for lunch? I've never been to London before."

"Leave it to me, then." She leans in closer to touch her forehead to mine. "Why didn't you want to tell me you're Desiree Lachance?"

"It's a long story, and I'll share all of it with you over lunch."

"Owen, I'm so sorry I told Chelsea and Dom about your pen name. I was upset, but that was still inexcusable. They wouldn't tell anyone else."

"Don't worry about it. Naomi has a talent for fucking up the life of anyone she meets, especially me."

"You still want to have lunch with me, then?"

"Damn straight I do."

She straightens and grins. "Brilliant. We'll take my car."

"The sardine mobile? Better bring a crowbar, or I'll never get out of that contraption."

Poppy gives me a sly smile. "Should I ring Dominic to come and help you?"

"Oh, no. He would probably drag me out of the passenger seat just so he could lock me in the trunk."

"The boot. That's what we call it here in England."

"I appreciate the language lesson. Mind if I browse your collection of books until lunchtime?"

She touches my cheek, rubbing her thumb over my lips. "Browse all you like. I'm glad you came back, and I can't wait to learn more about you."

"Ditto."

But how will she feel when I tell her everything? Poppy Goodburn is worth the risk of humiliation, because she is the most incredible woman I've ever met.

Chapter Seven

Poppy

CUSTOMERS WANDER IN AND OUT ALL MORNING, SOME BUYing, some only browsing. But I have trouble focusing on my work, thanks to the man who keeps glancing my way and smiling. Owen occasionally waves too, and once he blows me a kiss. He is the most unusual bloke I've ever met. How often had I wished I could find someone who loves books as much as I do? I'd never had any luck on that front. The men I've dated have all been more interested in football or cricket than reading. Well, they might pick up a newspaper to skim the sports section.

But Owen loves books. He writes them too. And he happily accepted my recommendation that he should try Tennyson. Owen actually read that book rather than pretending to be interested. Might Owen Metzger be the perfect man for me? It's much too soon to tell. But I get a fluttery feeling in my tummy every time I see him. I don't give a toss what his ex-wife says or does. I will spend as much time as possible with Owen.

I close my shop at twelve thirty so Owen and I can go to lunch.

As we're climbing into my car, he says, "You should hire someone to help you at the shop. Then, you wouldn't need to do everything yourself and you could keep the place open during lunch."

"I have thought of that. But I can't afford to do it yet. It's taken me years to get to the point where I'm earning a small profit."

While I navigate the streets of London, Owen watches me. "What did you do before you opened your bookshop?"

"I worked at Waterstones. That's the largest bookseller in the UK."

"So, it's like the Barnes & Noble of England."

"Yes, I suppose it is." I glance at him and raise my brows. "Aren't you amazed that a Brit like me knows about Barnes & Noble? That is a strictly American bookseller."

"But *you* are a bookseller, so I assume you know a lot about the global industry. You are a smart cookie, Miss Goodburn. I love that in a woman."

Owen assumes I'm intelligent and knowledgeable about more than what I sell in my own shop. Yes, he is definitely the most unusual man on earth.

"When did you decide to open your own shop?" he asks. "That sounds like a major undertaking."

"It was. But I wanted to strike out on my own, so I could offer more than books by famous authors. I wanted to promote independent writers too."

"Waterstones doesn't do that?'

"They do, somewhat. But I prefer to be the one selecting which indie titles are for sale. Chain stores are likely to choose only indie books that are already selling well, rather than promoting authors who need a boost." I've just pulled into a parking space at the restaurant, so I shut off the engine. "I hope that one day my shop might become a promoter of unknown authors."

"That's an amazing idea, Poppy."

As we walk into the restaurant, Owen opens the door for me. He pulls out my chair for me too, once we've been ushered to a table.

Owen fiddles with the collar of his shirt. "I hope I'm not offending you with my old-fashioned manners. My mom taught me to always be respectful toward women. That means opening doors, pulling out chairs, and all that other stuff that's completely out of fashion these days."

"I'm not offended. I appreciate your good manners and your deference toward women."

"My ex-wife thought it was annoying." He winces. "Sorry. I shouldn't talk about Naomi."

"I don't mind if you do, as long as that's not the only topic of conversation. Besides, if we want to get to know each other better, we will need to talk about our exes. Don't you think?"

He relaxes visibly. "Yeah, I agree."

We both begin browsing the menu, but we end up chatting to each other about what to order. It turns out that we both love steak and seafood as well as hamburgers, but we agree to go with seafood for lunch—lobster, crab cakes, and brown shrimp. All of the food is sourced from the UK, and we both love that.

While we wait for our food, we enjoy local wine too.

"How did you find this place?" Owen asks. "It's amazing, but I never came across it when I was searching for places to eat."

"One of Dominic's mates, Dane Dixon, invested in this restaurant. He and the bloke who owns it are old college chums."

"I assume Dane Dixon will want to kill me too, like your cousin Dominic."

"No, he wouldn't do that. Dane is soft-spoken. He used to design vibrators for women, but now he and his wife Rika have taken over Diana Sangster's business incubator enterprise. That means they help small businesses and startups."

"Are Diana and Rika British too?"

I take a sip of wine before responding, strictly because I love the flavor. "Rika is American, but Diana is British. Her husband, Derek Hahn, is American too, like his sister Avery. She married Hugh Parrish, Lord Sommerleigh."

Owen leans back in his chair and shakes his head slowly. "And I thought Munro's huge family was confusing."

"Munro?"

"Yeah, he's kind of my best friend. Just don't tell him I said that. Munro MacTaggart, that's his name. He edits all my books."

"Oh, that Munro." I pause while the waitress sets our meals on the table. Once she walks away, I tell Owen, "I've never met Munro MacTaggart, but Hugh Parrish is best mates with Callum, who is Munro's cousin. The MacTaggart clan is quite large, I hear."

"Munro has hinted at that. But I've never met any of his relatives." Owen eats a bite of his crab cake while his expression grows contemplative. "How many cousins do you have?"

"Only one—Dominic."

"I think Munro has way more cousins than you. A couple weeks ago, I was talking to him on the phone, and he called his family a 'horde' of Scots."

That doesn't sound inviting, but I doubt his friend meant it as a serious insult. Dominic has met quite a few MacTaggarts, but he hasn't called them a "horde."

For the rest of our meal, we talk about our love of books and make silly jokes just for an excuse to laugh. Talk of books leads into a discussion of movies, and eventually, music. We share many of the same tastes, which is a surprising discovery. Owen brings out his mobile to show me pictures of his home in the town of Yestermont in Wyoming, as well as the cabin where Munro used to live. His mate still owns the house, but he moved back to Scotland with his American fiancée. They're married now.

Over dessert, we finally broach the subject of our romantic pasts again. We didn't have the chance to discuss that in detail on the night when Naomi made her surprise visit. My previous relationships aren't much to talk about, but I tell Owen as much as he wants to know. The men I'd been involved with were never abusive or neglectful. They simply had no real interest in what matters to me, and the initial attraction had faded.

"My love life has been a lot like yours, with one notable exception," Owen says, once I've finished my story. "Naomi Hansen is the anomaly. She seemed like such a nice girl when we first met. We dated off and on for a while, even broke up twice. But Naomi always managed to worm her way back into my life. I fell for her hard and fast, but she kept breaking it off, only to beg me to take her back again."

"When did you get married?"

"Eight years ago." He consumes a bite of his dessert while his gaze goes distant as if he's remembering the past. "I was so into her that it was almost like I'd been brainwashed. Naomi can be sweet and charming when she wants to. On the night I proposed, I told her the truth about my writing career before I popped the question. She said she was fine with it. But eventually, she started to resent my job, though I still don't know why."

"I know it's none of my concern, but I can't help it. I want to kick that woman in the shin and throw a banana cream pie in her face."

He chuckles. "That's really sweet of you, Poppy. But I can handle myself. Naomi might've done a number on me, but none of that matters now. Being with you is like a breath of fresh air."

How could any woman treat Owen the way his ex-wife did? He's a wonderful man.

When we return to the bookshop, Owen decides to ring for a taxi and go back to his hotel. While he waits for the car, my curiosity gets the better of me.

"May I ask an impertinent question, Owen?"

"Go ahead."

"Are you wealthy? The hotel where you're staying isn't inexpensive."

He hunches his shoulders. "I do well enough with my books, but I'm not a billionaire or even a millionaire. Munro arranged the hotel for me. He has a cousin who's a billionaire and a few others who are millionaires. They ponied up the cash to get me a swanky hotel and first-class airline flight."

"I have two friends who are billionaires—Diana Sangster and Dane Dixon. Isn't it odd that we both know people who are unbelievably wealthy when neither of us belongs in that category?"

"Definitely, it's weird."

A horn beeps, and I see Owen's taxi waiting for him. "You should go. I have work to do, and you must want to relax."

"I'd love to have dinner with you tonight."

"That would be lovely."

He leans in close until our lips are almost touching. "Would you be interested in having dinner in my suite? It's okay if you aren't cool with that. We can find a restaurant instead."

"I would love to have a quiet dinner in your suite." Maybe I should have hesitated before blurting that out. But it's the truth, and I've never been good at lying.

He kisses me sweetly. "Be there at eight?"

"Perfect."

Owen pulls the door of the taxi open and turns partway to look back at me. He waves, and his lips curl into the sweetest expression. Then he climbs in, and I watch as the taxi disappears down the street.

I go back to work and try to focus on that, but my mind keeps showing me memories of Owen and all the things we've done together over the past few days. He makes me laugh, makes me smile, and makes me feel like nothing else in the world matters. I wish I hadn't legged it to Dominic's house after what happened last night, but I doubt there will be a repeat of this morning.

When my workday is over, and I've turned the door sign from "open" to "closed," I go upstairs to change into something more appropriate for a date. I don't have many outfits of that sort. I haven't dated much for quite some time. Oh, I need help. My first official, full-on date with a man I like so very much requires more than a skirt I bought at Marks & Spencer. So, I do what any sensible woman having a wardrobe crisis would do.

I ring Chelsea.

"Why don't you come over here?" she asks. "I've got some stuff that would fit you and look great."

"Is Dom there?"

"No. He went to the pub with his buddies." She lowers her voice to a sarcastic whisper. "But don't worry, even if he comes home early, I won't tell him where you're going tonight."

"Thank you, Chelsea. I want this date to go perfectly. Maybe I can't stop Owen's ex-wife from interfering, but I can make sure everything else goes smashingly."

"I love your attitude."

After a quick trip to meet with Chelsea, I'm ready for my date with Owen. I drive to the hotel, but as I walk into the lobby, someone calls out to me.

"Miss Goodburn?"

I stop and turn toward the reception desk. "Are you speaking to me?"

"Yes, if you're Poppy Goodburn."

"I am."

The young man behind the desk rushes over to me. "Mr. Metzger wanted me to tell you he moved up to the tenth floor, and he's in the Regency Suite."

"Thank you for letting me know. I can find it myself."

When I reach the suite, I've barely knocked before the door swings open—and Owen grins at me.

"Come in," he says. "Have I got a surprise for you."

Chapter Eight

Owen

MY JAW HAS FALLEN OPEN, AND MY EYES ARE PROBABLY bulging too, just like a cartoon character. Poppy looks incredible. Her red dress seems like it's plastered to her shapely figure, except for the skirt that fans out below her hips. Her green earrings match her eyes while her red lipstick goes with her dress. I can't resist skimming my gaze over her body from head to toe, loving the plunging neckline that draws my focus to her cleavage. Damn, she even has sexy ankles. Everything about this woman drives me wild with lust like no one else ever has.

She twirls for me, and I swallow hard when I see her dress is backless. Love those stiletto heels too.

Is it any surprise I switched to another suite? Can't have Naomi barging in again. I also left orders at the front desk that no one should give out my room number except to Poppy Goodburn. How did I make sure my orders would be carried out? I told the desk clerk not to share my info with any blondes.

Brunettes only for me.

I take Poppy's hand, backing away so she can enter the suite. Then I move around her in a circle. "You are one stunning bookshop owner."

"Tonight, I'm just a girl on a date."

"And I'm just a guy who wants to seduce you on our date."

She smiles, and that expression makes her emerald eyes sparkle. Lust rushes through me so hard and hot that I can barely breathe. But I promised her a real date, with food and everything. No ex-wife bullshit. Just me and Poppy in a swanky suite enjoying a romantic dinner.

I sling an arm around her waist and pull her close. "I have champagne. Seemed like a good way to start our date."

"Mm, that does sound wonderful."

"You are the most beautiful woman in the world. I thought you were gorgeous when I first met you in your shop. But tonight, you've cranked up the hotness meter to five thousand."

The lightness of her laughter makes my dick twitch. "I can tell you're a writer, Owen. If you keep talking that way, I might want to wait for dinner until after we shag."

"Seriously?"

Poppy nods and licks her lips. "You look rather incredible too. Your black suit reminds me of James Bond, even without the tie. You're the sexiest man I've ever seen. Maybe we should do what I said—have dinner after we shag."

I back away from her and wag my finger. "Poppy Goodburn, you naughty bookshop owner. I'm trying to be a gentleman and give you an amazing date at least once before I rip your clothes off."

"But seeing you dressed that way makes me want you like mad."

"Ditto for me." I rub my jaw as I take in the vision of her in that dress one more time. "Fuck, you're making it hard for me to say no."

She smiles again, but this time it's infused with heat. "Are you saying you want to have sex right now?"

"Hell yes."

"I'm glad you said that." She grasps the lapels of my jacket and starts walking backward, dragging me toward the huge, L-shaped sofa. "Sit down, Owen."

"Sofa sex? I'm up for that. Shit, I'll do anything you want, even pour honey all over myself and roll around in goose down feathers."

"That won't be necessary." She sidles past me. "Turn around, please."

"You're even polite when you're issuing orders. I love that."

When I turn around, she gives my chest a firm shove. That sends me plummeting onto the sofa cushions. "Just watch, Owen. This show is strictly for you."

"Are you about to strip for me?"

She bites her lip and nods.

That sends a sizzling-hot bolt of lust straight down my body and into my dick. Poppy Goodburn is about to blow my mind, and if I'm lucky, blow another part of me too. But I think I'd rather do that later, after I've fucked her mindless.

The sexy Brit slips her fingers under one strap of her dress, then slowly pushes it off her shoulder. I still can't see her tits, thanks to the way she bent her arm to hold the strap up. Next, she slips a finger under the other strap to push it down, down, down while not letting that strip of fabric fall away.

She hits me with a seductive smile, then turns her back to me so she can look at me over her shoulder. My pulse has already sped up, but it goes into overdrive while I watch this woman shimmying her hips to tease me. Admiring the elegant curve of her spine makes me want to lick my way up her back to make her gasp and shiver. But when she kicks her stiletto heels off, I forget all about my fantasy and sit up straighter. She bends her knees and spreads her thighs, shaking that sexy ass. Then she slowly rises again while swaying her hips like the goddess she is.

Damn, Poppy Goodburn knows how to do a striptease.

"How do you like this?" she asks, her voice now a sultry purr.

"Your striptease? I love it. Keep going."

Still facing away from me, she drops the straps that had held up her dress. It covers her from the waist down. I can't see her front side, but I know her torso is naked now since the backless design wouldn't allow for a bra. Yeah, I've undressed a few women in my time. I always love it when a woman shows me her backside, but I desperately want to see Poppy's bare ass. I want to see all of her naked, but I won't rush her, not when she's stripping for me in the sweetest, most sensual way.

Poppy sways her hips while she pushes the waist of her dress down, down, down until it finally slumps to the floor in a puddle of fabric around her feet. Still watching me over her shoulder, she bites her lip and releases it so gradually that I can't stop myself from stroking my cock through my pants.

I crook a finger at her. "Come over here, Poppy. I've got plans for that body tonight."

She shakes her head, and her sassy smile makes my dick throb. "It's my turn first. Just sit there and let me do this."

"Do what? You've already blown my mind."

The sexy Brit grins and wags a finger at me. "No interfering, Owen. I'm in control, so don't try to take over."

"Whatever you say."

Poppy sashays up to me and kneels between my legs, pushing them apart to make room for her body. She skates her palms up my thighs and over my hips, then moves them along my waistband until she finds the buckle on my belt. With deliberate slowness, she unhooks that buckle and leans in to grasp it with her teeth, drawing the belt out of the loops one by one until it's free. Then she tosses it over her shoulder.

I groan as she unzips my pants. "Who knew a bookshop owner could do the hottest striptease ever? You are so fucking beautiful, Poppy, and I want to be inside you so badly that I can hardly breathe."

Though she unzipped me, she doesn't pull my dick out. Instead, she leans forward to undo my tie as slowly as she'd removed my belt. "I have a confession to make. I hope you won't mind what I've done."

"I could never be upset with you. Tell me."

She flings my tie over her shoulder, then starts unbuttoning my shirt, completely focused on the task. "I started reading one of your books."

"Why would you think I'd be mad about that?"

"Because you're sensitive about the sort of stories you write."

I cup her chin in one hand, urging her to look up at me. "I'm glad you're reading one of my books, Poppy. Do you like it?"

She nods and smiles with her lips sealed.

"Did you like the steamy parts?"

Poppy nods again. "Why do you think I did that striptease for you? Your writing got me so randy that I couldn't think of anything else, only what I wanted to do with you tonight."

I freeze. "Is that the only reason you're doing this? Because of my books?"

"No." She presses her lips to mine. "I already wanted you like mad. But reading the words you wrote made me crave you even more—because you wrote those words. Your talent turns me on." She frees the last button on my shirt and tugs it out of my waistband. "*You* turn me on, Owen, more than anyone else ever has."

"It's the same for me. No woman has ever gotten me this worked up before. But it's your personality and your accomplishments that make me need to fuck you like crazy."

"Mm, I love the rough tone of your voice when you're aroused."

I must sound like a snarling demon right now, considering how intensely Poppy has aroused me. I can't even speak because I'm breathing so hard.

She lowers her head to my waist, then drags her tongue up my chest until she reaches my nipples. And she pinches one of them with her teeth.

"Holy shit," I gasp. "You'll make me go off before I've undressed."

"I'm just getting started." She rakes her teeth over my nipple while she pulls my cock out of my pants and begins to stroke my stiff length. "Mm, I want you inside me, Owen."

A laugh splutters out of me. "Yeah, I kinda want that too."

Poppy climbs onto my lap, kneeling so her bare tits dangle in front of my face. The sweet bookshop owner bends forward just enough that she can push my face between those luscious mounds and hug me to them while she rolls her hips forward and back, forward and back. I gaze up at her, stunned by how brazen and erotic this woman is, more than I ever would have guessed. When she lowers herself deeper onto my lap while still rocking back and forth, the motion makes my dick slide up and down her slick folds.

She jumps off my lap. "Get rid of your clothes, please."

I rush to obey her polite command, leaping up and struggling to remove my suit jacket. I trip several times while undressing and almost slam my head into the coffee table, all because I can't wait one second longer than absolutely necessary to be inside her at last.

By the time I get naked, I'm gasping and my chest is heaving.

"Are you all right, Owen? Your cheeks are pink."

"Uh, yeah, sorry about that. I've never been this excited about having sex with a woman before."

She presses her nude body to mine and slips her arms around my waist. "Shall we go into the bedroom?"

"I want to fuck you on every surface in this suite, but I can't decide where to start." Since I moved into a different suite today, I haven't explored it much yet. But a quick scan of the vicinity gives me an idea. "Ever done it outdoors?"

"No. Have you?"

"The idea never occurred to me until tonight. Wanna give it a try? I haven't actually gone out on the patio yet."

"Let's do it."

We hurry out onto the patio, holding hands the whole time, and stop just past the threshold. It's dark out here. Must be a light switch somewhere. I give up Poppy's hand so I can hunt around in the vicinity of the patio doors until I finally find the switch. There are several switches, actually. I flick one, which turns on all the patio lights. Shutting that off, I try the others until only the lights inside the jacuzzi are on. A raised platform houses the bubbling bathtub, while wooden chairs and a wooden table fill the rest of the patio. A hedge encircles it, providing just enough privacy, and there's even a little gas fireplace enclosed in glass.

"Where should we start?" Poppy asks.

I leave the patio doors half open and kneel in front of her. "You've read one of my books. Can't you figure out the answer?"

She leans back against the door and spreads her legs. "Something like this?"

"Oh, yeah, exactly like that." I comb my fingers through the hairs on her mound, making her gasp. Then I slide one finger between her folds, just so I can pull it out and suck on it to taste her. "Time for the appetizer."

I lift one of her legs to rest her knee on my shoulder. Then I dive in.

Chapter Nine

Poppy

OWEN GENTLY SEPARATES MY FOLDS WITH HIS FINGERS, then flicks his tongue out to tease my flesh. I'm so wet and swollen from my desire for him that the barest touch makes me cry out. I grasp his head and let him do what he will while my head falls back against the glass doors and my eyes flutter shut. The velvety texture of his tongue inflames me even more, and my breaths come in sharp gasps. The bubbling of the jacuzzi seems strangely arousing, or maybe that's only because of what Owen is doing to me.

He leans forward, which raises my leg even higher, and slides his hand down the underside of my thigh until he reaches my arse. As he splays his palm over my bottom, he begins to lick faster. Owen lifts his head just enough that he can gaze into my eyes, and I can't look away, not while he's doing this to me. My breaths grow shallower and faster, and my pulse accelerates, while my focus has become glued to the movements of his mouth as he shifts his head higher to seal his lips around my clitoris.

"Oh God," I breathe. "Owen, I—"

My words are cut off because he just plunged a finger inside me. I slap my palms onto the glass door behind me and keep watching the way his cheeks cave in every time he sucks on my nub, loving the hungry expression on his face and the way I can feel his fingers inside me, rubbing the walls of my vagina, stealing my sanity more and more with every swipe of his tongue and stroke of his fingers.

I can't watch him anymore, though. My eyes need to shut, preparing for the moment when he will drive me over the edge. I fondle my breasts and pinch the nipples, moaning and gasping while the jacuzzi gurgles in the background and a car horn blares far below us. I thrust my fingers into his hair again, unable to control my own body, because Owen has taken full control of me—and I love it.

The orgasm rises inside me like a wave on the ocean, mounting higher and higher, barreling toward the shore with inevitable force. Owen suckles my clit so fiercely that I cry out and scrape my nails on the glass door. My inner muscles tighten and pulsate around his fingers, but even when he pulls them free, I feel the spasms that keep going despite clenching nothing. The ecstasy makes me want to shout, but I can't summon my voice. Instead, I squeeze my eyes shut so fiercely that I see stars behind the lids and ride out the tidal wave of pleasure.

Once it's over, I can't move. My muscles seem to have melted, and the only thing holding me upright is Owen's body.

"Look at me, Poppy," he murmurs. "Look at me, please."

Somehow, I manage to pry my lids apart.

He gazes up at me with so much hunger in his eyes that it makes my clit pulse. "The look on your face when you came was the most beautiful thing I've ever seen. But the way you played with your tits, that drove me out of my mind. I need to fuck you right now."

"I want that too." My orgasm hasn't quite faded yet, and I know the remnants of it will make sex with Owen even better. But I realize something that might end our night of incredible sex before it's really gotten started. "Do you have a condom?"

He chuckles. "Of course I do. I knew I'd be seeing you tonight, so I made sure to have plenty on hand." He rises but wags a finger when I start to peel myself off the glass door. "Uh-uh-uh. You stay right there."

"But you need to open the door."

"It's already open. Don't you remember? You're plastered to one side of the glass doors." He smiles, then kisses me softly. "You're completely blissed-out, aren't you? Just wait, it's about to get better."

Owen disappears into the living room, though I can't see where he's gone. I am blissed-out, for sure. No other man has ever made me feel the way he does, whether we're talking or fucking.

He returns a moment later, breathing hard. "Had to hunt around for this. Almost forgot where I stashed it so the maid wouldn't stumble onto it."

"I'm sure a maid would have seen everything in her line of work." I finally look at the object he brought—a cardboard box emblazoned with the word CONDOMS in large, bold letters. "You didn't want to run out, did you? This is a fifty pack."

"That was all the store had. I'm not expecting us to get it on fifty times tonight."

Owen rips the box open, and the packets spill out across the patio. He grabs one and covers himself, then cages me to the door with both his palms spread on the glass at either side of me.

I hold my breath. Anticipation tingles through me. I've never before been this excited to have sex with a man, but Owen is different. Somehow, he makes me feel as if it's my first time again.

He wraps his hand around the back of my thigh, lifting gently until I can hook my leg around his hip. Then he pushes inside me so slowly that I can feel every inch of his cock as it glides through my flesh. I suck in a breath, loving the sensation of his hardness penetrating me until his balls brush against my mound, and I know at last he has gone as deep as he can.

He lays his cheek against mine. I grip his biceps.

And he begins to move, pumping his hips in a leisurely rhythm, his breaths teasing my cheek and fluttering my hair. The friction of my skin on the glass door creates a faint squeaking noise that mingles with the liquid sound of our bodies merging and separating, over and over. My skin is so sensitized that I know it won't take long for me to reach that peak again.

Owen freezes.

He gazes into my eyes for moment, then lifts his head to kiss me. While his tongue glides around mine like an erotic serpent, he grasps my other hip too and kicks the glass door open, then strides into the living room. Even while he keeps walking, he doesn't break the kiss or pull out of my body. When I peek out between my half-closed lids, I see he has his eyes wide open—to make certain he doesn't trip over any furniture, I'm sure.

Beside the long sofa, he halts. "Thought I wanted to do this outdoors, but I changed my mind. You deserve a nice, soft place to fuck."

He lays us both down on the sofa, never pulling out of my body. The fact he can do that impresses me, but also makes me even more aroused. With my legs framing his body, he begins to move again in the same languid motion as before, taking his time while we gaze into each other's eyes. He pushes up on one arm to latch on to my nipple and lave it with his tongue, swirling it round and round the taut peak until I'm digging my nails into his flesh and moaning because it feel so bloody incredible.

"Harder, Owen, please. I need to come."

"Me too. But I don't want to rush this and leave you feeling cheated."

"I won't feel that way. Please, go faster, do it harder."

"Yes, ma'am."

He pushes up with both arms now and pulls out until only the head of his cock remains inside me, then he consumes me with one powerful thrust. I grip his biceps harder while he pounds into me with enough force that my body bounces. Meaningless cries explode out of me. The wet sucking sound that our bodies create echoes through the suite as the sofa thumps and seems to slide across the floor, or maybe I imagined that because I can't tear my focus away from his eyes.

"Fuck," he snarls. "I can feel your muscles bearing down on me, and it's—"

He slaps his palms down on the sofa's arm behind my head and thrusts even harder, even faster, with his teeth clenched and sweat dribbling down his temples.

A shout explodes out of me while I come. My inner muscles pulsate around his cock, desperately trying to hold on to him, and the pleasure seizes me so hard that I can't even cry out anymore. My heart pounds like a jackhammer. I can't breathe, and I swear my eyes have rolled back in my head.

Finally, Owen collapses on top of me. He rolls to the side to keep from crushing me beneath his body. Then he sweeps hairs away from my eyes. "Damn, that was amazing."

"Yes, it was."

"I hope you don't feel cheated that we didn't finish the deed out on the patio."

"Not at all." I turn onto my side so I can look into his beautiful blue eyes. "That was a bloody fantastic shag."

"Ready for dinner now?"

I can't help grinning, though I suspect the expression is rather lopsided. "Yes, please. I'm starving."

"We burned a lot of calories." He sits up. "Room service?"

"Absolutely. I can't possibly be seen in public right now. Everyone would know we shagged like maniacs a moment ago."

Owen climbs over me to set his feet down on the floor. "Wanna put some clothes on for dinner? I mean, you did go to all the trouble of finding a sexy dress and fixing your hair and makeup. I think you're gorgeous with nothing at all on, not even lipstick. But I did promise you a nice dinner."

"I'll get dressed if you do." I swing my legs off the sofa. "But seeing you in that suit again might force me to rip it off."

He bends over to kiss my forehead. "Feel free to do that anytime."

"Even in public?"

Owen chuckles. "That depends. Will we be arrested for public indecency?"

"I think we would, yes."

He starts hunting about for his clothes while still talking to me. "My friend Munro told me that his relatives went to a nudist resort in Oregon a couple years ago. One of his cousins was getting married there."

I tuck my legs under me cross-legged and watch him gather his clothes. "Married at a nudist resort? I can't imagine anyone I know visiting a place like that."

Owen cocks one brow at me as he bends over to reach for his trousers. "But your British buddies *have* done that. Munro told me a bunch of them went to the wedding. They'd become friends with the MacTaggarts."

"What?" I gawp at him, thoroughly dumbfounded by his statement. My mates became nudists? Dominic never mentioned that to me. Perhaps he doesn't know. I'll need to ask him about that.

Owen zips up his posh trousers and searches for his shoes. "Munro told me that your friend Hugh Parrish played nude shinty when he went to Scotland last year."

"Nude shinty? That's a Scottish sport, isn't it? I know Hugh's best mate is a Scot, and I can't say I'm surprised Hugh would go nude. He used to be called Lord Steamy, after all."

"A lot of the other Brits in that gang played nude shinty too."

I can't stop myself from laughing. "And I thought I knew those blokes. Still, I'm positive Dominic would never take part in any sort of unclothed event. Shirtless is as far as he goes in public."

Owen pauses in buttoning his shirt. "You kind of hero-worship him, don't you?"

"Perhaps I do, just a bit. I don't have any siblings, and Dominic always felt he needed to look out for me. He is my brother in every way that counts, except for genetically."

"It's nice you have a surrogate brother. I'm an only child too, and I sometimes wish I had a brother or a sister."

Now that Owen is almost fully dressed, I jump off the sofa and gather my clothes. "It sounds to me like your friend Munro is essentially a brother to you."

"Yeah, I guess he kinda is. But he's the grumpy, growly type of brother." He taps one finger on his lips and squints as if he's thinking hard. "Come to think of it, he's a lot like your surrogate brother."

"Dom is not a grumpy, growly man. He's a sweetheart."

"I haven't seen that side of him. Maybe he brainwashed you to think he's perfect and amazing."

"Very funny." I grab a pillow and toss it at him. The pillow grazes his cheek. "Should I get a harder object to toss at you?"

He throws his hands up. "I surrender. Dominic Rigby is the reincarnation of Alexander the Great."

"You cheeky sod."

I hurl my entire body at him, knocking us both onto the sofa, and we start laughing.

Chapter Ten

Owen

WE ROLL AROUND ON THE SOFA FOR A MINUTE OR TWO, wrinkling our clothes and probably tearing a few buttons in the process. But we aren't trying to have sex. Poppy threw herself at me because I dared to make a sarcastic comment about her beloved cousin. I'm not annoyed, and I don't believe she really is either. A tussle on the sofa is fun, that's all.

By the time we order room service, we've moved on from discussing her cousin and his "mates," which I think is a strangely cute term for "friends." Poppy swears Dominic isn't a raging asshole, and I've decided to provisionally believe that. Now, we're talking about what books we like. Gotta do something while we wait for our dinner to arrive. And books are one subject we both love to discuss.

"I finished reading *The Idylls of the King* this afternoon," I tell her. "Got another reading suggestion for me?"

"You trust my recommendations?"

"Of course I do. I mean, about anything other than your cousin."

"Do I need to fling a pillow at you again?"

I raise my hands. "Nope, I surrender willingly."

She's wearing her red dress but not the stilettos, and her hair is kind of messy. But I love that. We're alone in my suite, so she doesn't need to look perfect. Actually, I don't care if she never looks perfect again because her mussed hair and naked feet make me want to kiss her.

"Do you want another quintessentially British book?" she asks. "If so, I have a wonderful suggestion for you."

"Fire away."

"This one is the polar opposite of the Tennyson book. It's a science fiction novel."

"Awesome. I love sci-fi."

She leans her sexy body into me and drapes one arm around my neck. "Are you ready for a cozy catastrophe?"

"Uh, what? I've never heard of that before. Catastrophe is, well, catastrophic. It's not cozy."

"But we Brits have our own way of handling a terrible event. Even if nearly everyone dies, it's not the end of the world."

"Uh-huh. So, what's the book you think I should read?"

She rests her chin on my shoulder. "*The Day of the Triffids* by John Wyndham. It's about carnivorous plants."

"I'll give it a try. Do you carry that book in your shop?"

"Yes, I do."

"Good. I'll grab a copy there tomorrow. Can't wait to find out what a cozy catastrophe is like." I sling an arm around her waist. "I have a reading recommendation for you too."

"Wonderful. What is it?"

"It's in keeping with the sci-fi theme you introduced. Have you ever read I, Robot by Isaac Asimov?"

"No, I haven't. Thank you for that recommendation. I should read that one, shouldn't I? It's a famous work of science fiction, and I even sell it in my shop, but somehow I've never actually read it."

A knock at the door ends our book discussion, and soon we're enjoying our meal out on the patio. The employee who brought our food even laid it all out on the table for us. I gave him a nice big tip, and he smiled when he thanked me. I might not be super rich, but I can afford to tip somebody well when it's deserved. Poppy smiles with her lips closed, so I assume that means she approves of what I did.

We talk even more during dinner, about everything from books to sports. Neither of us is very into that kind of thing, and Poppy admits she only watched cricket when Dominic was playing in a match. So when we discuss sports, it's to talk about how weird shinty is. I haven't seen a match, but Munro tried to explain the game to me once. Poppy doesn't know much about it either. She does, however, share a funny story about the time a few months ago when Dominic agreed to participate in a charity match after having been retired from cricket for years. The charity event also included a beefcake calendar that featured a dozen former cricket stars.

"Was this a naked calendar?" I ask. "That's what women like, right?"

"He wasn't nude. It was very sexy, that's all."

"Uh-huh. 'Very sexy' sounds to me like a euphemism for 'totally naked.' But then, I'm not British. You guys have weird terms for everything."

"Not everything. And our terms are no stranger than the things Americans come up with."

"Fair enough. We're all weird." I study her for a moment. "Did you look at the calendar?"

"Yes. I sell it in my shop." She scrunches up her face. "It was odd and somewhat uncomfortable to see the half-naked picture of Dom. I only looked at the calendar once, and then only because he wanted know if I thought it was embarrassing. I told him it wasn't, of course."

"He's lucky to have a cousin like you."

Poppy whispers into my ear, "I did enjoy looking at the photos of the other cricketers."

She really is the cutest.

After dessert—yes, I even remembered to order that—we sit on the sofa to talk even more. I can't remember the last time I chatted with anybody for this long. Maybe I never have. Poppy and I just clicked from the moment we met, which is something I assumed only happened in movies.

Finally, it's time to say good night.

I walk Poppy to the door and grasp the knob, though I can't actually make myself turn it. She might start to think I'm holding her hostage if I don't convince my muscles to function pretty soon. So, I decide to tell her the truth. "I'm having trouble opening the door. Don't want you to go yet."

She takes hold of my hand, the one not gripping the door knob. "I don't want me to go yet either. What should we do about that?"

"You could…spend the night."

Poppy chews on her upper lip for long enough that I figure she's about to turn down my offer. But then her lips gradually stretch into a bright smile. "I would love to stay with you tonight, Owen."

"Great!" I might have shouted that with a little too much enthusiasm. Yeah, it's been a really, really long time since I got serious about a girl—and I've barely known her for two days. Being circumspect about dating didn't do me any favors. Might as well dive right into the deep end and hope I'll grow some gills.

She grins and laughs.

I peel my hand away from the knob. "Shall we go into the bedroom, then?"

Poppy slips her hand into mine. "Lead the way."

We amble across the living room and into the large bedroom. I swear Poppy's jaw drops and her eyes bulge. I'm stunned too, though I'd checked out the bedroom earlier. Still, seeing it again makes me feel like I must have accidentally walked into the wrong suite. A guy like me doesn't sleep in a huge king-size bed with silk sheets and picture windows that overlook a second, smaller patio. The attached bathroom has marble columns that hold two suspended mirrors, one for each sink. And holy shit, even the shower is composed of marble tiles. We have a sofa at the end of the bed, as well as a ginormous walk-in closet.

Poppy swivels her head every which way, clearly having trouble with the concept that this is real and not a hallucination.

I nod toward the closet. "I think your cousin and all his former teammates could fit in there and still have enough room to do the boot scootin' boogie."

"The what?' she says with the cutest little laugh.

"It's a type of line dancing, which is something country music fans love."

"Ah, I see. My cousin Dane and his wife Rika have gotten interested in line dancing, but I've never heard of the boot scootin' boogie."

"Brits do line dancing? I thought you guys were all too uptight to bust a move."

She gives me a light punch in the arm. "Don't insult my country. Do I seem uptight to you?"

"Nope. And I'm very grateful for that."

We discuss the possibility of taking a shower before bed but agree we just want to go to sleep instead. I love crawling under the covers with Poppy and cuddling with her body nestled against mine. Naomi had never wanted to spoon or cuddle or anything like that. But Poppy seems to love the intimacy as much as I do, which is one more reason why she might be the perfect woman for me. The big question is whether she thinks I'm the right man for her.

For now, I'll simply enjoy this time with her.

In the morning, I wake up in the best way imaginable—snuggled up to Poppy Goodburn. Even in her sleep, she's cheerful, with a slight smile curling her lips. I lay here for a while to watch her, and I start to get an idea for a book about a sweet Brit who bumps into a lonely writer while he's on vacation in London. Yeah, that would be a big stretch. It's not like I've ever visited the city before. Maybe I should steer clear of ideas that are too close to reality.

Well, if I made the writer a country singer instead… Yeah, then I could have a sweet Brit who emigrated to America to take over a stud farm she inherited from a distant relative. Hmm, that story might actually work.

By the time Poppy wakes up, I've already got most of the story worked out in my head.

She yawns and stretches her entire body. Then she smiles and kisses me. "Good morning, Owen."

"Oh, I'd say it's better than good. This is a great morning."

"You're right. It's a brilliant day."

I wrap my arm around her and flip onto my back, taking her with me so she's now on top. "That's a British thing, right? 'Brilliant' means excellent."

"Essentially."

"Wanna take a shower together?"

Her smiles gets even bigger. "That's an irresistible offer."

After a shower that involves nothing more erotic than me shampooing her hair, we get dressed and order breakfast. While we wait for room service to come, I tell her about the idea I got in bed this morning.

"This character is based on me, correct? But I own a bookshop, not a stud farm."

"Well, my first idea was about a sexy bookshop owner, but I thought that was too on the nose. Besides, I can picture you in tight jeans and a flannel shirt with the top two buttons undone. You'd look hot in cowboy boots."

"Have you ever worn those type of boots?"

"No. But the hero in this story would be a country singer who has never been anywhere near a horse or a ranch."

She sets her elbow on the sofa's back, using it to brace her head on her hand. "Are you honestly going to write a book like that?"

"You don't approve of my plot."

"On the contrary, I think it's charming. But you do have quite a bit to flesh out before you can write it. You need a full-fledged plot."

"I'm a pantser, not a plotter."

She puckers her lips as if she's trying so hard not to laugh at me. "You're a what? I haven't a clue how your undergarments have anything to do with writing."

"It's a reference to pants, not underwear."

"Which are the same thing."

Poppy and I stare at each other for a moment, both wrinkling our brows.

"This must be a cultural difference," I say. "What does 'pants' mean to you?"

"Underwear."

"In America, it means these." I pat my jeans. "Or any other kind of pants, which are garments that have two legs."

"We call those trousers." She snuggles up to me, and the warmth of her body feels so good. "What is a pantser, then?"

"A writer who doesn't plot out the storyline meticulously before starting to write. I used to do the whole outline thing, but I eventually realized that doesn't work for me. My mind moves in random ways."

"So you never plan the story ahead of time?"

"Does it bother you that I don't? Authors who are plotters can sometimes look down their noses at the pantsers. But mostly, we all get along."

She rests her head on my shoulder. "I've missed a good bit of drama, haven't I? A bookshop owner doesn't get to see the seedy underbelly of the publishing industry."

"Writers aren't seedy, not usually. It's the agents, publishers, and marketing sleazebags who fit that bill. I struck out on my own to self-publish my books because of all that shit." I lay a hand on her knee. "You must need to get back to the shop today. But could we have lunch together?"

"I would love that. Meet me at the shop at one o'clock."

"Can't wait. But I will need a kiss before you go."

Poppy tickles my lips with her fingers. "How about a kiss before breakfast followed by a kiss before I go?"

"Now that's an even better idea."

I cup her cheek and lean in, aiming for her sweet, pink lips. Her eyes flutter shut, and my mouth grazes hers.

A knock rattles the door.

I groan. "That must be our breakfast."

Poppy smiles. "You can kiss me after our meal is delivered. And as often after that as you like."

"You're wonderful."

I race to the door and fling it open.

And my ex-wife smiles at me. "Good morning, Owen."

Chapter Eleven

Poppy

THAT HORRID WOMAN IS BACK. I LEAP OFF THE SOFA, IN-tending to race over to Owen's side to support him, but then I freeze before I've moved even a few feet. I shouldn't interfere. Should I? Owen and I are involved, in a manner we haven't defined or even really discussed yet. But that doesn't give me the right to butt into his private life. I might think Naomi is an evil witch and wish I could simply toss a bucket of water on her head to make her melt away into nothing, but I don't want to be the Other Woman.

"Go away, Naomi," Owen says firmly. "My life is none of your business anymore."

"Au contraire, *mon cher*." She breezes past Owen, who seems too stunned to react, and halts at the edge of the living room. Her gaze lands on me, and Naomi lifts her chin. "Husband-stealing sluts are early risers, eh?"

I open my mouth, but the only thing I can think of to say would betray the fact that I was here all night. It's up to Owen to decide if he wants to tell his ex-wife that.

He grabs Naomi's arm and drags her toward the still-open door. "Go home. We have nothing to say to each other."

"Didn't you appreciate my French rhyme? It was poetic."

"Fly home to America and go back to teaching overworked executives how to twist themselves into pretzels while saying 'ohm.' "

"You never took the time to understand my profession."

Owen huffs. "Like you ever cared to learn about my career."

Naomi shakes his hand off and sashays over to me. Her gaze roves my entire body, and her mouth kinks up at one corner. "Either you are the messiest librarian in London who moonlights as a hooker, or you screwed my husband last night."

"You are not married to him anymore." I shouldn't have spoken. Should I? But this woman makes me so angry. It's not like me at all.

"We'll see about that." Naomi, with her perfectly coiffed hair and perfectly polished nails plants her hands on her hips. When she smiles with predatory confidence, I can see her perfectly bleached teeth too. "I guess Owen has developed a fetish for chubby girls."

I start to speak, but Owen intervenes.

"Shut your mouth, Naomi," he snarls. "I don't love you anymore. You made sure of that. Wasn't it enough for you to destroy my life and demand alimony as the icing on the cake?"

Naomi keeps her focus intently and exclusively on me, which is rather unnerving. But I refuse to let her see that. Maybe I have never been in the middle of a love triangle before. Maybe I have minimal experience with girl fights too. But I care about Owen, and I will not let that slag ruin what has begun to blossom between us.

"Leave Owen alone," I say, sounding sterner than even I would have expected. "He's my boyfriend now, and he wants nothing to do with you."

"Oh really." She leans closer. "Listen up, Mary Poppins—"

"Enough!" Owen shouts. "Walk out the door now, Naomi, or I will throw you out myself."

She rolls her eyes.

Owen seizes her arm again, but this time, he doesn't let her wriggle away from him. He drags her into the hall, then slams the door in her face. Naomi bangs on it, but Owen simply shouts, "I'll call hotel security if you don't leave right now."

Silence follows.

Owen peeks out into the corridor, glancing left and right. His shoulders sag. He shuts the door and slumps against it. "She's gone."

I walk over to him and clasp his hand. "Why is she so determined to harass you? If she wants you back, she's doing a ruddy awful job of sweet-talking you into giving her another try."

He grunts. "I have no fucking idea what she's up to."

"You honestly did love her at some point. You said so."

Owen rubs his eyes and pulls me close. "Yeah, I did love Naomi. But she changed like flipping a light switch. I don't care about the past anymore, and I don't care what she wants now. How did she even find out which room I'd moved to? The concierge said he'd make sure she couldn't find me."

"Even with my limited contact with Naomi, I've gotten the impression she can be charming when she wants to be. She's over-egging the pudding, don't you think?"

"Uh, maybe I would agree if I knew what that meant."

"Sorry. It means a person is overdoing something to the point where it ruins whatever result that person had wanted to get."

"Yeah, that does describe Naomi's behavior." He touches his forehead to mine so we're staring straight into each other's eyes. "Let's forget about my ex-wife. Do you still want to spend time with me? In spite of Naomi's nonsense?"

"Of course I do. She wants to split us apart, so let's not allow her to succeed."

"You are amazing, Poppy."

I feather a kiss over his lips. "So are you. But I do need to go back to my shop, which means I can't be with you all day. Wish I could. Spending time with you has made me happier than I've been in ages."

"Would you mind if I hang out at your shop with you? We had agreed to go to lunch together."

"Of course you can do that."

Someone knocks on the door, and the vibrations rattle my bones. We step away from the door so Owen can pull it open enough to determine if the visitor is his ex-wife again. But he smiles and swings the door open all the way, making way for a hotel employee to wheel a cart of food into the suite.

Thank goodness it wasn't Naomi again.

After breakfast, I let Owen drive my car since he claims he now knows the route to my shop. He almost turns the wrong way down a street, but he doesn't get annoyed when I shout for him to go the other way before we crash into a double-decker bus. We arrive at our destination with all our limbs still attached and no head injuries. Owen stays in the shop while I go upstairs to change clothes.

Moments later, I trot back down the stairs and over to the door to unlock it and switch the sign from "closed" to "open." On my way, I hop up on my toes to plant a quick kiss on Owen's lips. He smirks. His gaze tracks my every movement, particularly when I bend down to pick up a small book that had fallen on the floor. I hadn't noticed that yesterday.

"Are you enjoying the view?" I ask as I straighten and set the book on the table.

"It's the best view ever. Mind bending over again? Can't get enough of your shapely ass."

"Yours is mouthwatering too." I jog over to him and give his arse a light slap. "But I prefer to see it in the nude."

"Likewise." He lodges his hands in his jeans pockets and hunches his shoulders. "I, uh, called the hotel while you were upstairs. They apologized profusely for letting Naomi find out which room I'd moved into. You were right. She sweet-talked a bellboy who didn't know my new suite number was supposed to be kept private."

"That bloody woman. Why can't she leave you alone?"

"Let's not talk about Naomi anymore. How about you sell me a copy of *The Day of the Triffids?*"

"I'd forgotten about that. Yes, I would love to give you a copy."

Though I offer to give him a free copy, he insists on paying since this is a business and not a charity shop. I grab a copy of *I, Robot*, though I won't have a chance to read it anytime soon. While Owen continues browsing the shelves and tables of books, the first customers begin to show up, and I don't have time to think about Naomi anymore.

I always take an hour for lunch, while sitting behind the sales counter, but I had never done anything during that time except eat and perhaps listen to the radio while staring out the window to watch for potential customers. Lunch had never been anything special. But now, with Owen, I look forward to my one o'clock break because it means I get to spend more time with the American man who has brightened my life more than he could possibly realize. I was happy before. But now, I feel exhilarated and excited for each new day.

In the mid-afternoon, an unexpected visitor arrives.

No, it's not that bloody woman again. It's Dominic.

No customers are inside the shop right now. As soon as Dom walks through the doors, making the bells jingle, Owen assumes a fighting stance complete with raised fists. I know he's teasing my cousin. But will Dominic believe Owen is serious? Of course not. He isn't that easy to fool.

"Put your dukes up," Owen says while making a ridiculous face. "I'm ready for you this time, Cricket Man. Chirp all you want. I'll squash you under my tennis shoe."

Dominic rolls his eyes. "I am not here to fight."

I come up beside Owen, who lowers his fists and relaxes. "Why are you here, Dom? I'm always glad to see you, but this doesn't seem like a casual visit."

"No, it's not." He leans against the wall beside the door and folds his arms over his chest. "We know about Naomi Hansen."

"How? I never told you."

He smiles with a touch of smugness. "We know everything. After all, you told Chelsea about Naomi, and she told Avery Parrish who told Kate MacTaggart. Soon, the American Wives Club was in full-on war mode."

"War? That's a bit extreme, don't you think?"

He shrugs. "It's not up to me. The British Branch is mobilizing, and I didn't want you to be blindsided when their plan is set in motion."

"Are you going to tell me what the plan is?"

Dominic winces. "I can't. My wife made me vow to keep my trap shut. Well, her exact words were 'keep your trap shut, Dom, if you ever want to have sex again.' I don't believe for one second that she'll refuse to shag me, but Chelsea made her point quite well."

"If you can't tell me anything, why are you here?"

"To warn you. The lovely ladies in the American Wives Club have set their sights on ensuring you three achieve your happy endings."

"Us three?" A chill washes over me, raising the hairs on my arms and nape. "Oh, no, you can't mean—They wouldn't do that to me."

Owen glances between me and Dominic. "What's going on? I don't get what you two are talking about."

"Meddling," Dominic says. "That's what we're talking about."

"What is the American Wives Club? I'm American, but I've never heard of any club with that name."

Dominic raises his brows at me. "Would you like to explain? Or shall I do it?"

"No, I should explain the situation to Owen." I turn toward the man who shagged me last night. "The American Wives Club is an informal group that started in Scotland and later spread to England. It began with the wives of three MacTaggart men. Emery, Erica, and Calli banded together to help other MacTaggarts find their happy endings. Then, after Catriona MacTaggart married Alex Thorne, a Brit, the club expanded into England."

"Okay. But that has nothing to do with me."

"Don't you understand? The club members think you and I need help to reach our happy ending."

"But we hardly know each other."

Dominic chuckles. "That doesn't matter. The beautiful busybodies have determined that their brand of meddling is needed. Naomi is interfering in your relationship with Poppy, and the club members and their husbands believe they can settle the matter."

"Settle what matter? Trust me, nobody can make my ex-wife give up her plot to drive me insane."

I sidle closer to Owen and clasp his hand. "Maybe we do need help. Naomi is obsessed with breaking us up. That's how it seems. Even if you and I don't wind up together in the end, wouldn't you say we owe it to ourselves to give our relationship a chance? This might turn out to be a holiday fling, or it might become something more. Don't you feel that way too?"

Chapter Twelve

Owen

HAVE I WALKED INTO BIZARRO LAND? I'VE HEARD OF MEDdling, of course. But it sounds like these Brits and Scots take interference to a whole other level. I guess the men in that club don't know how to say no to their wives. Munro never mentioned any such club to me, but then, he hadn't gone home in years. Maybe the club started up after he moved to America. I might need to call him later to grill my friend about this. He knew I was coming to England—it was his idea, for pity's sake—but he failed to warn me that his family and a bunch of British people might try to poke their noses into my life.

Poppy is gazing up at me while biting her lip, her expression expectant.

I glance at Dominic sideways, then turn to face Poppy. "I want to give us a try, of course. But with all your friends and relatives watching us? That's bizarre."

Dominic sighs. "Honestly, we aren't a bunch of voyeurs. No one will spy on you two while you're shagging. And our plan is designed to convince Naomi to stop behaving like a mad woman."

Good luck with that, pal.

Poppy swerves her attention to Dominic. "Did you just say 'our' plan? I thought you weren't involved."

"Well, I, ah, might be slightly involved." He throws his hands up. "My wife wants to do this, and I can't say no to her. You know that, Pops."

"How many times have I asked you not to call me that?" She rests her forehead on my arm and moans pitifully. "I understand if this is all too barmy for you."

I hook a finger under her chin and lift until our eyes meet. "Nothing is too barmy for me if it means I can spend more time with you."

"Are you sure? The American Wives Club often takes extreme measures. They had their husbands kidnap Hugh Parrish last year."

"Why the hell did they do that?"

"Because he and his best mate, Callum MacTaggart, were fighting over Kate Wagner. Everyone knew Callum and Kate belonged together, but Hugh was behaving like an arsehole and trying to get between them."

"Just like me and you and Naomi."

"Except she is the arsehole this time."

Yeah, that's for sure. "Will this crazy scheme involve me and Naomi sharing our feelings and crying it out? That's a little too daytime-talk-show for me."

"I doubt it will turn into a tabloid event."

Dominic clears his throat to get our attention. "I think my work is done here. Someone will ring you to provide the details and your itinerary."

"Itinerary?" Poppy says. "For what?"

"You'll see."

Dominic walks out the door.

How nice of him to drop that bomb and leave us to put out the fire. I'm beginning to wonder if the idea that Brits are super polite is nothing but propaganda.

Poppy is still gazing up at me with worry in her eyes.

So, I kiss her forehead and smile. "Don't worry. They can't possibly do anything too crazy. But even if your friends and family orchestrate a massive event, I doubt it would ever be as insane as when I helped Munro and Natalie catch a slew of bad guys."

"You should tell me the whole story sometime."

"And I would love to tell you."

Some customers arrive, and I try to fade into the background so I won't get in the way of her business. She does more than just sell books. Poppy gives advice and helps her customers find the perfect book for them. She even suggests other stores they could try if she doesn't have exactly what they want. If I hadn't already been falling for Poppy, I'm definitely feeling that way now. She is the perfect woman for me, and I hope she thinks of me the same way.

What were the odds I'd come to England and bump into the right girl? I've never believed in fate, but I might change my mind about that.

At closing time, I help straighten the shelves and tables of books while Poppy does whatever she needs to do with the cash register. I had used one of those when I worked at a movie theater in college, but I haven't touched a cash register since then. I might suck at ringing up purchases, but I rock the organization of books on shelves and tables.

When Poppy sees what I've done, she throws her arms around my neck and kisses me like she wants to "shag" right here on the nearest table. "Thank you for putting all those books back where they belong and for sweeping the floor. You are the perfect man."

But am I the perfect one for her? She was vague about that.

She nibbles on my bottom lip. "If you ever get tired of writing, a job is waiting for you at Goodburn's Literary Treasures."

"We could merge the two things. I can sit in a chair on the sidewalk typing on my computer to draw people into the shop. Then, you can reel them in to sell books."

"That's an interesting idea."

My cell phone rings. I want to ignore it and make out with Poppy instead, but I'm an annoyingly responsible person. So, I pull the phone out of my pocket and answer.

"We need to talk, Owen."

"Naomi? What the hell? You are genuinely stalking me now."

Poppy folds her arms over her chest and puckers her lips, but I can't tell if that means she's ticked at Naomi or if she's ticked at me.

"Please, Owen," my ex-wife says. "I need to speak to you alone. It's important."

"After the shit you've pulled this week, I don't feel like giving you the benefit of the doubt."

"I know. I've acted like a stalker, but that's not what is really going on here. All I'm asking for is a few minutes, alone with you, to explain."

She sounds completely different than she did this morning or the other night. Naomi seems...calm. Almost like a normal human being.

What's the etiquette here? Ex-wife wants to chat, but new girl-friend won't like that. Damned if I know how to handle this. "Let me think about it. I'll call you in a little while with my decision."

"All right. Thank you, Owen."

I stuff my phone back into my pocket and shift my weight from one foot to the other. I scratch my cheek too. Yeah, a writer knows what those signs mean. It's exactly the kind of behavior I've written about umpteen times. I'm anxious, but that's no surprise. I'm also feeling guilty, which is unexpected. What should I feel guilty about? Naomi being nice? Poppy seeming sweetly confused? Maybe it's all of that. And maybe I have no fucking idea how to handle the situation.

Poppy takes a step away from me. "That was your ex-wife. She wants to talk to you in person."

"How do you know that?"

"Because I'm not stupid. You said Naomi's name and told her that you'd call her later with your decision. That must mean she wants to meet with you."

"Yeah, that is what she wants."

Poppy hugs herself, staring down at the floor.

"I do not want to get back together with Naomi. But I do kind of feel like I should meet with her. We were married for five years, and then she just took off and filed for divorce. I need some closure, that's all."

Naomi had been sort of weirdly nice when she called me the other day. But then she went postal both times she saw me with Poppy. Maybe that's why Naomi followed me to London. She's…jealous.

Nah, that can't be it.

Poppy straightens and looks directly at me. Her determined expression makes me want to kiss her. "I understand that you need closure with that woman. And I realize you need to speak to her alone. But I don't like it."

"I know. I'm sorry. Relationships are damn complicated and confusing." I move closer and gently take hold of her upper arms. "But I do not want to get back with Naomi. That part of my life is over. All I want these days is to spend time with you and figure out how we feel about each other. Do you still want that?"

"Yes, I do."

"Do you trust me?"

"Of course."

I kiss her cheek. "Then don't worry. Everything will be fine."

"When will you meet with Naomi?"

"Right away. Might as well get it over with."

While my new girlfriend watches, I call my ex-wife. "Hey, Naomi, I'll meet you in half an hour at your hotel."

"No, Owen. We will meet at your hotel."

"I'm the one doing you a favor, so try being gracious about it."

"Sorry. I wasn't trying to be bitchy. But I would prefer to meet somewhere other than my hotel. Please."

"Fine." I rub my forehead while I rack my brain for a solution. Then it suddenly hits me. "One sec, Naomi."

I hold the phone to my chest.

Poppy raises her brows.

"This is awkward," I say. "But I need to think of a place where I can meet Naomi on neutral ground. She's trying to talk me into going to my hotel, but I won't do that. You're a London native. Got any ideas?"

"There's a pub just down the street. It has a casual, relaxed atmosphere." Poppy's lips twitch, and her eyes sparkle with humor. "Maybe you should get Naomi drunk so you can shove her onto a plane headed back to America."

"I know your buddies are into kidnapping, but I'd probably get arrested for that."

"Pubs are gathering places. You don't need to drink, though having a pint together might make her more amenable."

I tap my finger on my phone, considering her suggestion. "Hmm, that's not a half-bad idea. Actually, it's kind of genius."

"The pub is called The Crook & Nail."

"You Brits make up weird names for things." I hold the phone to my ear again. "Okay, Naomi. Meet me at The Crook & Nail—that's a pub here in London—and be there as soon as you can. Keep me waiting too long, and you'll lose your shot at apologizing or whatever it is you want to say."

"I understand. And I will be there right away."

"Good." I hang up. "It's all set."

Poppy nods. "I hope it goes well."

"Yeah, me too."

I walk Poppy to her car and kiss her goodbye. But when I start to walk away, she grabs my arm.

"Wait, Owen. May I drop you off at the pub? It's only a few blocks away, and it seems like a waste of time and money to ring for a taxi."

"Sure, I'd love a lift in your car. That would be great."

Once we've climbed in and I'm stuffed inside her tiny car, she smirks at me. "There's no lift in this car, Owen."

"Huh? Oh, is that an elevator jab? I know you Brits call that a lift."

"I like to confuse you. Your look of sheer bafflement is adorable."

"You can't embarrass me by calling me adorable. I write romance novels with hot sex scenes in them." I open the passenger door, then lean in to kiss her. "I'll call you once Naomi and I have signed our peace treaty."

"Good luck. I'll be waiting in my apartment above the shop."

I suddenly get a fantastic idea. Hopefully, she will agree it's perfect. "Why don't I give you the key to my hotel suite? Then you could wait in the lap of luxury until I get there."

"Are you sure you want to do that? I might order the entire room service menu plus five bottles of the most expensive champagne."

"Be my guest." I get out of the car, then bend over to smile and wink at her. "The MacTaggarts are paying all my expenses."

I shut the door and watch as Poppy's car rolls down the street and disappears around a corner. All my anxiety about meeting with Naomi had evaporated when I was in the car with Poppy, and it will not come back. I walk into the pub feeling confident and ready to weather Hurricane Naomi.

Yeah, I can do this.

Chapter Thirteen

Naomi

I WRIGGLE MY BUTT ON THE CUSHIONED BENCH BUT CAN'T get comfortable no matter what I do. Shoving my hands under my ass doesn't help either. I swear there must be pebbles inside the cushioned seat. When I clasp my hands on the tabletop, I suddenly realize I'm twiddling my thumbs. I never do that. No one does. An attractive man walks by and winks at me, but I can't even manage a slight smile in response.

No, I am not nervous. It's impossible.

My gaze veers toward the windows, though I hadn't meant to look in that direction. Where is Owen? I've been here for... I whip out my phone to check the clock. Eleven minutes, that's how long. I guzzle half of my glass of water and drum my fingers on the tabletop.

A flash of movement draws my attention to the windows.

Owen has just stepped out of the tiniest car I've ever seen. He opens the door, then talks to the driver. I can't see the other person, but I know it's that Flower Girl. Who else would give Owen a lift? He jumps out of the car and bends over to say something else to sweet little Poppy.

Finally, he shuts the door and saunters into the pub.

Owen glances around, clearly searching for me. So, I wave my hand wildly until he notices me. He nods and wends through the crowd until he reaches my table. Then he just stands there.

I gesture toward the opposite side of the booth. "Sit down, Owen. Unless you'd rather discuss things while shouting to me from the other side of the room."

He screws up his mouth, an expression I know means he's irritated, but then slides onto the bench. "What did you want to talk about?"

"Us."

"There is no 'us,' Naomi. You dumped me, remember? I've moved on."

How can I say this without turning into a she-devil again? Or worse, dissolving into a puddle of chilled cowardice. Owen believes I'm the worst harpy on the planet, but he has no idea how I feel about anything, especially not him.

"Well?" he says. "Are you going to explain why I needed to come here?"

"Yes, I am going to tell you everything." Well, almost everything. Even Owen doesn't need to know the whole truth. "I made a horrible mistake when I left you. I was scared, and I should have talked to you about that. But I took the easy way out."

He crosses his arms over his chest, leaning back against the booth. "You ridiculed my career. Made me feel like a wuss who didn't deserve a goddess like you."

"I acknowledge my bad behavior. And I apologize for all of it."

"That's nice. But you could have sent me a 'sorry I'm a raging bitch' greeting card instead of stalking me all the way to London."

I take another gulp of water and set my hands on my lap, gazing straight at Owen. "I'm still in love with you."

He freezes. The stark fear in his eyes sends a chill rushing over my skin. "Is this some kind of practical joke?"

"No. I'm being completely honest with you for the first time in far too long." My lips tremble, and that's no act either. "I love you, Owen. I want to spend the rest of my life with you and have those kids you always wanted."

"Uh-huh." His gaze narrows. "What's the catch?"

"There isn't one."

"With you, there's always a catch."

My throat feels tight, and I can't stop myself from averting my eyes. He is genuinely shocked by my statement. "Want a beer? I'd love one myself."

"No thanks." He rests his arms on the table, still squinting at me. "If you honestly want me back, there's one question you need to answer."

"Okay. Shoot."

"Do you like my books?"

I chew on my bottom lip while I consider how to respond. Lying would be the most advantageous response for me, but the truth is what Owen cares about. "You don't like yoga, but I love you anyway."

Yeah, I opted for deflection. It usually works for me.

Owen taps one finger on the table. "The difference is that I tried yoga. I went to your studio twice a week for two months."

"And then you gave up. Tell me, will you give up on the Flower Girl if her bookshop gets too dull for you?"

"No." He slants toward me. "Because I will never get tired of Poppy."

But he did get tired of me. That's what his statement implies. "That's bullshit, Owen. You loved having sex with me, and you would have stayed with me forever if I hadn't filed for divorce."

He slumps back against the booth, and the anger vacates his expression. For a moment, he stares down at his lap with one hand under the table. Is he doing something on his phone? I can't tell for sure.

Owen returns his attention to me and shakes his head slowly. "I would have ended things if you hadn't. We both knew it wasn't working anymore. You were miserable, I was miserable, and nothing was going to make our marriage better. We should never have gotten together in the first place, and you know it."

Maybe he's right. I won't give him the satisfaction of hearing me say that. We did have great sex in the beginning, but the spark began to sputter after we got married. Was it my fault? Or his fault? No, I think we both lost interest.

"We should never have gotten married," Owen says. "After two break-ups, we should've known better. But instead, we ran headlong into something that neither of us really wanted, all because we didn't want to be alone."

I drum my fingernails on the table and try to figure out what to do next. Give up? No, I never do that. Once I set my mind to something, I go for it with everything I have and don't stop until I've succeeded. Being pigheaded was one of the things Owen used to love about me. I'm losing this time, though. Should I confess the real reason I'm chasing after him?

"Face it, Naomi. You don't want to live my kind of life, and I don't want to live your kind." Owen sighs, and his shoulders sag. "We are not getting back together. Poppy makes me happier than you ever could, and I will do anything to make her just as happy."

He slides out of the booth and turns away.

"Wait, Owen."

"It's over, Naomi. Go home."

He strides out of the pub. I drop a tip on the table, despite not having ordered anything, and rush after him. I catch up to Owen quite easily since he's just standing at the curb.

"What are you doing?" I ask. "If you need a lift, I have a car."

"Don't need a ride. Already got one."

The Flower Girl's miniature car pulls up, and Owen gets in. He rolls the window down. "I texted Poppy ten minutes ago to tell her our little chat was over. Goodbye forever, Naomi."

He rolls the window up.

And the happy couple drives away.

What else can I do? My Machiavellian plan has skidded off the rails, but I can get it back on track. I deserve what's owed to me. My original plan might not have worked, but I always have a backup. Pouring my heart out to Owen was not part of my scheme, but I'd needed to improvise to get what I want. Now he at least might believe, in the back of his mind, that I genuinely want him back. Okay, that plan might have worked a little too well.

Because I honestly want him back.

I climb into my shabby rental car and go back to my shabby motel. The couple next door is getting it on like a pair of wild baboons, shouting and screaming and making the bed thump so hard the wall vibrates. Jeez, they need a tranquilizer. When was the last time I had hot, wild, mind-blowing sex? Pretty much never. Owen and I got close to that a few times. What if the years I spent with him were the last good thing I'll ever have? No, I am not the kind of woman who gives up on happiness.

Lying in bed, staring up at the ceiling, I can't stop thinking about what Owen and Poppy are doing. Fucking like crazed animals? No, they probably give each other hot-oil massages and screw like virgins who don't know what the hell they're doing. I toss and turn for hours while obsessing over those two. And when I finally fall asleep, I dream about throwing pies in Little Miss Poppy's face. Jeez, even my dreams have turned childish and bitchy. I wake up at three a.m. feeling tired and annoyed, but I know exactly how to cure myself of that.

I go straight to Owen's hotel, marching past the reception desk, ignoring the clerk's desperate shouts that I should stop. He catches up to me at the elevator, breathing hard.

"Mr. Metzger isn't in the suite anymore," the attractive young man tells me. "He checked out last night."

"Where did my husband go?"

"I have no idea." He grimaces. "But you aren't a guest, and you don't know anyone who is. That means you can't be here. I'm sorry, ma'am."

Did he just call me "ma'am"? I'm much too hot to be called that. "Thank you, sweetie. I won't cause you any more trouble."

Then I march out of the building. If Owen thinks changing hotels will stop me, he really doesn't know me at all. It's time to level up my efforts and become the badass ex-wife I've been pretending to be. How can I do that?

Step one, find out where Owen is hiding now.

Step two, crash the party.

Step three, show that Flower Girl who's the real woman in the room.

I drive back to my low-rent motel and change into my secret weapon, an outfit designed to drive men so crazy that they'll do anything I want. I'd spent too much money on buying that ensemble, but it's worth the price. I know what Owen likes, and his simpering little angel won't stand a chance.

Maybe I sort of admire Poppy. She's clearly a strong woman, running a business on her own and standing up to me. But girl power won't sway me. It's time for the real woman to lay down the law. How many metaphors am I mangling? I've lost count.

Time to blow away the competition.

Chapter Fourteen

Poppy

THOUGH I WOKE UP A WHILE AGO, I HADN'T WANTED TO disturb Owen or get out of bed just yet. So, I've been lying here on my side, facing him, watching Owen sleep. His lips are curled into a slight smile as if he's dreaming about something that makes him feel contented and relaxed. After his encounter with Naomi last night, I expected him to be tense or even upset. But he smiled during the entire drive back to my little flat above the bookshop, and he insisted on carrying me upstairs though I'm quite capable of walking under my own power.

I love that he does barmy things like that. It's romantic.

Owen stirs, moaning softly, but doesn't open his eyes.

Will he ever wake up? I need to get up and get dressed so I can start my day. A bookshop doesn't run itself. As much as I love to watch him sleeping, it's time to rouse the romance novelist.

"Wake up, Owen."

He stirs again and mumbles something that does not sound like words.

I give him a gentle shake. "Time to wake up, Owen."

The stubborn man peels his lids open, then squeezes them shut and moans. He mumbles what sounds like "five more minutes," but it's hard to tell for sure.

Time for tough love.

I roll onto my back and suck in a big breath to shout, "Wake up, Owen Metzger!"

"Ah!" He bolts upright, glancing around with wide eyes as if he expects the room to burst into flames. Once he realizes that won't happen, he aims a halfhearted scowl at me. "What the hell, Poppy? You almost gave me a heart attack."

"You were virtually comatose. Extreme measures were required."

"Oh, there will be payback for this."

"What sort of revenge are you devising?"

"This kind." He turns around to hover over me on his hands and knees, then gradually lowers his body onto mine. "There's no better way to start the morning."

"How is this payback? I want you to fuck me."

"Revenge isn't really my thing. I'd much rather make you come for me."

"That sounds wonderful." I glance at the clock and wince, having suddenly remembered the reason I woke him in the first place. "But we can't. I need to get ready for work."

He buries his face against my neck and moans pitifully. Then he rolls off me to lie on his back. "If Naomi hadn't begged me to meet with her last night, we could've had sex instead of falling asleep the second we crawled into bed."

"Let's not talk about her. Please."

"Right. She who shall not be named will not be discussed either."

Since we don't have time to shag, we rise and shine and begin our day. Owen helps me open up the shop, but then he informs me that has a "secret mission" to complete this morning. He kisses me goodbye and ambles out of the shop, casting me a secretive smile. I offered to let him drive my car, but he feigned extreme horror at the prospect, like a character in a silent film, just to make me laugh. He is utterly adorable.

A taxi had picked him up.

Now, I'm alone in my shop until a customer arrives. No one turns up until nearly ten thirty. Then, it's only one chap who is looking for historical fiction. He doesn't want my advice on which books to read, and he becomes a bit grumpy when he realizes I will be standing behind the counter while he searches the shelves. Finally, he leaves—without buying anything.

Yes, this is the life of a bookshop proprietor.

At noon, Owen returns.

I rush out from behind the counter and fling myself at him. Why bother restraining my joy? I've always believed I should remain calm and professional, even when I'm having dinner with a bloke. But that's complete rubbish. I've realized that ever since I met Owen. A woman should never feel ashamed of wanting to express her joy by throwing her entire body at a man and showering his face with kisses.

He pats my back. "Guess you're glad to see me, huh?"

"I'm happy as a pig in muck."

Laughter splutters out of him. "Is that a good thing?"

"Yes. It means I'm so bloody happy to see you."

"Well, in that case, I'm happy as a clam." He sets me down on my feet, which had been dangling above the floor. "You need to teach all the British sayings. They're so dang cute, but not as cute as you."

I glance around the empty shop. "Business has been nonexistent today."

"Maybe this will cheer you up." He snatches up a sack that had been sitting on the floor beside him. Now, he whips out an item and holds it between us. "This is for you, Poppy. Just because."

I accept the bouquet of flowers and thrust my nose into them to inhale the scents. "Mm, I love flowers. This bundle has roses, daisies, and... Are these poppies?"

"Yep. That seemed like your flower."

"No one has ever given me poppies before. No one has given me flowers, full stop." I hop up on my toes to kiss him. "Thank you, Owen. This is the sweetest gift."

He shakes his head. "The sweetest gift in the world is you."

"No need to go overboard with the compliments. You might begin to sound like a sappy romance film."

"Right. I need to maintain my manly attitude." He reaches into his sack again and brings out another item. It's a stack of papers held together with a paperclip. "I wrote this for you. It's only the first two chapters, but I want to turn it into a novel."

"About what? Cowboys? I remember you had an idea for a story like that."

He thrusts the papers at me. "Just take this and read it. If you hate it, you can tell me so. I've never written a story that was inspired by a woman I'm dating, but you have become my muse."

I take the sheaf of papers and read the title page. "*Love in the Bookshop?*"

"Yeah, I'll come up with a better title later." He averts his gaze and scratches his cheek. "Read it when I'm not around. Okay?"

"If that's what you want. I'm looking forward to reading these chapters." I kiss him again, this time with far more passion. "I'm honored that I could inspire your writing."

"Might change your mind once you read it."

Oh, I doubt that. But Owen is clearly anxious about how I might react, so I won't say anything more until I've read these pages. I trot over to the counter and set the paperclipped pages on the shelve underneath where no one will see it. Then I return to Owen.

"Might as well go out for lunch," I say. "Doesn't seem as if I'll have any customers for a while."

"Have you tried advertising?"

"Yes, but that's expensive and I would need to keep the adverts running on a regular basis. I gave up on that."

"Hmm." He surveys the shop as if he means to devise a solution to my problem. But even Owen can't make people visit my shop. "I might have a few ideas. Let me think about it."

"You don't need to try to help me improve my business. It isn't your problem."

"We're a couple, aren't we?"

I feel my brows tighten. His question seems to have come out of nowhere. "Yes, I would say we are."

He grins. "I love it when you're confused. It's adorable."

"Did you ask me that question strictly to confuse me?"

"No. That was a happy accident." He clasps my hand. "We're a couple, and that means we help each other. Right?"

"I would say so. That's how a relationship should be, though I'd never experienced that until I met you."

He squeezes my hand. "I want to help you, so please let me think about it. I promise not to bulldoze my way into taking over your shop."

"Of course you wouldn't do that." I sigh. "Go on, think about it. If you can come up with a solution to save my shop, I will be eternally grateful."

He lifts my hand to kiss it. "May I buy you lunch?"

"That would be lovely."

Owen insists on paying for my meal, including dessert, and he also insists on taking me to a restaurant that's out of my budget though hardly five-star quality. Still, the food is excellent. We enjoy a very nice wine as well. I've never been to a restaurant of this caliber before. Owen assures me that he can afford it, especially since the MacTaggarts paid for his travel expenses. The first time he mentioned that arrangement, he had seemed somewhat uncomfortable talking about it. Now, he doesn't care at all.

When we return to the shop, Owen offers to dust and straighten the shelves.

"You are not an employee," I say. "This is meant to be a holiday for you, not welfare for a struggling bookshop."

"I want to help you. And I have an ulterior motive." He whispers into my ear, "When you see me dusting and sweeping up, it'll get you so hot for me that you won't be able to stop yourself from ripping my clothes off and yours too."

"Only if the shop is closed. I'm not an exhibitionist."

"I bet you're wilder than you think."

He may be right about that. Being with Owen has awakened something in me that I never knew was there. I do feel wilder when I'm with him, and I absolutely lust for that man with a hunger that defies reason. Who gives a toss about being reasonable and rational anymore? I certainly don't.

Strangely, he was right. I don't know if it happens because he told me it would or if watching him do manual labor actually does make me randier than ever. Though I struggle to focus on browsing a catalog of upcoming books, so I can order some for the shop, my attention keeps wandering to Owen. First, he removes jacket and begins to sweep the floor. The task requires him to use his arms, which makes his biceps flex and stretch his shirt. Every time he leans forward to push the broom across the floor, his arse muscles flex and cause the denim of his jeans to stretch in the same manner as his shirt had done.

Has it gotten warm in here? Perhaps I need to turn the thermostat down.

But I can't tear my gaze away from Owen. He's begun to sweat, and droplets roll down his temples. He unbuttons his shirt rather more slowly than seems necessary, then removes it and tosses the garment onto a nearby table. He picks up a folded brochure map and fans himself with it. I can see the outlines of his chest muscles, and his arms are now on full display thanks to the fact his undershirt is a tank top.

I hurry to the thermostat and lower the temperature.

At last, he finishes sweeping the floor. Observing while he dusts the shelves won't get me aroused, surely.

Owen abandons his shirt, leaving it draped over the table, and picks up the feather duster. With swift, precise movements, he flicks the duster back and forth, beginning with the top shelf and making his way toward the lower ones. He bends his knees slightly deeper with every shelf he attends to, and that motion once again tightens his arse muscles. Good heavens, that man has the finest bum I've ever seen. Even with his jeans on, the sight of his derrière gets me outrageously randy.

I grab a cold bottle of water from the little fridge behind the counter and swig several large mouthfuls.

Two elderly women enter the shop. One woman notices the gorgeous man dusting the shelves and whispers to her friend. Both of them gawp at Owen while speaking to each other too softly for me to hear, and I'm sure Owen can't hear them either. They point at his arse and their lips form "O" shapes. Yes, that man is worthy of O's and oohs, and ahs too.

The ladies approach the counter, and one leans forward to ask a question in a hushed voice. "Do you have any romance novels with men like that in them?"

"I have a good selection of romance. If you're wanting the steamy sort—"

"Oh, yes, the steamier the better."

"Follow me."

Chapter Fifteen

Owen

I CAN'T HELP GLANCING OVER MY SHOULDER TO SEE WHAT Poppy's doing with those senior citizens. She must be taking them to a shelf of cozy mysteries or something. But no, she leads them straight to the display she had set up yesterday, which features the works of Desiree Lachance. My books. Those don't seem suitable for elderly ladies.

Poppy gestures toward the books on the table. "I think you'll enjoy this author's works."

All the covers feature half-naked men. Surely those sweet little old ladies will blush and hurry over to the shelf of crossword puzzles.

But no, the women begin sorting through the romance novels while commenting on the physiques of the male models on the covers. One woman says she'd love to "canoodle" with the bare-chested man on a certain cover, and her friend says "right you are," then adds that she'd love to see the "John Thomas" on that "geezer." But that model isn't old. Brits must use the word geezer in a different way. I have no clue what "John Thomas" is supposed to mean.

The sweet, cheerful, lustful ladies purchase five Desiree Lachance books, though they have no idea a man wrote all the torrid scenes they will be enjoying. I guess I had a stereotype stuck in my head, one that told me nobody over sixty gets it on or has any sexual desire. Not that I ever thought much about the sexual fantasies of the baby-boomer set. Maybe I need to write a romance novel about septuagenarians at one of those communities for older people. Or better yet, seniors at a Caribbean resort. I've always wanted to visit a tropical island.

Once those ladies are done shopping, it's time to close up for the night. I'm still shirtless, but I stayed that way mostly so Poppy would keep ogling me. She seems like she can't do anything except stare at my sweat-soaked chest while I amble up to her and casually wipe my face dry with my shirt. I use it to dry the back of my neck too, tipping my head side to side because I love the lustful look on her face.

I can honestly say I'd never been ogled by sweet, elderly, sex-obsessed women before. That means it's time I asked Poppy about those weird terms the ladies used.

"The phrase John Thomas refers to a man's penis," she informs me. "And a geezer is simply a man."

"What about 'canoodling'?"

"I'd love to do that with you, for starters." She leans that sexy body into me, tilting her head back to meet my gaze. "It means to kiss. But I want more than a bit of canoodling right now."

"Don't you want to salivate over those cover models? I'm nowhere near as ripped as they are."

"I love your body best. And I don't need a book. I have my own steamy, muscular romance hero standing right here."

As I rest my ass on the table's edge, my legs naturally spread apart just enough that her focus is drawn to my groin. I'm sure she can tell I've gotten turned on. The bulge of my dick has gotten bigger. "You okay, Poppy?"

"What? Oh, yes, of course I am."

Her breathless tone doesn't mesh with her statement. The hot bookshop owner is not okay. She's horny as hell. And she can't stop staring at my dick, despite the fact Poppy can't actually see it, only the lump it creates. We've seen each other completely naked and had sex twice, but she acts like this is the first time she has ever gotten a good look at my body.

"If you keep staring at my dick, you know what will happen."

She licks her lips. "Yes, and I want that."

"Right here? Right now?"

Poppy nods slowly, and her gaze lifts to my face. "Fuck me in the bookshop, Owen."

I pat the table I'm sitting on, the one that holds a pile of Desiree Lachance books. "Think this table can handle it?"

"Shall we find out?"

"Hell yeah." I slide off the table and sweep all the books off it. They tumble to the floor, some falling open, and a few scatter halfway across the aisle. "I'll pay for any damages, but it'll be worth it."

Poppy glances at the picture window and bites down on both her lips. A sweet little wrinkle forms between her brows.

"Would you rather we do this upstairs?" I ask. "If you're worried about somebody seeing us."

Her brows smooth out, and a wicked smile curves her lips. "I don't give a toss if someone sees us."

"All righty." I unzip my jeans and pull out my dick. "Let's do it."

Poppy shimmies out of her panties and flings them onto the table behind her. Then she hurries up to me and flips around to set her shapely bottom on the table I'd cleared. "Please tell me you have a condom."

I whip one out of my pocket. "Always prepared."

She snatches the packet away. "I'll do this for you."

"Okay." Is that a wise decision? Probably not. But even if I should get so excited that I come before I'm even inside her, I'll make sure Poppy feels all the pleasure she deserves.

She tears the condom packet open with her teeth.

Yeah, my dick throbs when she does that. Mild-mannered bookshop owner? No way. Poppy Goodburn is the hottest woman on earth.

She crooks her finger. "Come closer, Owen."

I shuffle toward her, drawn in by her sultry tone and the irresistible appeal of the woman who wants to me to fuck her in front of the picture window. Poppy spreads her thighs and hooks a finger inside my waistband, tugging me even closer. While I struggle to breathe normally, she rolls the condom over my erection so slowly that my ears start to ring because I'm not pulling in enough oxygen.

Once she's done covering me, she hikes up her skirt. "Fuck me, Owen."

Every time she speaks in that husky tone, I get instant amnesia. My brain wants me to keep staring at her exposed flesh, the slick folds that glisten with her cream and the silky hairs on her mound. My breathing has gotten so heavy that I know I can't wait any longer. But I need to taste her again first. So, I push her thighs wider apart and kneel before her.

Poppy plunges her fingers into my hair, her eyes drifting half-closed.

With two fingers, I separate her folds. Then I bury my face between her thighs and scrape my tongue along her cleft, up one side, then the other, devouring the flavor of her with every swipe of my tongue. She gasps and grips my head tighter. I seal my lips around her clit and suckle it, while I drag two fingers up and down her folds.

"Owen, yes," she breathes. "Please don't stop."

I keep teasing her with my fingers and my mouth until I feel that she's on the edge, ready to tumble off that cliff if I just keep going for a few seconds more.

But I stop and lift my head.

Poppy's tits are heaving, and she grips the table's edge hard.

I never leave a woman hanging. Surging to my feet, I grasp her hips and thrust into her deeply, holding that position for long enough that she grips my biceps and makes desperate, hungry little noises. I wrap my arms around her and start pumping. Our faces hover so near each other that my lips graze hers every time I pull out and thrust in again.

The table begins to quiver. Poppy cries out and locks her legs around my hips while I fuck her faster, diving in deeper, and seal my mouth over hers, plunging my tongue deep to consume her completely. She makes hungry grunting noises while our tongues tangle and the table thumps across the floor. I lower her onto the surface with her ass hanging partway over the edge and keep going, taking her body with abandon while the liquid sucking sound created by our bodies echoes inside the shop.

She throws her head back, severing our kiss. "Owen, yes."

The table creaks and thumps and seems like it might crack apart any second. In the back of my mind, a small part of me realizes Poppy might get hurt if that happens. I lift her off the table, hugging her body to mine without pulling out of her body, and stagger toward the nearest upright surface.

The picture window.

Her back smacks into the glass, and I keep thrusting. She bounces on my cock, crying out, clearly on the verge of coming. I'm so damn close to going off that I can't stop myself. The need takes control, and I can't think at all anymore. I pound into her again and again, snarling like a wild animal, and pump my hips faster and faster.

Poppy freezes, her entire body rigid. Her mouth falls open on a silent cry. Then her head snaps forward, and her inner muscles clamp down on my cock in pulsating waves. Those movements push me over the edge as electric shocks crackle down my spine and straight into my dick, and I grit my teeth hard. Half-strangled shouts explode out of me while I spend myself deep inside her body.

After two more thrusts, I sag against her. My head falls onto her shoulder. "Damn, Poppy. You're the hottest bookshop owner on earth."

She laughs, but it's a breathy sound as if she's still dazed.

I nuzzle her cheek. "I thought naughty librarians would be the hottest thing ever, but I was wrong. Bookshop girls are the absolute hottest."

"Mm, I think men who write romance novels are the steamiest of all."

"Better move away from the window before somebody sees us." I unwind her legs from my hips and set her on her feet. "How can we ever top this?"

"Oh, I'm positive we can. But not tonight. I'm knackered."

I think that means she's tired. I am too, so I don't argue about going upstairs to sleep. We undress and curl up together in the nude, simply because we love feeling each other's skin. I can still smell the scent of her cream, but oddly, that puts me to sleep faster. Of course, I dream about Poppy—naked, writhing beneath me, gasping my name. I've completely forgotten about Naomi and that wacky club for meddling. Nothing matters except being with Poppy.

We have breakfast in the little living room that's right next to the little open kitchen in her apartment. I have an idea that might help her business, but I'm not sure how she'll react. It might seem to her like I want to take over her bookshop, but that's not my intent. While we eat, I try to think of the best way to present my idea.

"Poppy, I want to talk to you about something. I've been thinking about the bookshop and how you aren't getting enough customers."

"You don't need to save my business, Owen. I'll survive one way or another."

"Would you listen to my idea? Afterward, if you don't like it, I won't ever mention it again. Okay?"

She nods. The mouthful of scrambled eggs she's eating prevents her from speaking.

Time to go for it. "I want to use my books to bring customers into the shop. I might not be a celebrity like Nora Roberts or E.L. James, but I have a lot of fans. A live book signing with Desiree Lachance could bring in a good amount of business."

She drops her fork and blinks rapidly. "Are you saying you want everyone to know you are Desiree Lachance?"

"Yeah. I think it's time to come out of the writer's closet."

"What if your fans abandon you when they find out you are a man?"

I shrug. "I don't think they'll do that. My fans have speculated about who Desiree Lachance really is, and a lot of them already believe a man actually writes those books. Maintaining a secret identity is hard work."

"Owen, it's so sweet of you to offer to do this for my shop. But you should think about it for a while before you commit to outing yourself."

She's right, I know. But my need to help her grows stronger every day.

Poppy's cell phone rings. She glances at the screen, then answers. "Dominic? What is it?" Her face tightens into a pinched expression. "I see. Thank you for letting me know."

She ends the call.

"What's wrong?" I ask.

"Nothing. Dominic rang to warn me that the American Wives Club has voted to meddle in our lives—beginning today."

Chapter Sixteen

Poppy

I FEEL THE WAY OWEN LOOKS—CONFUSED, SLIGHTLY AN-noyed, but mostly worried about what those women and men are plotting. I don't need anyone to meddle in my life. Owen and I are already a couple and quite happy together, though we do still have one critical hurdle ahead of us. He lives in America, and I live in England. A writer can do his work any-where. My shop is a physical location that I can't simply pick up and move to another country.

But I care about Owen. I care a great deal.

A little voice in my head whispers that I've only known him for less than a week, but I'm bloody sick of listening to every ir-ritating voice in my mind. Owen makes me feel so good, and I've never been happier than I am with him. Dominic knows this. He must have told his mates that too. Why, then, are they plotting to meddle in my love life? I see no reason for it.

Unless…Naomi has done something.

"Poppy, are you okay?"

I suddenly realize I've been staring down at my nearly empty plate of food and raise my head. "What? Yes, I'm fine. Just worried about what the American Wives Club is plotting."

"Seems like it must have something to do with Naomi."

"I agree. Not knowing what might be about to happen is sheer torture."

He puckers his lips slightly and taps one fingernail on the countertop. "Maybe I should call Munro and see what he knows about this."

"Oh, you don't need to do that. We'll find out soon enough."

"But you are anxious." He pulls his mobile out of his jeans pocket. "I'm calling Munro."

He dials the number and waits. And waits. And waits. Then he sighs. "Hey, Munro, it's Owen. Please call me when you get this message. It's important."

Owen sets his mobile on the counter. "Sorry. He didn't answer."

"Yes, I heard. But he will call you back, won't he?"

"Maybe. Munro is new to the world of cell phones."

I must look surprised because I am. "How could that be? I thought Munro was a relatively young man, in his thirties or forties."

"Forties, yeah. But he's been a bit of a Luddite for a long time. Munro only got a cell phone after he met Natalie, who teased him about not having one already."

"Oh, I see." I lean toward him. "Does Munro realize that you have to check your voice mail?"

He shrugs. "Who knows."

"Maybe I should ring Dominic and insist he explain what his cryptic warning meant."

Owen hops off his stool. "Why don't you do that while I open up the shop for you? If you trust me to do that."

"You know I do. Thank you, Owen."

"No problem."

While he goes downstairs, I grab my mobile and try to get in touch with Dominic, but I only get his voice mail. So, I ring Chelsea instead. She does answer.

"Hi, Poppy, what's up?"

"Dominic told me the American Wives Club are up to something. Do you have any idea what that means?"

"Um… Not sure I should say."

"You do know, don't you?"

Chelsea clears her throat. "It won't be horrible, I promise."

"That isn't terribly comforting."

"Don't worry. Anything we do will be strictly to help you and Owen and Naomi."

Why should anyone care about helping that woman? She has done nothing but cause trouble. Then again, if they want to meddle in Naomi's life and find a suitor for her, that would be brilliant. She wouldn't harass me or Owen anymore. But who would want to date such an abrasive woman? I doubt they could find someone quickly.

Since Chelsea won't give me any details, I say goodbye to her and go downstairs to see how Owen is doing. This is the first time I've ever let anyone open the shop for me, but I didn't even hesitate when Owen offered to do just that. And I was right to trust him. As I step off the last stair and detour around the counter, I can see that the sign on the door has been switched to the "open" side. I also note that he has returned the copies of his books to the table where they had previously been, arranging them in precisely the order they'd been in before. No one will ever realize we shagged on that table.

"Any customers yet?" I ask. Then I answer my own question. "No, there wouldn't be. We've only just opened."

He pulls me close and kisses me. "Things will get better. Especially if I hold a real-name reveal in this shop."

"Please wait a while and think hard about the consequences before you do that."

"What are you afraid of? It's not like I'll be arrested for writing under a false name."

"I know. But you're doing that for me. What if we break up later and you regret having outed yourself?" I fist my hands in his shirt, gazing straight into his eyes. "Please, Owen, wait a while."

"All right. I'll do anything for you."

Warmth blossoms in my chest, soft and sweet, while my cheeks warm too. No one has ever said to me the sorts of things Owen does.

He surveys the shop visually while still holding me in his arms. Then he twists his mouth into an odd expression that seems to indicate he's thinking. Suddenly, he smiles and slaps my arse. "Got an even better idea."

I pretend to be suspicious. "Do I want to know?"

"Yes, you do." His smile turns a touch smug. "Instead of me announcing that I'm Desiree Lachance, I can sign a bunch of copies of my books. You can then advertise the fact that you've got signed copies for sale. And you can also promote a giveaway."

"What will the prizes be?"

"Signed copies of my upcoming book that hasn't released yet."

"That is a wonderful idea. I'll need to order more copies."

"You can't get pre-release copies yet. I'll handle that." He gives me a squeeze. "Consider it a donation."

Owen won't let me pay for the books, of that I'm certain. He wants to help, and I can't say no when he's so earnest about doing that. So, I agree. He grins when I tell him that and immediately gets on his mobile to order the books. Fortunately, the distributor he works with has a facility here in the UK which means he can get the books quickly.

After that, he insists on staying with me in the shop. No matter how strenuously I encourage him to explore the city, since this is his holiday, he refuses to leave. Even when I tell him that I can't close the shop for lunch today, he still won't leave—except to jog across the street a little fish and chips shop and bring food back to me. I give in and eat with Owen, then let him hang about in the bookshop, browsing the shelves while he straightens them. I had asked him for recommendations for romance novels I could stock, in addition to his, and he gave me a two-page list. It includes everything from sweet to steamy, and historical to paranormal, and all the varieties in between.

I finally have some customers in the late afternoon, and they actually buy books. Owen is sitting in the corner, on a chair he dragged down from upstairs, reading *The Day of the Triffids*. He seems genuinely engrossed in the story.

When the customers leave, he approaches the sales counter, leaning against it while he smiles at me with a sparkle in his eyes. That means he believes he has a brilliant idea. "You've got paperbacks and hardcover books, but you're missing one very important format."

"Board books?"

"No. You already have some of those."

"What, then?"

He taps his hear. "Audiobooks."

"This is a *book* store, the sort where people purchase actual books and read them."

"Are you a snob about audiobooks? They're super popular these days and are the only segment of the publishing industry that has seen consistent double-digit growth year-over-year."

I must be gawping at him because Owen has stunned me. I shouldn't be surprised that he can quote industry statistics, but I'd never met an indie author until Owen walked into my shop. Maybe all of those kinds of authors have in-depth knowledge of the publishing industry. But I have a suspicion that most don't. When I ask Owen about that, he chuckles.

"No, most writers don't take the time to learn about the industry. They want to be artistes, not run a business."

"Surely a write can be both."

"Yeah, we can. But it's damn hard work and not at all glamorous."

I'd already known that Owen was an unusual man, but now I realize he is truly the cleverest, most determined, and hardest-working man I've ever known.

"So," Owen says slowly, "what do you think about audiobooks?"

"I would be willing to give it a go. But where would I shelve those? My shop is already stuffed to the gills."

"Hmm. Let me think on that."

Every time Owen says that, I know he's about to come up with a big idea. I hope he doesn't go overboard again, like he had with his idea to reveal the true identity of Desiree Lachance. But I'm grateful to Owen for wanting to come up with a plan to resurrect my dying bookshop. I just don't know if anything is going to change the fact that my business is gradually sinking toward the bottom of the ocean. Once it hits the seafloor, I'm done.

At the end of the day, I flip the door sign to "closed" and move around the shop switching off each light one by one. Owen waits for me at the sales counter.

"Shall we have dinner here?" I ask. "Or would you like to go out?"

He rests his elbow on the counter and rubs his chin. "That's a tough decision. Is there someplace nearby, besides the fish and chips joint, where we could have a decent meal?"

"There's a candy shop. That's all."

"Could we order pizza?"

"Yes. There is a good pizzeria several blocks away, and they do offer delivery."

"Perfect. Now we just have to argue about which toppings to put on the pizza."

Out of the corner of my eye, I notice a figure has approached the glass door of the shop. I instinctively turn in that direction—and my brows shoot up.

"That looks like Dominic." Owen says. "Is he a peeping tom?"

"Of course not." I race to the door and unlock it to let Dom come inside. As I shut the door behind him, I ask, "What are you doing here at this hour?"

"Have you two eaten yet? If not, you should come to ours for dinner. Chelsea and I would love to get know your new mate."

Dominic rolls his eyes toward Owen without actually looking at him.

"I assume you mean my boyfriend." I glance at Owen. "Would you be comfortable with having dinner at Dominic and Chelsea's house?"

"Sure. Sounds like fun." Owen smirks at Dom. "How about a wrestling match in your living room first? You know, to work up an appetite. You seem to like showing off your muscles."

Dom feigns a scowl. "Careful, lover boy. If you annoy me, my mates and I will have you shanghaied to the Arctic Circle."

"Uh-huh. I've been through way worse shit than that."

"He's not joking," I say. "Owen has had truly harrowing experiences. And if you're sweet to him, he might share those stories with you."

"Sweet to him?" Dominic shakes himself in an exaggerated shiver. "That's a horrifying suggestion. I'm married, Pops. My sweetness is for my wife only."

Before either man can utter another syllable of sarcasm, I grab my purse and rush out the door. Dom and Owen hustle out behind me, and I lock up after them. Luckily, Dominic drove his car here, instead of taking a taxi, so we won't need to squeeze ourselves into my "turtle shell on wheels," as my cousin likes to call it.

Will Dominic behave himself? Will Owen?

Dom rests one hand on the wheel as the car rolls down the road. "So, Desiree, do you write BDSM romance?"

"You know about that subgenre?" Owen says. "Didn't think you actually knew how to read. But I guess you asked your wife to spell out BDSM for you. At least you know the alphabet now."

"If you try to turn my sweet cousin into your sex slave and hold her hostage in some sort of torture chamber, I will castrate you."

Oh, bollocks. There's a better chance that the moon is indeed made of cheese than there is that Dom and Owen will stop harassing each other.

Chapter Seventeen

Owen

I MIGHT HAVE SORT OF MAYBE A LITTLE DECIDED THAT Dominic Rigby isn't a total asshat. We guys have our own language that involves verbal harassment as well as the physical type. I'm not the least surprised when Dominic slugs my arm and threatens to take his hands off the wheel "to make the soft American squeal like a little piggy." I can handle that kind of bullshit. In fact, I can give as good as I can take. But his behavior does not mesh with what Poppy keeps telling me about her cousin.

Sweet? No, Dominic is not like that.

Well, okay, maybe I haven't spent much time around the guy. Poppy is the smartest person I've ever met, and I trust her opinions on pretty much everything. Dominic must be a decent guy underneath all the weird British razzing. I watched a British TV comedy series once, and it was totally bizarre. That might explain Dominic's behavior.

Despite his incessant threats to kill me and "dump the body in the woods where animals can gnaw on the carcass," I'm still alive and kicking when Dominic parks the car in the driveway of his house. Once we've all climbed out, I have to ask a question.

"Are you going to lighten up on the death threats yet? It's getting old."

"Can't handle it, eh?"

Poppy steps between us, facing her cousin. "Of course Owen can handle your morbid and rather juvenile humor. But I want him to see the real you. Owen can't get to know you if all you do is threaten him."

"But my mates do the same thing. You should have heard the things Derek Hahn said to Hugh Parrish when they first met."

"I expect you to be the mature one. And besides, 'my mates are all doing it' is a ridiculous excuse." She jabs a finger into his chest. "Would you want your students to see you acting this way?"

He sighs. "No, you're right. It's all in fun, but I see your point. I'm making a bad impression on Desiree."

Poppy flattens her lips and plants her hands on her hips.

Dominic throws his hands up. "Yes, yes, I know. I'm behaving like an arse again. Sorry. Owen, I do not actually want to murder you. In fact, you are the last person I would want to feed to a school of sharks."

"Wow, thanks. I'm flattered. But it's a shiver of sharks, not a school."

"Shiver?" He can barely say that without laughing. "I'll trust the writer to know the proper term, but it sounds ridiculous. Who on earth came up with that term?"

"No idea. But I've always wondered if it was someone who was terrified of sharks. You know, they shiver when they see them."

"That would make sense."

Poppy drums her fingers on her hips. "May we go inside now? I'm starving."

Dominic winces. "Sorry. Let's go inside. Chelsea made dinner while I went to retrieve you two."

"Thank goodness. I thought I'd literally starve if you didn't stop talking. I'm glad you were having a chin wag instead of insulting each other, but I want to eat."

Poppy grasps my hand as we follow Dominic into the house. Wow, I finally get to see where the murder-happy former cricket player lives. His wife rushes up to greet us the second the door shuts. Though she already knows Poppy, she still hugs her like they haven't seen each other in months. Then she turns to me.

Our hostess offers me her hand. "I'm Chelsea, Dominic's wife. And I'm American like you, so I'll be happy to translate when they start spouting British-isms."

"Thanks, I appreciate that. I'm Owen Metzger, by the way. Just in case your husband told you my name is Desiree."

She laughs. "Yeah, Dom and his friends love to rib newcomers, especially if they're American."

"Did your husband tell you what I do for a living?"

"No. He said that would be up to you. If you want to tell me, great. If not, I'm fine with that too."

Hmm, the guy who lifted me off the floor to glower in my face did not blab my secret to his wife. Maybe he is a nice guy after all.

Dominic and Chelsea lead us into the dining room, where we enjoy a good meal and good conversation. When I tell Chelsea that I write romance novels as Desiree Lachance, she doesn't laugh or make the "ugh, romance" face. She wants to know about my books and seems genuinely interested in reading them. Poppy pipes up with a glowing recommendation, though I had no idea she'd read any of my books yet. Maybe she's being supportive and lying so nobody will realize she has no interest in my novels.

No, that's Naomi's influence making me think that way. She only ever tried to read two of my books, and both times, she informed me that I should write something "meaningful" instead of "silly tripe."

Chelsea invites us to spend the night, and her husband agrees we should. Dominic doesn't even vow to toss me out the window while I'm sleeping. Poppy and I share a bed, but we don't have sex. We're guests, and it seems rude to get it on while our hosts are sleeping across the hall from us.

In the morning, we go out onto the patio behind the house to relax in a swing and wait for Dominic and Chelsea to make breakfast. They wouldn't let either of us help, though we offered. I can honestly say that I've changed my mind about Dominic. He's a nice guy.

Poppy leans against me, nestling her head on my shoulder. "You seemed uncomfortable when I told Dom and Chelsea that your books are wonderful."

"I kind of was. You didn't need to pretend you love my books."

"But it's not pretending. I do love your novels." She raises her head to look at me. "I've read two this week and started another one yesterday."

"What? You never told me."

"I had a feeling you would be uncomfortable knowing I'd read them. Naomi convinced you that your writing is rubbish, didn't she?"

"Yeah, but it's not all her fault. I made the choice to believe what she said."

"That's bollocks." Poppy turns her whole body toward me. "Did Naomi make little comments that seemed innocuous but were actually jabs at you?"

"Well, yes. How did you know?"

"I've seen that happen before. My best mate at university dated a boy who made her feel like she wasn't good enough. He made small comments that added up gradually until she believed it was her fault that he didn't love her."

Did I let Naomi do that to me? Not sure. It's hard to look back into your past and see a pattern when you lived through those events. I can't be objective about it. But Poppy can.

"You may be right," I say. "It's hard to remember when the little jabs started and how long that went on. Naomi hated my books, that's all I can remember now. She said the love scenes were the bits everyone skips over. That's bullshit. Readers of steamy romance love those parts."

"Do you love those bits?"

She places her mouth over my ear so her lips tickle my lobes while she speaks in a husky tone. "I adore those bits, Owen. They make me want to shag you anytime, anywhere. If you read me a scene right now, I'd mount you on this swing."

"I love it when you get naughty."

"Do you believe me now when I say I adore your steamy books?"

"Yeah, I do. Poppy Goodburn doesn't lie."

She slumps against the swing, frowning slightly as she stares straight ahead at nothing. "I might not lie, but I'm rubbish at running a bookshop."

"Your shop is amazing, and all your customers love your recommendations. You need to find a way to market your business to more people, that's all." I take her hand, covering it with both of mine. "I had the same problem with my books. I'm no marketing genius, but I've learned enough that I think I can help, if you'll let me. What do you say?"

"I say you're a wonderful man, and I'm grateful for your help. But I don't know if anyone or anything could save my shop."

"Aren't Brits supposed to keep their chins up or something like that?"

Poppy laughs. "I guess we are. I did tell you about how cozy catastrophe stories usually end with the plucky hero surviving."

"See? There's always a silver lining."

The patio doors whisk open, and Chelsea pokes her head out. "Breakfast is served. Hurry, before Dom gobbles it all up."

Poppy hops off the swing. "He still eats like a cricketer, eh?"

"No, he eats like a newlywed."

What on earth does that mean? I won't ask because it's none of my business. Besides, I don't really want to know the answer. It probably involves the two of them doing the nasty.

Damn, thinking about that makes me want to drag Poppy into the bushes and make her scream. In a good way, not a creepy horror movie way.

After breakfast, our hosts drop a bombshell.

"We're all going to Scotland," Chelsea says. "The travel plans are already in motion."

"Yes," Dominic agrees. "A trip to the Highlands will be a cracking holiday."

Poppy smiles politely. "Oh, that's nice, Dom. You and Chelsea deserve a real honeymoon, one that doesn't involve attending a cricket match."

"You misunderstood, Pops. You and Owen are going with us."

"What? No, I can't take time off. My shop will crumble if I shut it down for even a few days."

"I can't go either," I say. "My vacation is only for two weeks, and it sounds like you guys want us to stay in Scotland indefinitely."

Dominic lifts his brows. "Did I give you the impression this was optional? Sorry. I should have been more clear." He leans forward and narrows his gaze. "This is mandatory."

"You are ordering me to go on vacation in Scotland? I'm not your wife, so you can't command me to do anything. And Poppy can't leave her shop, which means I'm not leaving London."

He leans back in his chair, folds his arms over his chest, and shakes his head. "I told you, Owen. This is mandatory—for you and for Poppy. You're coming with us whether you like it or not."

"I know you and your buddies kidnapped that Lord whoever guy, but I'm an American citizen. My country will kick your asses if you abduct me."

Dominic smiles with wicked glee. "This is for your own good. Can't have you dragging my sweet cousin through the muck while you and your ex-wife bicker."

Poppy jumps up, and her chair topples over backward. "This is sheer bollocks, Dom. No one is kidnapping anyone, and Owen and I are staying here in London."

"Take it easy, sweetie," Chelsea says. "If you're worried about the shop, we've got that covered."

"How?"

"A substitute will fill in for you. He's highly qualified and almost as knowledgeable about books as you are."

Poppy squints at Chelsea. "Who is this bookshop genius?"

"Kendall."

My girlfriend's jaw drops. She gapes at Chelsea but seems incapable of speaking, even to yell at her friend.

I clear my throat to get everyone's attention. "Who is Kendall?"

"The butler at Sommerleigh House," Dominic says. "That's the home of Lord and Lady Sommerleigh, also known as Hugh Parrish and his wife Avery."

"A butler is an expert on books?"

"He has an undergraduate degree in literature and a master's in library science. Kendall worked at a library for several years before he went to work for the Parrishes."

Poppy smacks her palms down on the table. "This is rubbish, Dom. You and your mates are plotting something, and I don't appreciate being included in your meddling nonsense."

"We're doing this because we love you." He smirks at me. "And we've decided we can tolerate Owen in a 'we don't want to murder you anymore' sort of way."

I can't help chuckling a little. "Gee, thanks. That's a really tempting offer, but I think I'll pass on the kidnap vacation. Will we have our mouths duct-taped shut? What about our hands? No, you'll probably use cuffs for that."

"Unless you behave like Hugh did, we won't need to restrain you. Cooperation is required."

I suddenly realize what Dominic said a few minutes ago. "Are you kidnapping Naomi too?"

He smirks again. "Naomi has already been taken care of."

"In what way?"

"You'll see."

Chapter Eighteen

Poppy

DOMINIC AND CHELSEA HAVE LOST THEIR MINDS. KIDNAP-ping? I know they did that to Hugh, but he had been acting like a monumental arsehole back then, trying to break up Callum and Kate. Naomi might be the most annoying woman I have ever met, but I don't believe she sincerely wants to steal Owen away from me. After his meeting with Naomi the other night, we both agreed that she has an ulterior motive. Seducing him into taking her back is nothing more than a distraction, like something a magician might do to stop the audience from seeing how his trick works.

Yes, Naomi is a trickster.

"Sit down, Pops," Dominic says. "Let us explain a bit more."

Owen clasps my hand and gives me a reassuring smile.

And I sit down again. "I thought you hated this barmy plan of theirs."

"I'm not crazy about it. But maybe we should at least let them explain before we storm out of the house with our cloaks of righteous indignation billowing behind us."

My lips tick upward a little bit, though the smile can't quite take root. Only a writer would say something like what Owen just said. It's oddly adorable. So, I sigh and slump in my chair. "All right. Let's hear it."

"Thank you," Dominic says. "First, there will be no kidnapping."

"But you called this a mandatory holiday."

"I didn't phrase that in the best way. Sorry. What I meant was that we are paying for this holiday for you and Owen, and we've made all the arrangements so that your bookshop will not wither away. We've also ensured that you and Owen will have plenty of time alone to continue getting to know each other."

"And Naomi?"

"She will be there too, but we have plans for her. Trust me, Naomi will not ruin your holiday in Scotland."

Owen stares at Dom with a skeptical expression. "You still haven't said exactly what you will do with my ex-wife. I might not want to be with her anymore, but I don't want her locked up in a dungeon or something."

"There is no dungeon where you're going. Naomi will have luxurious accommodations, as will you and Poppy." He glances sideways at Chelsea. "We've assumed that you two will share a room."

"Yes," I say. "We are a couple now, after all."

"And we're very happy about that. The whole gang is."

"Why should all your mates be thrilled that I'm with Owen? They've never met him."

"No, but Chelsea and I vouched for him. Everyone is chuffed to bits that you've finally met a man who appreciates you."

Owen chuckles. "I guess that means you're happy about it, huh? Brits use weird idioms, but it's a treasure trove for a writer."

"I'll ignore that comment for now and not point out how bizarre American idioms are. It's time to lay out your travel plans and what will happen once we all arrive in the Highlands. Are you ready?"

"Yes, Dom, we're listening," I say. "Owen and I understand the English language."

"Speak for yourself," Owen says. "You Brits only kinda sorta speak English."

When Dom opens his mouth to complain about that statement, I hold up a hand to silence him. "Let's move on."

I can tell he wants to sling another insult at Owen, but Dominic heeds my command and moves on with the discussion.

"We'll begin with the logistics of getting there." Dominic glances at his wife. "Chelsea, do you have the map?"

"Oh, no. I forgot to grab it." She hurries into the living room, returning a moment later with a large sheet of rolled-up paper in her hand. She gives it to Dominic. "Here you go. The Dom commands, and I obey."

Owen snorts. "Your wife actually calls you The Dom?"

"Everyone does. It was my nickname back when I was a pro cricketer. They used to say I dominated the field, and I was The Dom for that reason."

"Uh-huh."

I point at the rolled-up paper. "May we get on with the explanations? I assume that thing Chelsea has is part of your plan."

"Absolutely." Dom takes the rolled-up paper from Chelsea and spreads it out on the table. "This is a map of the Scottish Highlands."

"Yes, we can see that."

"The red line shows the route we will take from Inverness to Dùndubhan. That's the medieval castle owned by Rory and Emery MacTaggart. It's now mainly a museum but has recently become a bed-and-breakfast too." He winces. "Of course, they had a rather unfortunate incident there a few months ago."

Chelsea jabs her elbow into Dominic's side. "We agreed not to mention that."

"What happened?" Owen asks. "Did somebody die?"

"No," Dom says slowly. "A guest went missing."

"Seriously? I hope you're not suggesting we should stay there."

"Well, yes, we are. But that incident was a one-off. Dùndubhan has hosted a good number of guests since then with no issues."

I fold my arms on the tabletop and study the map. "No trace was ever found of the missing guest?"

"That's all we know about the incident. Rory and Emery might know more."

Chelsea gives her husband an exasperated look. "Honestly, Dom, we weren't supposed to talk about that. It might scare away Poppy and Owen."

"No, it won't," I announce. "If you want us to stay at Dùndubhan, we have no qualms about that. Do we, Owen?"

"I'm fine with it. Maybe we'll meet a ghost. Of course, the missing guest might just have skipped out on paying their bill."

"That is possible," Chelsea says. "We shouldn't assume the worst."

Perhaps I should feel odd about sleeping in a medieval castle where a guest vanished, but for all anyone knows, that person simply walked away from paying the bill as Owen said. There are any number of rational explanations that don't involve foul play. Besides, Dùndubhan was once a fortress that experienced countless battles. I know that because Hugh Parrish told me. He has been to Dùndub-han many times.

"Does the castle have any ghosts?" Owen asks. "That would be a great thing for a writer to experience."

"I'm not aware of Dùndubhan having ghosts," Dom says. "But you can ask the MacTaggarts about that once we get to Scotland."

"Will Munro be there?"

Dom grins. "This plan was his idea. Of course he'll be there to greet you."

I grin too. "I'll finally get to meet Owen's best mate. I've heard all about him, and I can't wait to get to know the man who did all the wild things Owen told me about."

"They do call him the Wild Man," Owen says. "His own family gave him that nickname. And he proved he deserved that moniker when those jackass criminals laid siege to his cabin."

"Brilliant. I would love to hear Munro's side of the story."

"He loves to talk about it. The grumpy bear has become a local celebrity."

I lean forward to examine the map more closely. "You've forgotten something, Dom. I see the route from Inverness to Dùndubhan, but I don't see the one for how we get to the Highlands in the first place."

"That's because we are not driving the whole way."

"Are we riding on broomsticks?"

Dominic rolls his eyes. "No, you cheeky chit. We're flying on Rory MacTaggart's private jet. A limousine will take us to Heathrow, and from there, we'll be whisked away to Inverness. Another limousine will then ferry us to Dùndubhan."

"Aren't you lot going a bit overboard? This isn't a gigantic reunion of all the MacTaggarts and all our British mates gathered in one place."

He laughs heartily—and so does Chelsea.

"What is so funny?" I squint at Dom. "There's something you haven't told us yet. Spit it out now."

"Can't tell you, pet. It's a surprise."

"At least you can tell me when we're leaving."

"Immediately after breakfast."

My jaw drops. "That's not possible. I have to go home and pack my bags. Owen needs to pick his up too. What's the rush? Surely another day won't matter."

Dominic walks around the table to kneel beside my chair. "Relax, Poppy. This will all work out, and you'll be glad we did the things we're going to do. We had planned to stop at the bookshop anyway, so you could talk to Kendall and reassure yourself that he can handle everything in your absence."

"I don't know…"

"Either you trust us or you don't. But you'll need to decide right now."

Owen claims my hand. "I'm in if you are."

I pull in a deep breath and blow it out. "I'm in too."

Chelsea leaps out of her chair and grins. "That's wonderful! You won't regret this, Poppy."

Oh, bloody hell. What am I getting myself into? I trust Dom, but this event or whatever it is involves more than just him and Chelsea. His group of mates and an entire clan of Scots will be there for whatever mysterious things they have planned.

Dominic rises. "Time to go. Chelsea and I already packed our bags and stowed them in the trunk of the limousine."

"When did you do that? You were making breakfast when we came downstairs."

"The car was hired yesterday by Hugh and Avery. It was scheduled to arrive at nine a.m., and we had time to stow our bags while you and Owen were swinging in the backyard."

"Oh." My goodness, they really have planned every moment of this bizarre excursion. I'm wearing the same clothes as yesterday, and so is Owen. "Let's go, then. We need to change and grab our suitcases."

"No need to hurry. The jet will wait for us."

We wash the dishes, then rush out to the limo where a smartly dressed man is sitting in the driver's seat doing crossword puzzles. Dom knocks on the window. The gent nods and sets his crosswords aside, then starts the engine. Dom opens the door for us, and Chelsea climbs in first, waving for me and Owen to take the seat opposite her. Dominic slides in beside her.

And we're on our way.

Our first stop is the bookshop. Kendall is already there, as promised, waiting for customers to arrive. I've seen Kendall many times, though I never said much to him other than to request a certain drink or ask where the loo was. Sommerleigh House is quite large. I don't even know the man's first name.

Kendall hurries out from behind the counter to greet us. "Mr. Rigby, sir, so glad to see you again. And you as well, Mrs. Rigby. These two must be the guests you mentioned."

I'm not sure "guest" describes our situation, but Kendall is always tactful and polite.

Dominic shakes Kendall's hand. "Good to see you again. Yes, these are the two we told you about. Meet my cousin, Poppy Goodburn, and her beau, Owen Metzger."

We all shake hands, and Kendall gives us the polite, professional smile he always wears at Sommerleigh House.

"I hear you're a trained librarian," I say to Kendall. "And that you have a degree in literature. You'll be in seventh heaven here at my shop. But don't be alarmed if hardly anyone comes in to buy something."

"Yes, ma'am, I've heard sales have been slow of late. I'm terribly sorry to hear that."

"No worries. Nothing stays the same forever. Should I show you around the shop?"

"Lord and Lady Sommerleigh have already done that. They even carried my bags upstairs for me, though I tried to stop them from doing that. It's my job."

I lean in and touch his arm. "For the time being, you are not a butler. You're a bookshop proprietor."

Hugh and Avery have visited my shop occasionally over the past year or so, but I had no idea they knew enough about it to get Kendall up to speed. Still, I trust they know what they're doing. They wouldn't have shown Kendall what to do if they had no clue.

Footsteps on the stairs cause us all to glance in that direction. Hugh and Avery appear, smiling when they see us. After the obligatory hello hugs, we return to the limousine and head for Heathrow. The ride isn't a long one, and soon we're crossing the tarmac and mounting the stairs that lead directly into the jet. I can't deny it is lovely not to have to go through security.

Soon, the jet lifts off.

Owen and I sit on a sofa that lies against one wall of the cabin, with windows behind us. When I twist around to gaze out our window, I can see the city shrinking away from us until, eventually, it disappears altogether. I keep gazing out the window, though, while I wonder what awaits us in Scotland. Scots and Brits and one bloody annoying American woman, that's all I know. The secret part of this forced holiday still makes me a bit uneasy. But a larger part of me has begun to feel rather...excited.

It's completely barmy, but I don't care anymore. This is the most exciting thing I've ever done.

Chapter Nineteen

Owen

I ROTATE MY WHOLE BODY TO FACE POPPY AND REST MY arm on the sofa's back just like she's doing. Stepping onto this jet changed her whole demeanor. She's no longer worried, but excited instead. I can tell that because I've seen her get excited before, though for different reasons. She gets a special glint in her eyes when she wants to get wild with me, whether we're about to fuck or about to be swarmed by wacky Scots. According to the stories Munro told me, his family is the definition of wacky.

Maybe I should have come to Scotland with Munro and Natalie a few months ago when they invited me to hide out at the castle with them. I missed the big siege there, and I didn't get to see Munro scare the shit out of Natalie's ex to make him confess to his crimes. I also missed watching Natalie pick Elliot's pockets to divest him of his weapons.

Instead, I hung out in a safe house that was even more sparsely furnished than Munro's cabin. I'd been too uneasy about leaving America. But that experience eventually led me to England and Poppy, so I can't complain. It'll be great to see Munro and Natalie again and to meet his other relatives.

The story Dominic told us about a guest at the castle vanishing had intrigued me and stimulated my writerly instincts. That might be a mystery I need to solve in real life. Yeah, right, like I'm a police detective. I have zero skills for hunting down a missing person. But the story still fascinates me.

Right now, though, something else fascinates me more.

I run my fingers up and down Poppy's arm. "You're a cloud-lover, hey?"

"Not particularly. But I've never been on a private jet before."

"Yeah, neither have I. Did you see there's a big-screen TV too?"

She smiles and laughs, finally tearing her focus away from the window. "I didn't see that, but it doesn't surprise me. The pilot did say there's a chef on board and a bedroom."

I shake my head and sigh. "I could've had a ride on a swanky jet months ago if I'd accepted Munro's invitation."

"Why didn't you?"

"I'd never been outside the US before. Plus, the siege at Munro's cabin left me reeling for a while after that."

"Can't imagine what that must have been like."

"It was a thrill ride for sure, but the adrenaline rush wore off pretty fast once it was all over." I slide a little closer. "Are you still worried about Kendall running your store? He seemed to have it all in hand."

"Yes, I know. But I've never handed my shop over to someone else before. It's a bit nerve-racking."

"Want some help relaxing? We could join the mile-high club."

She laughs and kisses me. "Not with my cousin and his wife on the plane too."

"But I told you there's a bedroom. It has a door and everything."

"Maybe later. I'm enjoying the clouds right now."

"Okay. You keep doing that."

The flight to Inverness doesn't take as long as I'd thought. I had no idea how far Inverness is from London, but on a map, it looked a lot farther away. When the pilot announces we'll be landing soon, Poppy gets even more excited. She grins like a little girl and kneels on the sofa to stare out the window. Far below, the Scottish country-side flies past us as the jet sinks lower and lower. I can't help myself. I kneel right beside Poppy and curl an arm around her while we both watch the earth seem to rise up beneath us as the jet descends.

Finally, I see the airport.

"Please remain seated while we make our final approach," the pilot announces through the intercom.

That means we're minutes away from touching down at Inverness. I'm in Scotland for the first time ever. It's strange to realize I became friends with a Scotsman without ever leaving America. But now, I'll be surrounded by Highlanders.

I keep my arm around Poppy while the jet taxis down the runway and stops at its designated spot. Then we descend the stairs to set foot on the tarmac. We're in Scotland now. Poppy grins and grabs my hand, dragging me away from the jet like she knows where we're supposed to go. Dominic and Chelsea hurry to get ahead of us. They must know where we're going, and they lead us to the edge of the tarmac where a limousine waits for us.

Once we've all piled into the car, it begins to roll down the road.

"How far is it to that castle?" I ask. "You guys didn't tell us."

"It's about three hours to Loch Fairbairn," Dominic says. "Then it's another half an hour to reach Dùndubhan."

"What kind of a name is Dun-doo-in?"

"It's Scots Gaelic. Don't ask me what it means in English. I've met a few MacTaggarts, but I never asked for a primer on their language." Dominic eyes me with suspicion that I'm sure is pure sarcasm. "Didn't your Scottish best mate force you to learn Gaelic? From what I've heard, the MacTaggarts are devoted disciples of their mother tongue."

"Munro uses the occasional Gaelic word. I asked for translations once in a while, but Munro would snarl and call me an American heathen."

"He sounds like a lovely chap."

"Actually, he is a great guy. You have to get to know him, though, before he'll really talk to you. Munro got used to living alone in the woods."

Our trip to the castle involves multiple stops to get out and stretch our legs. Poppy loves to admire the scenery, so a few times we stop to let her have a look around. I love the scenery too. Wyoming has mountains and rivers, and it's equally as beautiful as Scotland. But the terrain is different here. The mountains are craggy and sharp, unlike the Rockies back home, and the slopes tend to be more spread out. The lochs look deep and dark. When we'd pulled over just outside Inverness to admire Loch Ness, I found myself imagining that the famed monster in this very deep and dark lake might spring up out of the water at any moment.

"I imagined that too," Poppy says after I share my fantasy with her. "Doesn't everyone? Nessie must be the most famous legendary creature in the world."

"She probably is. But I'm more interested in selkies."

Poppy gives me an odd look. We're sitting in the limo right now, barreling down the highway, so Dominic and Chelsea look at me funny too.

"Don't you guys know about selkies?" I ask. "Munro told me about them, but I don't know if his version of what they are matches the real myths. He pretended to be a selkie once to scare a bunch of criminal jackasses."

"You were there when he did that, weren't you?" Poppy says. "Munro tricked them into diving into an underground tunnel."

"No, I wasn't there for the selkie skit, though I was around for the underground tunnel incident. But Munro was with his cousin Errol and Ashley Hartman when he scared the shit out of antiquities thieves."

"He sounds like a fascinating man. I'm looking forward to meeting him."

"Munro is pretty cool if you can see past his grumpy exterior."

When we reach Loch Fairbairn, we pause only long enough to gas up the limo. I want to see more of the village, since I know Munro and Natalie bought a house here and a lot of his relatives live in the little town. But Dominic informs me that we are not sightseeing today, despite the few stops we made so Poppy could admire the scenery.

"Tomorrow, you can explore the area," Dominic say. "Today, everyone is waiting for us at Dùndubhan."

"Can't they wait a little longer so Poppy and I can enjoy the view out the window? If the driver went a little slower—"

"I'm afraid not. The event is already planned and will begin as soon as we arrive." Dominic sighs. "Sorry. This wasn't my idea. Chelsea and I are the messengers and the minders."

"Minders of what?"

"You and Poppy. To make sure you arrive on time."

"What kind of event will we be walking into?"

He smirks. "That is above my pay grade, mate."

Terrific. A mystery event awaits us.

Poppy goes on staring out the window. I roll it down so she can get a clearer view, which means it gets windy inside the limo, but I don't care. Poppy is having so much fun, and that means I'm having just as much fun watching her.

Finally, we turn down a two-track that Dominic says is the driveway to Dùndubhan. The somewhat bumpy road seems to go on and on, though it probably feels that way only because the driver had to slow down to avoid us cracking our teeth because of the potholes. I had the impression, from what Munro told me, that his cousin Rory is rich. Why hasn't the guy ponied up the cash to redo the driveway?

Gradually, the two-track smooths out and becomes gravel. as we approach a metal gate that hangs open. Dominic tells us that he'd been informed ahead of time that the gate would be open and we should drive right through it, and he also says the main gateway will be ready and waiting for us. How many gates does this place have? It's not like an army is going to invade the castle. But if it's partly a museum, I guess they keep everything as close to original as possible.

The dense forest around us limits what we can see as the car rolls down the gravel driveway, but then the trees give way to a large grassy area that seems to surround the castle and its walls. The gray sky above us can't diminish my awe of the structure before us because I have never seen anything like it before. We don't really have castles in America. I wonder how many are still standing in Scotland and how many existed in the past.

My writerly instincts urge me to document everything, but I don't want to do that. This is a time to enjoy everything in the moment.

Poppy leans her head out the window, her eyes wide and her lips parted. When she glances at me, the brilliance of her smile gives me a pang in my chest that I recognize. I felt it once before, back when I'd fallen for Naomi. But this time, the feeling is stronger and based on more than lust. Naomi and I had pretty good sex, but we argued too much because our relationship was difficult. With Poppy, everything feels easier and better. I don't worry about when our next argument might happen. Sure, every couple bickers once in a while, but with this woman, I know those quibbles won't turn into agony.

The driver parks inside the gravel courtyard near the "house," which is apparently how Scots describe a castle that has high stone walls and massive wooden gates. Yeah, that's not how I would de-scribe it. This place was clearly a fortress at one time, and it has other buildings that probably served the army that must have lived here. I don't know much about medieval architecture, but even I recognize the turrets.

Poppy jumps out of the limo and starts racing around the com-pound while still grinning. I catch up to her and grab her hand to slow her down a little. We wander around the courtyard and see another building that currently serves as a garage for a Mercedes and a Jaguar. I wonder what that structure was originally. The garden is the most stunning part of the castle, though. A wall surrounds it on three sides with the fourth side being part of the outer wall. The garden overflows with flowering bushes and vines of many different colors and shapes. Poppy drags me through the whole enclosure and through the little arbor that's covered in vine roses.

She wants to go through the wooden door in the outer wall to see what's out there, but I convince her to delay that excursion. Dominic and Chelsea are standing just outside the inner garden doorway. Poppy is trying to haul me over to a huge bush, but her cousin raises his brows which I'm sure means "get your butt out of there now because everyone is waiting."

I tug her hand. "Think it's time to go, Poppy."

"Oh, but I haven't smelled the roses yet."

Dominic glowers at me, though I don't think he really knows how to seem angry. He strikes me as an easygoing guy. Still, I get the point. We're holding up the festivities.

I throw my arms around Poppy's waist and throw her over my shoulder, marching out the garden door.

Chapter Twenty

Naomi

SOMEONE BANGS ON MY DOOR SO FORCEFULLY THAT IT sounds like the door might explode. I pluck my earbuds out and toss my phone onto the table. Maybe I had been playing my music a little too loud. But what else is there to do in this castle? I'm not a fan of museums, and I don't like walking in the woods, especially not alone. They must have wild animals in Scotland, probably the kind that bite. I imagine they have insects too.

That fist pounds on my door again. "Naomi! Come out here, please!"

How anyone can sound polite and demanding at the same time baffles me. I don't know which MacTaggart is hollering at me, but it hardly matters. I don't appreciate being relocated to Scotland against my wishes.

I amble over to the door and pull it open a few inches. "Is the castle on fire? That's the only reasonable excuse for trying to break down my door with your fist. Who are you, anyway?"

"Pardon me for not introducing myself." He offers me his hand. "I'm Alex Thorne. I do apologize for the caveman-esque method of getting your attention, but you ignored my civilized attempts."

Well, at least they sent a hot guy to kick my door down. Alex has fantastic muscles and gorgeous brown eyes. His British accent turns me on too. Maybe getting kidnapped to the Highlands isn't so bad after all.

"I was listening to music. A steamy song with a pulsing rhythm." I swing the door wide open and rest one hand on the jamb, cocking one hip. "Are you single, Alex?"

"My wife Catriona is out in the courtyard with Munro and Natalie as well as Errol and Ashley."

"Are there any single men on the premises?"

"This is not a spa holiday, pet. It's an intervention. For the moment, it will remain an easygoing event, but if you persist in harassing Owen, this will become a radical intervention."

I inch a little closer to him, putting on my seductress routine out of habit, not because I want to steal him away from his wife. Despite what other people might think, I'm not a man-eater. "Radical intervention? That sounds hot."

He folds his arms over his chest. "That won't work. I'm immune to your charms, which means you're wasting your time. And a radical intervention is not sexy. Just ask Hugh Parrish."

Who the hell is Hugh Parrish? And who are Munro and Natalie? I don't know who Errol and Ashley are either. "What about my husband? Is he here yet?"

"Since you don't have a husband, he can't be on the premises."

"Owen is my husband."

Alex bends his head to stare into my eyes. "You are his ex-wife. Do you have an odd version of dyslexia that makes you forget you're divorced?"

"I take it back. You aren't hot, you're a jackass."

"You haven't called me hot, so you can't take it back." He smiles with saccharine sweetness and pats the top of my head. "Now, behave, pet. You can play in the sandbox later. It's time to greet everyone."

I want to say something snide, but I have no idea how this obnoxious man will react to that. So, I give in and follow him down the hall and out into the courtyard. I'm not blindly rushing after a stranger. My so-called hosts brought me here early this morning and let me wander around the castle compound until they got word that Owen and the Flower Girl would arrive soon. I did have a chaperon trailing me too, so I couldn't poke my nose into anyplace they don't want me to go. Still, I've seen enough to know my way around.

Alex halts behind a limousine.

Hey, why didn't I get one of those? They stuffed me into a crummy old van and made me sit on the floor for three and a half hours. Okay, maybe they offered me a sleeping bag that had nice padding, but I was still essentially on the floor. Owen and his new sweetheart got the top-of-the-line treatment.

Alex cups his hands like a megaphone and shouts, "We're ready now!"

The two people who have been standing in the garden doorway with their backs to us now turn around and step aside. Owen and Poppy walk through the doorway and stop. They talk to the other couple, and Owen seems a touch annoyed. Probably because he noticed me standing here. The other man says something that makes my ex-husband relax and nod. His Flower Girl smiles and nods too.

The four of them head for me and Alex.

I adopt a casual posture like I don't give a hoot if they talk to me or not. Of course I care. I'm getting a flutter in my tummy with a hint of nausea, and my pulse is quickening. I know Owen won't take me back, so why on earth am I trying so hard to make him dump his new girl toy? I've always been pigheaded. I guess that's the reason.

Owen stops a couple of yards away from me. And he's holding Poppy's hand. "Hi, Naomi."

I lift my chin and play the cool bitch. "Hello, Owen. I had no idea you would be here."

"Sure you didn't. Dominic told us his buddies tricked you into getting on a plane and then tricked you into getting into a van for the ride to this castle."

I rake my gaze over the other man, the one who had blocked the garden doorway. "You must be Dominic. Damn, Owen, you never used to have such hot friends. Is this one married like your friend Alex over here?"

"Alex isn't my friend. I've never met him." Owen turns to Dominic. "I still don't get how bringing Naomi here will do anything other than tick me off and cause chaos. Hurricane Naomi loves to do that."

I set my hands on my hips. "When did I become a hurricane? I thought writers tried to avoid hyperbole."

"No writer who ever met you would agree with that statement. Hyperbole is absolutely necessary when we're talking about you."

"Oh, please. You always—"

"Enough!" hollers a loud male voice. The sound echoes off walls of the castle and amplifies it. Everyone has fallen silent except for the figure wending his way through the crowd. I hadn't even noticed when that crowd gathered in the courtyard, too focused on Owen and Poppy to see anything else. Are all those people MacTaggarts? Are there more Brits in the group too? I'll find out soon, I suppose.

The bearded, long-haired man dressed in army-like fatigues, who had shouted that single word, now halts between me and Owen. "I want everyone to haud their wheesht right now."

I put on my best haughty attitude. "Who are you? I mean, other than being a scruffy wannabe tough guy. Didn't anyone tell you a man needs to do more than buy a pair of olive-green pants to become a commando?"

The Scot squints at me, and I can tell he's about to snarl something nasty.

Owen steps between us. "Back off, Munro. Naomi is trying to piss you off because she loves to cause trouble. I'll let you know when it's time to throw her over your shoulder and cart her off to the dungeon."

"There is no dungeon," Alex declares. "Rory doesn't like it when anyone implies there might ever have been one at Dùndubhan. Oddly, he's perfectly fine with nudism on the premises."

The man Owen had called Munro continues to squint at me. This must be Owen's friend.

I think it's time I stirred the pot until it boils over.

Chapter Twenty-One

Poppy

I'VE SEEN THE MYSTERIOUS MUNRO AT LAST, BUT I HAVEN'T had the chance to speak to him. I haven't spoken at all since we left the garden. What can I say? I've met Naomi twice and dislike her intensely, but I can't think of anything I might say that would contribute to the conversation. I want to smack the woman hard, but I'm not the sort who does that.

Munro's nostrils flare. I swear they do. Never in my life have I seen anyone actually do that. I thought it was something straight out of a children's cartoon. But this man has proved me wrong.

He finally tears his steely gaze away from Naomi and holds out his hand to me. "You must be Owen's lass. I'm Munro Mac-Taggart."

"I'm Poppy Goodburn. It's lovely to meet you, Munro."

The Scot pulls me into a brief hug, then throws his arms around Owen and thumps him on the back several times. "*Bod an Donais,* it's about time you found the right lass."

Naomi rolls her eyes. "He had the right woman—a *real* woman—but he didn't know what to do with me."

I bar my arms over my chest and lift my chin. "Owen knows what to do with me. He didn't want you, but no one can blame him for that."

"Oh, please. *I* dumped *him*, Flower Girl. You're the consolation prize."

"Then why hasn't Owen taken you back? You did beg him to do that, after all, which is rather pathetic."

Naomi balls her fists and opens her mouth. But before she can utter one syllable, Owen moves between me and his ex-wife.

"Let's act like adults, okay? Poppy is my girlfriend now, and it's time you accepted that, Naomi. You know damn well our marriage never would've worked long-term, and you're just trying to make trouble because you're jealous and hurt that I don't want to be with you anymore."

Naomi turns her head away.

"Act like a baby, then," Owen tells her. "Poppy and I came here to settle things between the three of us. If you won't cooperate, there's nothing else to say."

Though I hadn't been there at the pub when Owen talked to Naomi, I know from what he told me that she was upset. She tried to brush it off as nothing, but Owen could tell she genuinely wishes she hadn't thrown him over simply because of his chosen career. But he also mentioned that he sensed she was hiding something too. An ulterior motive? If so, neither I nor Owen could figure out what it might be.

How can we uncover the truth? I'm a bookshop owner, not a psychologist. But Owen must be a student of human nature, almost a psychologist, to write the sort of characters that appear in his books. They aren't flat caricatures. They're real people with problems who sometimes get involved in outlandish situations. But somehow, Owen makes even the most unrealistic moments feel completely believable.

Is it any wonder why I love him?

Oh, I can't believe I thought those words. I love him? We've barely known each other for a week. My heart might have pounded briefly when that idea popped into my mind, but I can't accept that it's more than a fleeting thought. Not yet. Perhaps in a few more days or weeks… I don't know. I've lived inside a whirlwind since the day Owen first stepped into my shop.

"Are you okay, Poppy?" Owen asks. "You look sort of dazed."

"Dazed?" I say with a slight laugh. "No, I'm not feeling that way. I'm still recovering from the shock of finding myself inside a medieval castle, that's all."

He must realize I'm telling a porky, but I don't care to speak the truth in the presence of Naomi Hansen.

Owen slides an arm around my waist, pulling me close. But he speaks to his ex-wife. "The three of us need to have a serious talk, but only after you've calmed down and decided to behave like an adult."

"Dinnae worry," Munro says. "We will take good care of the lass. She won't be left alone for a moment."

Was that a threat or a promise of friendship? I can't say for certain since I don't know Munro. When I look up at Owen, he winks. That must mean that Munro and his mates have a plan to…do something.

Naturally, Naomi does not want to cooperate. She lodges one hand on her hip and rolls her eyes. "Oh, yes, I'm terrified by the wannabe commando. He'll probably try to drive me insane with bagpipe music."

Munro leans in close to stare straight into her eyes. He speaks in a menacingly soft voice. "I am no wannabe, unlike you. I served as a commando in the British Army and learned all the ways to sneak into enemy territory and take them out before they even see me. If I can do that, what makes ye think I cannae do that same to you?"

"You don't need to sneak up on me, genius. I'm standing right in front of you."

He smirks. "I should let my wife tell you how we terrified a band of criminals and took them down without laying a finger on the laddies."

Alex, who I had almost forgotten was there, moves out from behind Naomi. "Don't deprive me of the pleasure of showing off my skills to our guest. And I'm sure both Jack and Luke will want to have their turns."

"Oh, aye," Munro agrees. "Everyone will get their turn."

From somewhere in the crowd, an American man shouts, "Don't forget, you've got a certified gypsy here to lend a hand too."

"Thank you, Damian. We are all well aware of your talents." Alex lays a hand on Naomi's shoulder. "Lest you think we have only a handful of skilled grifters on hand, let me disabuse you of that notion. We also have a former MI6 agent, a bounty hunter, three Wiccans, a computer genius, several lawyers, a bodyguard, a former World Cup winning football star, and a former US Marine. Those are only the ones I can recall off the top of my head."

"Don't forget the former cricketer," Dominic says. "If Val Silva gets a mention, I should too. Cricket is far deadlier than football."

Naomi shakes her head. "You just called those morons 'grifters.' That means you're all a bunch of liars who belong in jail. I'm so impressed."

Alex shakes his head. "You are as daft as a bush if you can't comprehend the situation."

"Which is what? You morons think you can scare me? I'm not a bookish little girl who flutters her lashes at every man who walks into her shop."

And of course, she made the word shop sound as if I shag every bloke who wanders into my bookshop. I have gotten a leg over with a man there, but I won't admit that to Naomi. Owen and I had a cracking shag on the table and up against the window. I still can't believe I did that, but I'd love to do it again.

"Ladies," Alex shouts, "come and get your charge. She clearly needs your help. A polite conversation isn't doing the trick."

Several women separate from the crowd and surround Naomi, gently urging the rest of us to back away. I recognize Diana Sangster, a fellow Brit, as well as Avery Parrish. But the others are strangers to me. As these six women lead Naomi into the castle that everyone here calls a "house," I grow more confused.

"Who are those other women?" I ask. "I know Diana and Avery. But are the rest all MacTaggarts?"

"No," Alex replies. "Two are the American wives of MacTaggarts—Piper and Natalie, who married Magnus and Munro, respectively. Then we have two from the gang at the Au Naturel Naturist Resort in Oregon. Those ladies are Heidi, the wife of our resident gypsy, Damian, and Eve, the wife of the aforementioned Val Silva. They own the resort. All of those women are clever and formidable. They'll know how to handle Naomi."

"I don't understand what they mean to do."

"Talk to her." He pats my arm. "Don't worry. If the ladies can't resolve the situation, we have several contingencies."

"What sort of contingencies?"

"If you keep repeating what I say as a question, we will never get the ball rolling. You trust Dominic and Chelsea, and they agree with our plan, so you should trust that. Fair enough?"

Not really. But I suppose I'll get my answers eventually, so I just need to be patient. "Yes, fair enough. Thank you, Alex."

"Good girl."

"What are Owen and I meant to do in the meantime?"

His lips curve into an enigmatic smile as he turns and walks away. Most everyone heads into the castle, leaving me and Owen alone.

"That was rather rude," I say. "They abandoned us."

Owen slides an arm around my waist. "No, they didn't. We still have chaperons."

He points toward the garage.

I swerve my attention in that direction and see two people standing beside the Jaguar I'd noticed earlier. "Is that Munro and his wife?"

"Yep."

"Do you know why they're waving to us?"

"Nope. But I'm guessing they want us to go over there." He starts walking toward the garage while keeping his arm around me as we approach the other couple. "Hey, Wild Man, what's up?"

Munro whispers something to his wife, and she nods.

"Neither of you has been to Scotland before," Natalie says. "Munro and I agreed we should give you a tour of our favorite places."

"That would be wonderful," I say. "Would you like to do that, Owen?"

"Yeah, sounds great."

Munro opens the driver's door of the Jaguar, which seems like an older model since it has a backseat. He reaches inside to fiddle with something. The roof of the car raises and folds itself up and out the way.

"It's a convertible," I say, possibly sounding more excited than a grown woman should. "I've never been in a luxury sports care, much less a convertible. I assume we'll be riding in this car."

Natalie grins. "Of course you will. We can't wait to show you around, and there's no better way to do that than in a convertible with the top down. Luckily, the sun is coming out, so you'll get a great view of everything."

"This is brilliant. Thank you both for doing this."

Munro smiles but does not speak. He spoke earlier, so I know he doesn't have laryngitis. I'm sure he will say something eventually.

Natalie waves for us to climb into the backseat. "Munro and I will sit up front since we know where we're going. But if either of you gets car sick, we can switch places."

"Not a problem for me," Owen says. "What about you, Poppy?"

"I don't suffer from that problem either."

Owen grasps my waist and lifts me up and sets me on the back-seat. Then he jumps in beside me. Munro leaps into the car to take the driver's seat while Natalie gets into the convertible the normal way. She makes a joke about her husband letting Owen outdo him, since Munro didn't lift her into the car. Munro simply shakes his head, starting up the engine.

As we drive through the open wooden gateway, the vehicle's engine purrs like a kitten. I've never heard a car that sounded like that before. I'd assumed it was an exaggeration. But no, this car does purr. I'm beginning to understand why men love sports cars.

When we leave the long driveway and turn onto the paved road, the trees no longer shade my eyes. I hadn't thought to bring sunglasses. Owen didn't either, clearly, since we're both squinting.

Natalie twists around in her seat to see us. "How are you guys doing? Looks like you forgot your shades."

"Yeah, we did," Owen says. "Or at least I did."

I wince from the glare coming off the windshield. "I did too. Could we stop somewhere to buy sunglasses?"

"No need for that." Natalie roots about in the glove compartment and brings out two pairs of sunglasses. "Here you go. I hope they fit."

Owen and I slip on the glasses and smile.

"They're perfect," I say. "You were very clever to think of having extra sunglasses for us."

"Don't be too impressed. It was actually Eve Silva's idea. She is co-owner of a nudist resort, so she's used to thinking of everything guests might need when they're outdoors."

"That does make sense. I'll need to thank her later."

Owen drapes an arm across the seat behind me, moving closer. The wind whips my hair, the plush leather seat cradles us, and the sunshine warms our skin. Life couldn't get more perfect.

Chapter Twenty-Two

Owen

THINK THE SUN CAME OUT TODAY BECAUSE IT KNEW POPPY was here and wanted to shine its light and warmth onto her. That might be the sappiest idea I've ever come up with, but I don't care. Poppy can't seem to stop smiling. I can't stop watching her instead of the scenery. She's beautiful. But more than that, she has a light inside her that makes even the smallest smile feel like a gift from heaven.

Yeah, I've definitely turned into a sappy moron.

When we get to the village of Loch Fairbairn, Natalie suggests we should stop at the one and only café in this town. She swears it has great food, and I believe her. I got to know Natalie back when she first met Munro in Wyoming, and the siege at the cabin showed me how strong and trustworthy she is. That means I trust her food recommendations too. I trust her, period. There's nothing like a life-or-death experience to solidify a friendship.

Munro parks along the side of the street directly in front of the café. It doesn't look like many people are here yet, which is great. It means we won't need to shout to talk to each other. Of course, this quaint little village doesn't seem like it ever becomes a bustling metropolis.

Natalie and Munro lead the way into the café. I hold Poppy's hand while we follow them. Once we're seated a table in the outdoor section, Poppy leans in close, her mouth almost touching my ear, and whispers to me.

"Why hasn't Munro spoken since we all got into the car? Doesn't he like me?"

"Of course he does," I whisper as softly as she had. "Why would you think he doesn't? And he has spoken. I think."

"No, he hasn't."

I rewind my thoughts to the trip from the castle to this café and realize something. "You're right. He hasn't spoken. That's weird. Munro is never a chatterbox, but he does talk, and he was looking forward to meeting you and getting to know you."

"He spoke to me when we first met. But not since then."

"There's one way to find out what's up with the Scottish bear." I clear my throat to get Munro's attention. He and Natalie have been studying their menus. I wait until they look up at me. "Hey, Munro, why haven't you spoken since we left Dùndubhan?"

I hope I pronounced that right.

Munro scowls and goes back to studying the menu.

So I kick his shin under the table. "What's up with you? Your behavior isn't making Poppy feel welcome."

Natalie bites her lip as she stares at her husband. "He's right, Munro. You haven't said a peep since we got in the car? Aren't you feeling well?"

He scowls again and slaps his menu down on the table. "When we were getting the car ready, ye told me to try not to confuse Poppy with my Scottish words."

"I didn't mean you should never again speak in her presence." Natalie jabs her elbow into his side, though not very hard. "Honestly, you can be so dense when you want to be."

"Dense? I was following your orders."

A laugh bursts out of me. "Munro MacTaggart following orders? That's got to be a miracle or something."

My best friend squints at me and growls. I swear he actually does that, like an angry dog. "*Falbh a ghabhail do ghnùis airson cac.*"

I laugh again. "Nice try, Munro. If you wanted to flummox me with that Gaelic phrase, you should never have told me what it means."

He freezes, his unblinking gaze aimed directly at me. "Dinnae remember telling you that."

"Ah, but you did. It means 'away and take your face for a shit.' Gotta say, I like that curse. It's inventive and descriptive at the same time."

"I didn't create the phrase."

"Yeah, I know. But you deliver that line better than anybody."

"Haud yer wheesht, ye *fanaidh bàlaichean*." He crosses his arms over his chest and lifts his chin a touch, smiling with smug satisfaction. "I'm dead certain I never told you what those phrases mean."

"You got me, Munro. What do they mean?"

"I said 'shut your mouth, ye fannybaws.' And a fannybaws is a very annoying person."

"You called me annoying?" I hold my hand to my chest and make a phony expression of pain. "You've wounded me deeply."

"Like hell I have."

Natalie grins. "Owen, you are a miracle worker. You convinced Munro to start speaking again without him realizing what you were doing."

"I wish I could say I had a genius idea, but I wasn't actually working from a plan. Poppy thought Munro didn't like her, and I couldn't have my girl believing my best friend won't speak to her."

Poppy leans her head against my shoulder. "You are so sweet, Owen."

Munro grunts. "Aye, he's a sweetie-pie. That's what Emery calls Rory. If it's good enough for the Ogre of Loch Fairbairn, it's good enough for Owen."

I shake my head. "Do you think that will embarrass me? You should know me better than that by now."

"Aye, I do." Munro folds his hands on the table and looks directly at Poppy. "I apologize for my behavior. But I honestly thought I might confuse you so much that you might leave Owen."

"Leave him? Don't be silly." Poppy lays a hand over Munro's. "Nothing will scare me away from Owen. And your Scottish words won't make me feel out of place."

"If I say something you dinnae understand, just ask and I'll explain."

"Thank you, Munro. I appreciate that."

Natalie kisses his cheek. "That's my sweet grumpy bear."

Munro rolls his eyes and twists his mouth into an expression I've seen a lot since he met Natalie. It means he's a little embarrassed, though he would never admit to that.

Now that we've solved the mystery of speechless Munro, we start to have a real conversation peppered with plenty of jokes at each other's expense. We manage to order our lunch even while laughing. The waitress doesn't miss a beat, and our food arrives quickly. Munro ordered a bottle of genuine Highland whisky—single malt, of course. I know he never drinks anything but single malt, and when he was living in America, he used to have bottles imported so he could enjoy a dram now and then.

I can't deny Scottish whisky is damn good.

Poppy likes it too, though she tells me she doesn't drink alcohol very often. I don't either. It's a special-occasion thing for me. Seeing my best friend again after months apart feels pretty special.

When the ladies go to the restroom, I decide to take advantage of the fact we're alone. "I've been meaning to tell you something."

"Go on."

"I'm sorry I missed the wedding. After what the three of us went through together, I should have made the time to come to Scotland for your big day."

He shrugs. "Dinnae care about that. We got married at the registrar's office, so it wasn't a big event."

"A registrar's office? Why would you do that?"

"Because we didn't care about all the wedding rubbish. We just wanted to be married."

"How come you never told me about that?"

Munro shrugs again. "It didn't seem important."

"Did you even ask Natalie if she would've preferred to have a regular wedding ceremony?"

He flashes me a scowl. But before the Wild Man can complain about my question, the girls come back from the restroom. I'm sure Munro feels like he got pardoned from a death sentence, but he must know I won't give up that easily. We've been friends too long for him to believe I'll let him get away with not explaining. Of course, I do have another option for getting an answer. It's underhanded. But then, he hasn't left me any other choice.

Poppy sits down beside me, and I'm forced to kiss her. Okay, I wanted to do that. But it's the polite thing to do when the woman you worship sits down beside you.

Natalie settles onto her chair again.

Munro saw me kissing Poppy, so naturally, he feels compelled to do the same with his wife. What a copycat.

I wait until we've ordered dessert, then go for it. "Natalie, Munro mentioned that you two got married at a registrar's office."

Munro narrows his eyes and flattens his lips. "Dinnae do it, ye *cacan*."

He just called me a "wee shit." That's all the permission I need.

Natalie kisses Munro's cheek, then turns to me. "We agreed to get married right away without all the fuss."

"I can believe Munro would do that. But didn't you want a real ceremony?"

She hunches her shoulders and stirs the ice cubes in her lemonade with the straw, intently focused on the task. "Well, I don't know."

That means yes, she did want a wedding. I've spent years studying women so I could write realistic female characters for my books. I had a feeling Natalie wanted more than a quickie marriage. She might not care about having a huge wedding, but she wanted to walk down the aisle and have a nice little reception. I bet they didn't even have a cake.

When Munro puckers his lips while glaring at me, I raise my hands in surrender. "I'm not trying to be obnoxious. But you do tend to bulldoze people into doing what you want. You lived alone for a long time. Take it from me, that lifestyle isn't good for a man. Natalie loves you, and you really should have let her decide how she wanted to get married. That's all I'm saying."

Just when I think he's about to leap over the table to strangle me, Munro slumps in his chair and sighs. "You're right. I should have asked. I'm sorry, Natalie."

His wife wraps her arms around his neck. "It's okay, honey. I'm happy we got married, however it happened."

"But you would've liked a more traditional ceremony. Owen didn't even get to be there."

"Well, he is your best friend. I was surprised when you didn't invite him to be there on the day."

Munro rubs his neck. "We should have a real wedding. With our families and friends. That's what you want, isn't it?"

"Only if it's what you want too."

He clasps her hand to his chest. "It's what I want. After the way my first marriage ended, I was afraid you'd change your mind. So, I, ah, rushed things a bit."

Natalie smiles. "Oh, Munro, you know I would never run out on you."

"Aye, of course I do. But I, ah…"

"Panicked?" I offer. "Yeah, did you ever."

"Haud yer wheesht. I'm talking to my wife." He winks, letting me know he isn't annoyed. Then he clasps both of Natalie's hands in his. "Will ye marry me again, *gràidh*? In front of everyone?"

"Yes, I will."

Munro grins. Natalie does too. And Poppy and I just sit here like we can't decide if we should sneak out to give them some alone time or clap to show our support for their decision. I sort of orchestrated this, but I didn't expect Munro to pop the question—again—right here in the café.

The waitress has noticed us and guessed that something romantic is happening. Munro absolutely won't want everyone in town to know what's up.

"Why don't we get back on the road?" I ask. "You guys can hash out the details later."

"But we haven't had our dessert yet," Poppy says. "I was looking forward to trying *cranachan*."

The waitress stops at our table carrying a tray that holds four glasses of *cranachan*. The menu told me it's a dessert made with oats, cream, and whisky. It does look good.

"Could we get that to go?" I ask.

"Aye."

The waitress leaves with the loaded tray. No more than five minutes later, she returns carrying a paper bag and hands it to me. I peek inside and see four plastic cups that hold our dessert, as well as plastic spoons and napkins.

"This is great," I tell her. "Could we get the bill too?"

She pulls a ticket out of her pocket and hands it to me. "You can pay at the counter."

"Thank you."

Within minutes, we're in the car again and enjoying our desserts while we leave the quaint village of Loch Fairbairn. Munro insists on driving, of course. But somehow, he manages to eat his *cranachan* while navigating the roads, all without spilling even one drop of cream. He and Natalie talk about what kind of wedding they'd like to have in between telling me and Poppy about the sights we see along the way.

I can almost forget that his family and a bunch of Brits are waiting back at the castle to do who knows what. It's all in the name of meddling. But are they helping me and Poppy? Or Naomi?

Either way, we'll find out soon.

Chapter Twenty-Three

Poppy

AS WE DRIVE THROUGH THE GATES OF DÙNDUBHAN, I don't see anyone around, though I do see the limousine and multiple cars parked where they had been when we left this morning. The Mercedes is still in the garage. Where has everyone gone? The women can't still be doing whatever they'd wanted to do to Naomi. They won't try anything too outrageous. I've heard tales of the wild things my British mates have done over the past few years, but I think the MacTaggarts enjoy even more outrageous stunts.

We get out of the car and stretch our legs.

Owen glances around the courtyard. "Munro, do you know what happened to the guest who disappeared here? Was a body ever found?"

"She's not dead. The lass left a note that everyone had overlooked until weeks later. It must have fallen onto the floor under the bed or what have you. The note said she went home and no one should worry because she's well taken care of."

Natalie shakes her head. "Alyssa's belongings disappeared long after she did. That has never made sense to me."

"Women can be irrational."

Owen winces. "Oh, Wild Man, you stepped in it this time. Natalie won't let you 'have a poke' tonight."

"Let's go inside and talk about something else."

As we walk into the vestibule, we still don't meet anyone. The entire ground floor seems vacant. Munro leads us into the kitchen so he can use the landline there to ring someone. He didn't specify who that might be. I can faintly hear the line ringing at the other end, but no one picks up. He sets the handset in the cradle and shrugs.

"What now?" Owen asks. "Everybody must have gone home."

"That seems unlikely," I say. "After all, they wanted to meddle in our lives and took Naomi off to somewhere inside the castle."

Munro leads us out of the kitchen and back into the vestibule, but then he veers toward the spiral staircase to go up to the first floor. As we trudge up the stairs, I still can't hear any sounds that might suggest someone is inside the building. At the first floor landing, we turn right to head into the great hall. I still see no evidence of anyone being here.

"This is very odd, isn't it?" I say. "Maybe I should ring Dom on his mobile to find out where everyone went."

Natalie hooks an arm around mine. "Let's check the long gallery upstairs before we resort to extreme measures."

"I don't think contacting Dominic is extreme."

She clears her throat loudly, the sound echoing through the first floor, and announces rather too loudly, "Let's go up there anyway. If we don't see anybody in the long gallery, then we'll call someone."

"If you think that's best."

She leads me up the spiral staircase while Munro and Owen trail behind us. The long gallery is, as its name suggests, a large room that takes up most of the second floor, which is actually the third level. The long gallery houses the museum portion of the castle. I would love to get a good look at the antiquities in the glass cases in the center of the room or the historical artworks on the walls. But Natalie ushers us straight to the third floor which is the fourth level. Castle architecture is bloody confusing.

The top level houses bedrooms. Of course no one is there. Did Natalie think everyone was hiding under the beds?

She and Munro tell us to "wait over there," by which she means the end of the hall. Her hand gesture made that clear. Owen and I linger near a closed doorway to what must be a bedroom and wait.

"What are they doing?" I ask Owen.

"Not a clue. Munro isn't the cagey type. He blurts things out even if that offends someone."

At last, Natalie and Munro finish their secret conversation and approach us.

"Back down the stairs," Munro says gruffly. "Into the great hall."

"We were just there. What are we meant to see in an empty room?"

"Just follow us, would ye?"

Munro and Natalie march down the spiral staircase and stop at the first floor landing, where we can see only a sliver of the great hall. It seems as empty as it was the first time we stopped on this floor. Our hosts—or perhaps captors is a better word—block the doorway, preventing us from craning our necks to see more of what lies beyond the landing.

I stand on my tiptoes. "What is going on in there that you don't want us to see?"

Natalie smiles, though her expression seems a bit mischievous. "Close your eyes. Both of you."

"Why must we do that?" Yes, my tone is full of suspicion. I'm not the suspicious sort, but the bizarre behavior of our hosts makes me antsy.

Munro scowls. "Just do it, ye daft woman."

"Hey," Owen says, "don't call my girlfriend stupid. She's right to be suspicious of what you two have in mind."

Natalie laughs. "Oh, it's not *our* plan."

"Then who the heck's plan is it?"

"Close your eyes and you'll find out. Or do I need to get my husband to growl and snarl at you some more? He's really good at duct-taping people's mouths shut too."

Duct-taping mouths shut? That's what she said, I'm sure of it. Her statement makes no sense, but I assume it has something to do with the cabin siege Owen had mentioned.

Natalie and Munro both cross their arms over their chests.

I sigh. "Might as well do what they want."

"Yeah," Owen agrees. "They're both stubborn mules."

He slips his hand into mine, and we shut our eyes.

"No peeking," Natalie says.

Odd noises emanate from the great hall. It sounds like shuffling and whispering and other things I can't identify.

"Keep your eyes closed," Natalie says. "We will lead you where we want you to go."

A hand grasps my arm, urging me to walk. I shuffle along, but it feels very strange to let another person guide me. I worry that I might trip over something, but Natalie wouldn't let that happen. I assume she is the one leading me into the great hall.

Finally, we stop.

"Open your eyes, Poppy," Natalie says in a singsong voice. "And you too, Owen."

I open my eyes.

Natalie and Munro step back, leaving me and Owen to face the crowd that has gathered inside the great hall.

"Surprise!" they all shout at once.

Clapping and cheers erupt, along with a few whoops and various kinds of noisemakers of the sort only used at a birthday party or a similar event. Since I'd kept my eyes closed for only a short time, my eyes don't need to readjust to the lighting. Owen and I glance at each other, and he seems equally as confused as I am. Why have our mates thrown a big do for us? We aren't getting married. It's not my birthday, and I assume it's not Owen's either.

Dominic emerges from the crowd, grinning as he trots up to us. He tries to speak to us, but the noises reverberating through the great hall make it impossible to hear anything he says.

I point at my ear and shake my head.

He nods, then turns toward the crowd. Dom raises his hands above his head and claps, but that doesn't work. So, he shoves his fingers into his mouth and blows, creating the loudest, most piercing whistle I've ever heard. I need to plug my ears because the noise is that deafening.

Everyone falls silent.

"Thank you for quieting down," Dom says. "It's time we explained to Poppy and Owen what the devil is going on here at Dùndubhan tonight."

The crowd nods and murmurs their approval.

Dom turns to face me and Owen, though he speaks loud enough for everyone to hear. "We are chuffed to bits that you two have found each other, and we all agree that you're a lovely couple."

Should we thank him for the compliment? I have no ruddy idea. This is the strangest situation I've ever found himself in, and I don't know how to respond. Owen seems to be suffering from the same confusion.

Chelsea walks out of the crowd to stand beside Dominic. "The American Wives Club welcomes you to Dùndubhan. This party is for you guys. But it's also the start of a five-day marathon of meddling designed to help you sort out your feelings for each other. And we mean all of you."

"All of us?" I say. "No, you can't mean—"

"Naomi will participate in the meddling marathon too. She's already begun her journey toward finding peace and happiness, though she doesn't know it yet. Now it's your turn."

Owen twists his mouth into an odd expression. "I never signed up for meddling camp."

"This will be good for all of you. Munro agrees."

We both glance at Munro at the same time. The Scot shrugs and smirks.

Dominic claps a hand on Owen's shoulder. "This will be fun. It's a holiday in Scotland with a side order of well-intentioned meddling and sundry insanity."

"Insanity? Oh yeah, that sounds fantastic."

Chelsea prods Dominic with her elbow. "You weren't supposed to phrase it that way. Did you practice your speech at all?"

"Yes. But I decided to improvise."

"Honestly, Dom." Chelsea smiles at me. "Don't worry, sweetie. It won't be as bad as Dominic makes it sound."

"I might feel relieved by that statement if Dom hadn't used the word insanity."

"Let's enjoy the party tonight. Then in the morning, we can discuss the details of our five-day regimen."

First, it's insanity. Now, it's a regimen. Oh yes, this sounds more enticing every moment. But I know they mean well, and they've gone to a great lot of trouble to arrange a big do in this castle for us. When I glance at Owen, his lips curl into a soft smile, and he shrugs. Yes, we might as well both give in to the madness.

"Ready for the party?" Dominic asks. "I promise you'll have a good time."

"We would love to join in. Thank you."

"Brilliant!" He whirls around to face the crowd. "Let the revelry commence!"

For the next three hours, we have a jolly good time in the great hall. Buffet tables positioned along every wall offer a variety of foods, everything from fish and chips to stovies, which I learn is a traditional Scottish dish. We also enjoy a variety of desserts and various beverages, most of which are alcoholic. I try not to drink too much. I don't like feeling dizzy, and alcohol will trigger that unless I curb my intake. Owen doesn't like to drink much either. That's another thing we have in common.

We also both decline an invitation to try haggis.

Music fills the great hall, emanating from speakers at one end of the room. It's mostly modern music at first, but then someone announces that it's "ceilidh time." I can't see which man said that. I know a ceilidh is a dance party, but I know nothing about Scottish dancing. Owen doesn't either. Munro and Natalie assure us that we can pick up the steps quickly and that no one cares if we aren't proficient. This isn't a competition.

I must admit I enjoy the Scottish dances, especially the ones that require everyone to spin round and round in a group. In the one-on-one dances, I get to chat to various men, some I know, some I've never met before. I spin round and round with Brits and Scots and even a few Americans. Gavin Douglas and Luke Turner both married Scots lasses while Derek Hahn is married to Diana Sangster, the British billionaire.

Thankfully, the do winds down before I'm too exhausted to move. Natalie and Munro urge us to go upstairs to the bedroom on the left and they will meet us there in a few minutes. The room is large and beautifully decorated, plus it has a big window that overlooks the courtyard. The curtains are closed right now for privacy. The four-poster bed seems large enough for several people.

A knock rattles the door, and Munro shouts, "We're coming in."

"Yeah, fine," Owen says. "We're not naked or anything."

The door swings open, and Natalie and Munro carry in two trays full of leftovers from the big do. They set the trays down, bid us good night, and leave. Munro winks at Owen on his way out.

At last, we are alone.

But what "sundry insanity" do our mates have in store for us?

Chapter Twenty-Four

Owen

I YAWN AND STRETCH, SMILING BEFORE I'VE EVEN OPENED my eyes. The sunlight filtering into the room through the lace curtains glows behind my lids, and I have no inclination to get out of bed yet. The warm, sexy woman snuggled up to me either hasn't woken up yet or, like me, doesn't want to crawl out from under the covers. Poppy has one arm draped across my torso and her luscious body pressed against me. I'm lying on my back, holding her to my side with one arm wrapped around her. We're both naked, and I love feeling her soft skin on mine.

Is there any better way to start the morning? Absolutely not. This is perfection.

Poppy moans softly.

Though I want to kiss her, I can't tell for sure if she's awake or just moaning in her sleep. We did have an amazing time last night in the great hall, and we gobbled up all the leftovers Munro and Natalie had brought us. That included two glasses of Glenfiddich Scotch whisky. After that, we had showered together, though that didn't involve any steam other than the waterborne kind. We had washed each other's bodies with a soft sponge. So yeah, I'm feeling very relaxed and contented this morning.

My years of friendship with Munro taught me that in Scotland, whiskey is spelled without the E.

Poppy moans again, wriggling her sexy self against me. "Are you awake yet?"

"Yes, I am. Are you?"

"Mm-hm."

"Doesn't sound like you're awake."

She stretches, yawning as she scrunches up her whole face. Then she aims those beautiful green eyes at me. Even in muted sunlight, they sparkle like emeralds. "Good morning, Owen."

"Good morning, gorgeous." I give her ass a light squeeze. "How about a morning fuck to wake us up."

"That does sound like a wonderful idea." She rolls on top of me. "Mind if I'm on top?"

"Are you kidding me? I don't mind if you're on top, on the side, on the floor, or hanging from the bedposts."

She laughs. "You can't shag me if I'm hanging from the bedposts."

"I write steamy romance novels. That means I've thought of every way a man can screw a woman and then some."

"Show me one of those positions, please."

"The way you're polite even during sex is the cutest thing ever." I slide out from under Poppy and kneel beside her. "Roll onto your side, then bend your elbow to prop your head up."

She follows my instructions, then wriggles her ass.

"That wasn't part of my directions." I slap her ass. "But I like it. Now, bend both your knees."

Poppy complies with that command too.

I lift her thigh, the one on top, and turn her leg so her bent knee faces down. Then I set her heel on the mattress. Now it's my turn. I crawl closer until my hips are lined up with hers. She catches her lower lip between her teeth while she watches my every movement. When I push one leg under her bent knee, she raises her brows, releasing her lip little by little. I have my cock positioned near her entrance, and with her leg bent over my hip, I'll be able to get deeper penetration. She'll love this, I know it.

Luckily, I left a few condoms on the bedside table. Once I've rolled one on, we're ready to go.

Setting my hands on the mattress at either side of her, I start thrusting. I take it slow at first, easing my cock in and out while I keep my gaze trained on Poppy's face. I love the subtle changes in her expression that tell me she loves what I'm doing to her. I bet no other guy has ever shown her this position. I learned it from a book. It seems appropriate for a writer and a bookshop owner to try a position from a sex manual.

Her tits jiggle every time I push inside her, and her lips fall open with every soft gasp that whispers out of her. When I plunge into her sheath, I can hear her slickness gliding along my length. She lays a hand on my hip, watching me the entire time, licking her lips, while I can't stop staring at her breasts and the way they move, their stiff nipples begging to be sucked. My breathing quickens more and more every minute, and suddenly, I need to taste her nipples right now.

I bend forward and down until I can catch one peak between my teeth. She cries out, arching her neck. While I suckle that rosy bud, her breaths grow heavier and her sheath grows slicker. I ease my middle finger into her anus, just to see if she likes that, then pull it free.

"How did that feel?" I ask. My voice has gone rough, but that has never happened to me before. I want this woman like I've never wanted anyone else.

"Do that again. Please."

I push that finger into her again, slowly, while I use my other hand to rub her clitoris in delicate circles that make her breaths shorten and her mouth fall open while she lets out soft little grunts. Maybe I should've put some lube on my finger before I tried doing this to her, but the way her body feels wrapped around me erases any other thoughts that my brain might have tried to form.

A string of languid, half-whispered cries tumble from her lips. "Go deeper, Owen, please."

"With my dick or my finger?"

"Both."

I pull my hips back and thrust inside her even more deeply, adjusting the angle so she'll feel everything even more. I've never tried this before, but I read about it once while researching a book. Damn, it actually works. When I hit that sweet spot, she lets out a sharp cry that echoes off the walls, arching her back as much as she can in this position and gripping my biceps so hard that it stings. I don't give a shit about that, not even if she cuts me with her nails. I slide my finger deeper too and swirl it to tease her.

"Oh God, Owen, yes!"

"Fuck, you're so hot and wet and responsive. You're killing me, baby, but I don't care."

I pound into her, accelerating the pace with every thrust until the wet suction of our bodies merging fills the room along with the creaking of the bed frame. I can't speak anymore because I'm gasping and groaning and grunting. Poppy's cries turn into babbling nonsense.

Then she comes. I keep my finger inside her while I punch into her even harder, so wild from the need to fuck her mindless that I have no idea what I'm doing anymore. The spasms of her inner muscles milk my cock, and I can't stop myself from spluttering because this feels so fucking good. It's like I'm strapped to a rocket that's about to launch, the pressure building second by second as the cloud of smoke and fire pushes me up, up, up into the sky and through the atmosphere into outer space.

I let out a strangled shout, then collapse beside her. "Shit, that was amazing. I hope I didn't hurt you."

She drapes herself over half of my body. "I loved it, especially when you put your finger inside me."

"I read about that in a book. Never tried it before, but I'm glad you liked it."

"That position was quite something too. You're very inventive. But I shouldn't be surprised since you are a writer."

I trail a fingertip along her arm, making her shiver. "You make me feel even more creative. Being with you has stimulated more than just my sex drive, but my imagination too. Good thing I brought a big box of condoms with me on this crazy Scottish vacation."

The landline phone on the bedside table rings. I reach over Poppy to snatch up the handset. "Yello."

"I'm not yellow, ye *baltan*."

"Good morning to you too, Munro. 'Yello' is another version of 'hello.' My dad likes to say 'yello' instead. Don't ask me why."

"I see. Then I reckon I'm sorry I called you a pussy."

"When did you call me that?"

He clears his throat. "Just now. *Baltan* means 'pussy' in Gaelic. Sorry for insulting you. Thought you were calling me a coward."

"Thanks for the apology, Munro. And for the record, I would never call you a coward. It was a cultural misunderstanding."

"Glad we cleared that up. Breakfast will be served in twenty minutes. So if you're needing to shag Poppy first, best get to it straightaway."

I glance down at Poppy, who is lying on her side underneath me, and my lips curve into a sly smile. "Don't worry about that, Munro. See ya soon."

Poppy grabs the phone out of my hand, setting it in its cradle. "Did Munro ring you just to insult you?"

"No, that was a misunderstanding. He called to let us know breakfast will be served in twenty minutes." I check the clock on the table. "Make that eighteen minutes. If you want a shower, better hop to it."

She slings a leg around my hip and rubs her foot on my ass. "Let's take a shower together."

"That might lead to more sex, which would make us late for breakfast."

Poppy jumps off the bed. "I'll have a shower by myself, then."

I study her ass while she sashays across the room to the attached bathroom. Her swaying hips transfix me. She has the most beautiful body I've ever seen, and I love making her come. Though I shouldn't do it, considering how powerfully I want her, I rush into the bathroom to join her.

Fortunately, or maybe not so fortunately, I stop myself from seducing her.

We walk into the dining room with three minutes to spare. Natalie and Munro sit on one side of the long table with Luke and Kirsty beside them. I'd met almost all of the MacTaggarts last night at the big bash. Kirsty is a Wiccan who owns a metaphysical shop in Loch Fairbairn while Luke is a psychophysicist, though I don't fully understand what his job entails. Rory and his wife Emery have taken the chairs at opposite ends of the big table. Poppy and I end up seated next to yet another couple—Errol and Ashley Murdoch. Errol is another of Munro's many cousins, and he's a treasure hunter by trade. His wife, a former librarian, now goes on expeditions with him.

And of course, Munro went on an expedition with Errol and Ashley too.

Breakfast is fantastic. They could have set it up as a buffet, considering how much food they put on the table. I'm ravenous this morning, but I try not to rudely gobble up my food. Nobody seems to care, though, not even when I shove a whole slab of Lorne sausage into my mouth.

"Glad you're enjoying the meal," Rory says. "I've never seen anyone eat as heartily as you do, except for Aidan perhaps."

"Who is Aidan? There are so many MacTaggarts around here that it's hard to keep track."

"Aidan is my younger brother. He owns a construction company."

"Oh, right. I do remember bumping into him last night."

The conversation continues in a different direction, and I finally have my fill of all this tasty Scottish food. While everyone else goes on eating, since they didn't scarf it down the way I did, I ask a question that I know has made Poppy curious.

"About that b&b guest who disappeared. That was a really strange note she left."

Rory shrugs. "Aye, it was. But she said she was fine, and her belongings disappeared. So she must have gone willingly."

"Did you ever report the disappearance?"

"The police couldn't find anything. She mentioned to us that her parents are still alive, but after she vanished, no one could find them either."

Holy shit. The story keeps getting weirder. I'm no detective, but the mystery of a woman and her parents disappearing has triggered my curiosity. "This might sound weird, but would you mind if I did a little digging? Just to satisfy my curiosity?"

"Digging about what?"

"The woman who disappeared."

"Why would ye want to dig into that? You don't work for the police."

I poke at the crumbs on my plate. "You're right. It's none of my business."

But the mystery has burrowed into my brain. What did happen to that woman?

Chapter Twenty-Five

Poppy

NEVER EAT A LARGE MEAL RIGHT BEFORE WALKING INTO something that has been described as "sundry insanity." If I'd known what would happen this morning, I would have eaten light. But there was no warning. I think I might be more anxious about the "well-meaning meddling" than the insanity part of the day's events. As much as I love and trust Dominic and Chelsea, I can't help feeling slightly terrified by what they've organized.

Owen and I don't need to have anyone meddle with us. We're already a couple.

"Are you?" Dom asks when I say that to him after breakfast. We're walking down the hall, headed for the vestibule. Chelsea and Owen went outside. "You and Owen met a week ago, and you haven't had a great deal of time together. His ex-wife has stuck her nose in between you two. Are you sure you want to get involved in a relationship with a man who has that sort of baggage?"

"It's not Owen's fault that Naomi followed him here."

"Fair enough. But you haven't responded to the rest of what I said."

Do I want to get seriously involved with Owen, that's what Dom asked. "I like Owen very much, and I want to be with him. But is it forever? I can't answer that question, not yet."

"You aren't sure about him."

"I'm positive Owen Metzger is a good man who makes me feel happier than I ever have before."

"Glad to hear it. That should make what we're about to do less…taxing."

"I don't understand. What 'taxing' thing are you planning to put me through?"

He gives me a tight smile but does not answer my question. Instead, he leads me upstairs to the great hall. Dominic halts at the top of the stairs, where we can just see into the large room in which, last night, a huge party had taken place. Now it's once again an open space with sunlight streaming through the tall windows.

Dom pats my shoulders. "Good luck. I'm off to help with the Owen side of things."

"But wait—"

He bounds down the stairs, leaving my sight before I have the chance to finish what I'd been about to say. *But wait, I don't know what you're throwing me into, Dom.* That's what I'd wanted to say. The fact that he scurried away like a rat about to get caught in a trap doesn't ease my anxiety.

I can only see part of the great hall from the stairwell doorway, so I shuffle into the first floor and walk straight into the hall, having no idea what awaits me. The first thing I notice is the mats on the floor. Yoga mats. Seven of them. Well, that's odd. But I keep walking and realize that, in the far corner, a small portable stereo system has been set up there.

"Hello?" I call out. "Is anyone here?"

A woman trots out of a doorway I hadn't noticed before. As the door swings wide open, I can spy a narrow stairwell that goes up to another floor.

The woman who greets me is Elena, the American wife of Chance Dixon. She gives me a quick hug. "It's wonderful to see you again, Poppy. Chance and I don't get to hang out with our British friends as often as we'd like, since we live in New Hampshire."

"Yes, it is wonderful to see you again. But why are there yoga mats on the floor?"

She grins. "Because we're all going to do yoga together. We have an expert instructor to teach us."

"I don't understand. Dom implied that whatever you lot mean to do with me, it will be somewhat taxing."

"Well, it doesn't have to be. That's up to you two."

"Us too? What are you talk—" The truth smacks into me like a wet towel to the face, and I shake my head slowly. "No, you can't mean that this is part of the meddling and that—Oh, bollocks. You invited Naomi to this yoga session, didn't you?"

"Yep, we did. It wouldn't be meddling if we didn't force you girls to broker a peace treaty."

My jaw drops open. I want to speak, but the only sound that emerges from my mouth is an odd little squeak. I sound like a ruddy mouse. I'm not afraid of crossing paths with Naomi again, but I'd hoped my mates wouldn't get me involved in whatever rubbish they have planned for rehabilitating Owen's ex-wife.

"Are you ready for this?" Elena asks. "We can cancel it if you aren't comfortable with the setup."

It is definitely a setup. Will I run away like a coward? No. I will show Naomi that she doesn't bother me at all. So, I straighten and roll my shoulders back. "I'm in."

"Great! Let me call in the rest of the gang." She shoves two fingers into her mouth and blows, creating an ear-splitting whistle. "We're ready to go, ladies!"

That door bursts open again, revealing the narrow stairwell. A horde of woman rushes down the stairs to flood into the great hall.

I feel my brows crinkling. "Elena, what is going on? There are only seven mats on the floor, but I count twelve women in the room now."

"That's right. The others are observers who will jump in if you and Naomi get in a cat fight."

"Never in my life have I engaged in any sort of fighting."

The last woman who enters the great hall is Naomi Hansen. She strides past me with her chin held high and a smug little smile on her lips. Though I try not to stare at the bloody woman, my eyes insist on tracking her as she approaches the mat that lies in front of the others. It's the only mat that isn't next to another one.

"I can't do yoga, Elena. I'm wearing jeans."

"No problem. We brought an outfit for you." She waves to someone in the crowd who approaches us. It's someone I don't know. "Poppy, this is Piper, the American wife of Magnus MacTaggart. She's in her last trimester of pregnancy, like Maddie, so she won't be doing yoga with us today. But she did bring workout clothes for you."

"Thank you. I appreciate that. And it's lovely to meet you, Piper."

Piper gives me a brief hug. "We're all so happy to help you and Owen. Any friend of Munro's is a part of the family. That includes you too."

My new mate ushers me to the narrow stairwell, which she informs me leads up to the tower bedroom. That room is between floors. Inside the bedroom, I'm pleasantly surprised to find beautiful decor and a plush bed. I suppose I expected to find medieval torture devices in a place called the tower bedroom, but it's nothing like that. I change into the new yoga outfit these wonderful women had bought for me and return to the great hall.

Elena drags me to the mat that lies directly in front of Naomi. "Here you go. Let me introduce our instructor, Naomi Hansen."

"I bloody well know who she is." Why am I getting snippy? I never do that. The sight of *that* woman turns me into a lunatic.

"Relax. Naomi is a certified yoga instructor. Didn't Owen tell you his ex-wife does this for a living?"

"No, he never mentioned it."

That woman smirks. Naomi must love finding out that Owen didn't tell me about her career. Honestly, I don't care what she does for a living. And I'm certain Owen never mentioned it because it doesn't matter.

Maybe yoga will help me relax. I'd felt fantastic before Dominic brought me to the great hall.

Naomi claps her hands. "Get on your mats, ladies. It's time to start the class. Stand straight and tall, and we'll begin."

Once the others have taken their places, Maddie Hunter sits on a wooden chair someone had dragged in from another room. She turns on the stereo, and soothing music begins to play at a low volume.

"Stand near the back of your mats," Naomi says, "and hold your hands in front of your chest with your palms together."

I follow her instructions. She studiously avoids looking at me

"Now, kneel and sit back on your heels. Very good, ladies. Bow down and rest your forehead on the mat, then stretch your arms out above your head. Go slowly, there's no rush. Keep your palms and forearms on the mat."

As much as I dislike Naomi, I can't deny she does her job very well. Her soothing tone and calm smile are perfect for this sort of exercise.

"Let's move into downward dog. First, get on your hands and knees. Then straighten your legs while keeping your palms on the mat. Perfect."

The yoga session flows onward, and I find myself getting into the rhythm of the movements, almost forgetting that I'm in a room full of women, some strangers, some old friends. The ones who are spectators only sit on the floor or on chairs they dragged into the hall and occasionally offer encouragement. I think that's mostly for my benefit. I have the impression that everyone else in the room has done yoga before.

Naomi honestly does do an excellent job. She might be the most obnoxious person I've ever met, but she doesn't let her dislike for me color her work. At the end of our session, we all return to the first position, standing upright with our palms together in front of our chests.

Naomi bows her head. "Namaste."

We all bow our heads too.

"Great work, ladies," our instructor says. "I hope you feel relaxed and at peace. Yoga always has that effect on me. Thank you for a great session."

Everyone claps. Even I do that. Naomi earned it.

Yes, I would much rather continue to despise her, but that would be childish. I will never be best mates with Naomi Hansen, but at least I've gotten to see another side of her. Her attitude and demeanor during the yoga session hadn't seemed like an act. She is genuinely more relaxed and at peace now. I can tell she loves what she does. I love my work too, and it gives me peace and personal satisfaction. I suppose that's one thing we have in common.

Is that why these women forced me to attend Naomi's yoga session?

We all change back into our everyday clothes. Then Elena announces, "Time for snacks, ladies!"

The women all race down the stairs. Well, all but the pregnant ones. They take the steps more carefully. I walk with Elena, Piper, and Maddie. Though I've known two of those ladies for years, Piper is a new friend. I enjoy talking with her and getting to know more about how she met her husband, Magnus, when she was falsely accused of murder. As a bounty hunter, Magnus was hired by a wealthy man to hunt down Piper and deliver her to the authorities.

"Magnus isn't technically a bounty hunter," she tells me. "The UK doesn't really have those. My husband is a certified private investigator, but bounty hunter sounds sexier. And since he does track fugitives, it's more accurate to call him a hunter."

"Don't the police frown on regular citizens hunting down fugitives?" I ask. "I've been wondering about that ever since Alex mentioned the MacTaggart family includes a bounty hunter."

"Magnus was in the army. He already knew most of the cops at the Met and in the Scottish police. They know he was a decorated soldier, though my husband doesn't like to talk about that." We've just reached the vestibule, and Piper pauses here to tell me the rest. "Magnus also has a cousin, Logan, who is a former MI6 agent. With Logan's recommendation, the cops gave Magnus the unofficial status of a bounty hunter. Honestly, these days police departments are understaffed, especially in the Highlands, and they're glad to have the help."

"The police pay Magnus for his work?"

"No. Private citizens hire him, though often the police refer those people to Magnus."

"How fascinating. I hope sometime you'll tell me all about your time as a fugitive and how you met Magnus."

Piper smiles. "Absolutely. It's an unbelievable story but all true."

Elena and Maddie had gone out into the courtyard while Piper and I were still on the stairs. Now, we head outside too.

And I have to ask a question. "Why did you lot want me to attend Naomi's yoga session?"

"We hoped it might show you another side of her. We've spent a lot of time with Naomi over the past two days, and we think she's hiding something. It seems like it's to do with Owen, though she's been mum about the details."

I follow Piper out the door and into courtyard. "That doesn't fully explain the yoga session. I didn't have a conversation with Naomi, so I have no idea what she's hiding."

"But now you realize she isn't the Wicked Witch. That means you're primed to help us tease her secret out of her."

Oh, that sounds like so much fun. But I think I understand what Piper and the other women hope will happen. They want me to "tease" secrets out of Naomi, and in the process, convince her to stop harassing Owen. That sounds like a much bigger job than one person can handle.

But for Owen, I'll do anything.

Chapter Twenty-Six

Owen

MUNRO HAD TOLD ME STORIES ABOUT HIS WACKY FAMILY, most of which he heard secondhand from his cousin Errol. But I never could have imagined exactly how crazy these people are until I met them and saw the kinds of things they love to do. What have I gotten myself into? I might die if I participate in the events these nutjobs have organized for today.

Don't get me wrong. I like the MacTaggarts and the Brits. They're fun and dedicated to helping others—with meddling, not charity. But if they're trying to solve my Naomi problem, they're going about it ass-backwards.

Munro jogs up to me, shirtless and covered in sweat.

"Sure you don't want me to help you guys?" I ask. "Looks like hard work. I might not be as insanely muscular as Magnus, but I'm no wimp."

"Let us do the setup. You need to rest before the insanity begins."

"I wish you people would stop using the word insanity to describe what's going on today." I squint at him. "And it's about time you gave me the details."

He shakes his head. "I can't do that. I'm sworn to secrecy."

"But I can see trees over there that had their branches removed. Those must be cabers. That means you want me to toss them."

"What makes ye think we'll be tossing cabers? Maybe there's another reason why we have those on the green."

"Yeah, sure, that's believable." I jab a finger in his direction. "You shouldn't have blabbed to me about caber tossing back in Wyoming. You can't fool me now."

"Dinnae worry about the cabers."

I'm leaning against the wall of the castle with a panoramic view of the green, which is another name for a lawn. As I let my gaze wander over the activity happening on the green, I still can't figure out the plan. "If you don't want me to toss cabers, what are you people plotting?"

"You'll find out soon enough."

The garden door bursts open, and the women pour out onto the green. As they pass by Munro, they make catcalls. My best friend smirks and flexes his biceps.

"How does Natalie feel about you preening for other women?" I ask. "I'd think a man who wouldn't give his wife a real wedding wouldn't want to poke the beast by showing off."

"Are ye calling my wife a beast?"

"Only in the sense that she might not appreciate your display."

Munro grins with feral glee. "I think you're jealous."

"Buzz off, Wild Man."

"Aye, now I'm dead sure you're jealous." He grasps one of his biceps. "You could have these muscles if you worked out more."

"I'm in good shape. Don't care about growing outrageously big muscles."

He slaps my arm. "Are ye ready for the day's events?"

"Ready? How could I be? Nobody has told me a damn thing about what you're plotting."

"We're turning things upside down."

I employ all my willpower not to growl like Munro does whenever someone annoys him. "Tell me what you and your pals are up to or I'm getting in a car and driving out of here."

"You don't have a car. And no one will give you the keys to any of our vehicles."

"Well then, I'll walk to the road and hitchhike."

He chuckles. "Dinnae care what happens to Poppy, eh?"

"She'll come with me. I'll carry her if necessary."

Munro settles a hand on my shoulder. "You need a dram of whisky, Owen. That'll relax you very well."

"I'll feel a lot less tense if you'd tell me what's going on."

"All right." He squeezes my shoulder. "We've arranged a series of events designed to test the lasses' commitment to you. Whichever woman wins, she gets to keep you."

"That's not funny."

"I was only partially joking. The events are real, but it will be up to the lasses to decide how far they'll go for you."

"What if I don't want Poppy and Naomi to fight over me? It's crazy. I'm going inside to find Poppy and get the hell out of here."

"Had a feeling you'd say that." Munro reaches into his back pocket and brings out a roll of duct tape.

"Oh, hell no. You've completely lost your mind, Munro."

I sprint away from him, heading for the garden doorway. But powerful arms lash around my midsection and stop me from fleeing. "Let go of me, Munro."

A different voice responds. "I am not Munro, ye *cacan*. He brought the tape, but I caught you."

I crane my neck to see who's speaking. "Who the fuck are you?"

"Domhnall Sterling."

"Are you another of Munro's cousins?"

"No. I'm the *tolla-thon* who's dating Fiona MacTaggart, sort of."

"What the hell is a *tolla-thon?*"

Munro comes up beside me, shaking his head and clucking his tongue. "You shouldn't have tried to escape, Owen. This is all for your own good. Domhnall, give him a wee bit of leeway so I can bind his wrists."

The hulking bastard who has an iron grip on me loosens his hold just enough that my former best friend can pull my wrists together and secure them with tape. Then he kneels, ready to secure my ankles too.

I kick him in the shin.

Munro chuckles and straps the tape around my ankles.

I glower at him. "You won't be getting a Christmas present from me this year."

"You'll be thanking me by the time this is all over."

This time, I do growl just like Munro. "I'm going to tell everyone what you do for a living."

"If ye do that, I'll reveal the same information about you."

Damn, he's got me on that one. But that would mean nobody else knows about either of our chosen professions. Has Munro really not told anybody that he edits books? I assumed his whole family knew by now. I've been embarrassed to tell anybody about my career because I write steamy romance novels under a woman's name. Munro doesn't have that impediment.

"Carry him to the chair, Domhnall. Owen will find out soon enough what we have in mind."

"Can I talk to you alone for a minute, Munro? I won't try to escape. I mean, I can't move my feet, so there isn't much I can do."

He sets his hands on his hips and sighs. "Leave him with me, Domhnall."

The other Scot, who's much bigger than Munro in terms of muscles, saunters away to join a crowd of Scots and Brits.

Munro lifts one brow at me. "What did ye want to say?"

"Have you not told anybody that you edit books?"

"So what if I haven't? It's not your business." He slants toward me, narrowing his gaze. "Have you told everyone about the sorts of books you write?"

"Well…no. Not exactly. I told Poppy, obviously. And also Dominic and Chelsea."

"But no one else."

Damn, he noticed that. Most people assume that Munro is stupid since he likes to growl and snarl and generally act like a caveman. They don't get that he behaves that way on purpose. I'd figured out his game not long after we met. Munro is smarter than most anybody else I've ever met.

Right now, I wish he were a dummy.

I throw my head back and moan. "Yeah, all right, you got me. I haven't told anybody else. But since you haven't revealed your secret, I don't think you should be criticizing me for doing the same."

"You haven't told your parents, have you?"

"No. They still think I write technical manuals."

"Haven't told my parents either." He sighs. "We should both talk to our families."

I rub a hand over my eyes. "I know I should do that, but I don't want to break the news to my mom and dad over the phone."

Munro's mouth slides into a devious grin. "Dinnae worry, Owen. That won't be a problem at all."

Yeah, I don't like it when he smiles that way or when he sounds way too pleased with himself. But he can't mean what I think he means. That would be the lowest, sneakiest, most underhanded way of forcing me to confess. My best friend wouldn't do that.

What am I saying? Of course Munro would absolutely do that.

I bow my head and groan. "Where are they?"

"Where are who, Owen?"

"You need some acting lessons, Munro. You suck at pretending to be clueless."

"Natalie says the same thing." He grasps my upper arms and turns me around since I can't easily do that myself while bound with duct tape. "Are ye ready for the festivities to begin?"

"Might as well get this over with."

"That's the spirit, laddie."

I shuffle across the green with Munro but quickly start to have trouble walking, what with my wrists and ankles bound. "Can you cut the tape off me, please? I won't run away."

"Sorry, I can't do that. I'm under orders to deliver you to the tribunal bound and ready for your trial."

"What in the world are you talking about? I'm not a criminal."

"No, but ye need a wee bit of help." Munro throws me over his shoulder. "Dinnae fash. It'll all be over soon."

I hear his footsteps and the sound of grass brushing against his boots. But I can't see a damn thing, not while I'm upside down with all the blood rushing into my head.

Finally, Munro stops and sets me down on my feet. "The prisoner has been remanded to your custody, Luke."

The only Luke I've met here is the one married to Munro's cousin Kirsty. But Luke Turner is some kind of psychologist or physicist or something.

Jack MacTaggart, who I know is a psychologist, ambles over to us. "We'll take it from here, Munro."

While my friend walks away, I suddenly realize I'm surrounded by a crowd of Scots and Brits that has formed around a circular area on the green. Jack leads me into the middle of the circle, where Luke waits for us.

A chair waits there too.

Jack pushes me down onto the seat. "Should we tape him to the chair too, Luke?"

"Couldn't hurt. Better blindfold him too, though not until the other participants arrive."

Participants? What are these people up to? "I promise not to run away or move from this chair, so there's no reason to duct-tape me to it or blindfold me."

Luke approaches us, halting between Jack and Munro. "The experiment won't work unless he's blindfolded. I suppose we could forgo restraining him in the chair."

"You're the expert on psychophysics," Jack says. "We'll do what you suggest."

Well, at least I won't be hogtied or bound with chains.

Luke pulls a bandanna out of his pocket, rolls it into a long strip, then marches up to me. "Just relax. This won't be too painful."

He ties the bandanna around my head, blindfolding me.

I hear shuffling sounds, then a voice I recognize.

"This is bloody ridiculous," Poppy says. "I don't care what your barmy test shows, it won't change my mind about anything."

Another familiar voice laughs. "Oh, come on, Flower Girl. If you can't handle a little test..."

"Why is Naomi here?" I demand. "What kind of half-assed test have you lunatics cooked up?"

"Stay where we put you, lasses," Munro says. "And be quiet, or we'll tape your mouths shut."

A long silence follows.

"I think we're good to go," Luke says. "Dominic, would you mind helping me wheel that cart over here?"

"Stay where you are. Nick will assist me."

The sound of creaking wheels emanates from my left. I hadn't noticed which Brits were in the crowd, but I'm not surprised Nick Hunter is taking part in this insanity. I met him yesterday, and he seems like the type who loves a good round of shenanigans, the wilder the better.

When the creaking stops, Luke announces, "We need silence from the crowd, please. Any little noise might throw the test off. Dominic, here are your instructions. Nick, you can go. Dom agreed to help me with the test."

"Good luck, mates," Nick says, and I assume he walked away.

"Bring the first subject over here, Munro. Good, that's perfect. Keep the subject right there."

More noises. I can't tell what they might indicate, though.

"Just try to relax, Owen," Luke says. "I'm about to put some electrodes on your fingers."

"Electrodes? I think it's time you explained what you're doing to me."

"You have leads trailing down from the electrodes, and those leads hook into my computer. I'm going to gauge your emotions under a specific circumstance."

"Sure, that explains everything."

"Haud yer wheesht, Owen," Munro growls. "Let the laddie do his job."

"Okay, I'm ready," Luke says. "It's time to run the experiment."

I want to growl too, but that would make me a copycat. "What the fuck is this experiment?"

"Oh, it's pretty simple. We call it the true love test."

Chapter Twenty-Seven

Poppy

RUE LOVE TEST? WHAT IN THE BLOODY SODDING HELL IS that? It sounds like sheer bollocks to me. I'd known that these people love to concoct bizarre tests to help a couple realize they belong together, but I already realized that I want to be with Owen. What do they hope to achieve with this ruddy test? I think they've lost their minds, utterly and completely, at long last.

Luke puts a hand on my back and urges me to move closer to Owen's chair. Then he hands me a small piece of paper that's been folded in half twice. "Follow these instructions."

I take the paper and unfold it. My eyes widen. When I open my mouth to speak, Luke holds up a hand and shakes his head. I did agree to take part in whatever insane game they're playing, so I'll follow the instructions I've been given, though I don't see how this will help anything.

"What are you doing?" Owen asks. "I agreed to this cockamamie test, but you're dragging it out just to be dramatic. Aren't you?"

"Be quiet," Luke says. "Unless you want to be gagged."

Owen huffs but does not speak.

Luke nods at me. "Go on. Do what the paper says."

I read the instructions again, hesitating because this is barmy to the extreme. It's not as if I've never done it before. Being ordered to do this in front of a crowd is a bit unnerving. But I pull in a deep breath and exhale it slowly. Time to do it. I lean in and touch my lips to Owen's mouth. My instructions were explicit, though, which means I must go all the way.

So, I crush my mouth to his lips and hold that position while I wait for him to respond. Since I've kept my eyes open, I can see it when his facial muscles relax. I can feel his lips softening too. When his jaw slackens, I know that means he wants to kiss me deeply, and I slip my tongue between his lips. But when I raise my hands, about to grasp his face, Luke seizes my wrists to stop me.

"Uh-uh-uh. Remember your instructions."

He releases my wrists, and I go on kissing Owen. At first, it feels odd to do this while he can't see me and has no idea if it is me. But then I relax too, and our kiss grows deeper, more sensual, and soon the rest of the world recedes from my perception.

Luke taps my shoulder. "That's enough. Back to your original position."

I pull away and walk toward the spot where Naomi still stands. I can't believe I made out with Owen in front of a crowd of virtual strangers. But I still have no idea what that was meant to prove.

Munro urges Naomi to walk over to the cart that holds Luke's equipment. He waves for her to step in front of Owen.

No, he can't mean for her to kiss Owen too.

Well, they had asked us both to remove any lipstick we might've been wearing and any perfumes too. I wasn't wearing either.

Naomi leans over Owen, then pauses to smirk at me and lick her lips.

What a showoff.

Finally, she presses her mouth to his. Presses hard. He doesn't react at first, but while she continues with her desperate attempt to make him enjoy the kiss, he winces and holds that expression until Naomi pulls away. She takes a step backward and sets her hands on her hips, frowning at Owen.

"Phase one is completed," Luke says. He whips the blindfold off Owen's eyes. "Now on to phase two."

"How many phases are there?" Owen asks. "And what was the kissing about?"

"You'll find out once we're done."

"And when will that be?"

"When I'm done." Luke pats the top of Owen's head. "Be a good boy and cooperate. No more complaints."

Owen rolls his eyes.

Luke waves toward his cart. "Ladies, please come over here. Stage two is about to begin."

Naomi and I approach Luke, who grabs a clear plastic bag from the cart. I can see it holds more electrodes. He proceeds to attach them to our fingers, leaving the wires to dangle from our hands.

Luke gives us each a clipboard with a single sheet of paper attached to it as well as a pen fastened to the metal clip. Though the paper appears to be blank, I suddenly realize there seems to be writing on the other side that's barely visible. I can't read what it says. Luke warns us not to peek at what's on the "flip side" of the paper until the experiment has officially begun. He then orders us to stand at opposite sides of the cart while facing away from each other. I don't understand this test either. I think Luke Turner might be slightly insane.

The mad scientist attaches our electrode wires to small boxes that sit on the cart.

"Here are the rules for this experiment," he says. "Look straight ahead at all times. Do not move from the spot where you are currently standing, not even one inch. When I tell you to do it, you will turn your paper over. Understand?"

We both voice our agreement with everything he said.

"Turn your paper over and secure it with the clip again, then pick up the pen."

I flip my sheet over and stare at the words printed on the page. What on earth? It's series of lines, each denoted with a number. This looks like a list, but I have no idea what we're meant to write on each line.

"Here's how this will go," Luke says. "I will ask a question, and you two will write down what you think the answer is. Got it?"

I nod my agreement, and I assume Naomi has done the same.

"Munro, please hold this umbrella right here so the ladies won't be able to see me or Owen."

A shadow falls over me as the Scot unfurls the umbrella. It's quite large and definitely will prevent us from getting even a glimpse of Owen. I can't see Munro, only his shadow that stretches past me and beyond the reach of the umbrella.

"Perfect," Luke says. "Now for the test. Question one, what is Owen's favorite color?"

I have no idea, so I guess: Blue.

"Question two, what is his favorite kind of movie?"

Fortunately, Owen and I had a lovely discussion about movies at dinner the other night, so I know the right answer. As the test goes one, Luke asks several more questions including Owen's favorite book, his favorite dessert, and other rather innocuous queries. The final question makes my heart skip a beat.

"Do you love Owen? Truly, undeniably, without reservations, come hell or high water, and place his happiness above your own?"

I write my answer, and I can't believe what I've confessed. I didn't realize it was the truth until Luke posed the question, then I suddenly knew.

Why did Luke's question sound like a marriage vow? Maybe that should bother me, but it doesn't.

"Don't answer that question," Owen says. "It's idiotic. What kind of a question is that, anyway? Doesn't sound very scientific. You shouldn't put them on the spot like that."

"Be quiet," Luke says. "Or we'll have to gag you after all. What are you afraid of? This is only a silly test, right?"

Since Owen does not respond, I assume he nodded or made some other gesture to agree with what Luke said.

Munro takes our clipboards and closes up his umbrella, then hands the lot over to Luke, who skims through our answers. Once he's done, he reminds us not to turn around and face Owen, who had seemed quite confused or perhaps annoyed, possibly both, a moment ago.

"Now for the real test," Luke says. "I will remove the duct tape from your wrists and ankles first."

I hear the ripping sound of the tape being torn away.

"All done. You're going to use this pen to write your answers on the blank sheet of paper attached to this clipboard, while I read the questions. Got it? Good. Let's get started."

"How am I supposed to write while I have electrodes on my fingers?"

"Carefully, that's how. Stop procrastinating, Owen, and listen to the questions." Luke recites the same sequence of questions that he'd asked me and Naomi to answer. When that's done, Luke announces, "The test is completed. Ladies, you may now turn around. Owen, you may now stand. I'm going to collate all the data you three gave me, and once I'm done, I'll share the results with everyone."

I turn around and see Owen is indeed as annoyed as he had sounded. His mouth is twisted into an expression I can only describe as part scowl, part puckered lips. I start to move toward him, but Munro throws an arm out in front of me to prevent it. I don't see any electrodes on Owen's fingers anymore, so at least that part of this bloody annoying event is done.

"Not until the results are given," he says. "Those are my orders."

I glance at Owen, who shrugs.

Luke hunches over the metal cart, tinkering with some sort of box that looks like it must be an electronic device. I have no idea what it does. He plugs the device into his laptop computer with a cable of some sort. I assume he's collating the data, as he said he would do. Several minutes elapse. Or it might have been thirty seconds. My brain might have tricked me into thinking an eternity has gone by.

The psychophysicist shouts "ah-ha!" and whirls about to face us, throwing his arms up above his head. He quickly lowers his arms but now grins at us. "Would you like to hear the results?"

Owen squints at Luke and puckers his lips. "No, I don't think I want to hear that. This whole cockamamie test accomplished nothing except to piss me off."

"You can go into the house and wait there while I share the results with everyone else."

"Just get on with it, Einstein."

Luke lifts his chin and raises a clipboard above his head. "I have collated all the data, including the answers to the written questions and the data from the electrodes. The purpose of this experiment was to determine the answers to two questions. First, who does Owen love. Second, which woman truly loves him."

Owen seems as if he's about to erupt like a human volcano.

"Take it easy, pal. I'm about to share the results, and I think you'll appreciate what you learn." Luke raises his clipboard again and speaks loudly enough that everyone will be able to hear. "My psychophysics experiment has revealed that Owen and Poppy are the perfect couple who truly know each other despite having met a short time ago. Owen got ninety percent of the questions correct, while Poppy's answers were ninety-two percent correct. Sounds like true love to me."

Naomi plants her hands on her hips. "What about my answers? I was married to Owen for years, which means I know him better than the Flower Girl does."

"Afraid not. Your score was only twenty-eight percent. You don't know Owen as well as you think."

Her eyes flare wide. For a moment, she simply stands there like a statue. Then she hugs herself briefly, her gaze downcast, before she resumes her usual haughty demeanor. "That's bullshit. But I want to hear the results of your other test."

"Sure thing. I was about to share that data." Luke studies his clipboard, then holds it up, though not as high as he'd done before. "The electrodes gather data based on the skin conductance response. It's similar to what is colloquially known as a lie detector test, though my experiment involves a lot more than detecting lies. The small boxes attached to each of you gathered the data remotely, and I collated it all on my computer."

No one speaks or moves, not even the men and women in the crowd. It feels as if we're all holding our breath in anticipation of Luke's conclusions.

He sets the clipboard down on the cart. "The results are stunningly clear. When Poppy kissed Owen, both their heart rates accelerated, and their pupils dilated. Owen was blindfolded, but the fabric was a high-tech blend that had a network of tiny photographic cells embedded in it. That let us detect that his pupils had dilated. For both of you, your skin also warmed slightly. Poppy also licked her lips after kissing Owen, and his posture relaxed."

I can't stop myself from staring at Owen. My heart pounds. A delicious thrill tingles over my skin.

"Face it," Luke says. "You two are made for each other."

Chapter Twenty-Eight

Naomi

THIS IS COMPLETE BULLSHIT. OWEN LOVES ME. WHEN WE were married, he couldn't stand to be away from me for more than a night, and he would always make love to me on the night before I had to go on a business trip. He called it "love insurance." I thought that was goofy, but it proved that Owen did love me deeply and I know he was devastated when I filed for divorce. We had years of history between us. He met the Flower Girl last week.

I try for a casual posture but can't quite achieve it, so I settle for a forced air of confidence instead. "You haven't said what those ridiculous electrodes revealed for me."

Luke gives me a sympathetic smile which seems genuine. "Sorry, Naomi. Owen had virtually no response to your kiss. And I think I should tell you about your physiological results in private."

My confident stance falters, and I even stumble sideways a little, though not enough for anyone else to notice. I think. No, I'm not devastated by what Luke said. It doesn't matter to me at all. A lump has formed in my throat, but that means nothing. I'm a tough bitch and everybody knows it. So what if I begged Owen to take me back a few days ago? He rejected me, and I moved on. The fact that I'm still here has nothing to do with him. I have other reasons for hunting down my ex-husband.

"Let's go into the sitting room," Luke says. "Just me, Naomi, and Owen. I'll tell you the rest of your results, then let you two talk."

"Whatever." Just like my haughty attitude, my confident tone has faltered too. "Let's get it over with."

Luke leads the way as the crowd disperses to let us pass. Owen glances at Poppy as he walks past her, and the love on his face makes my chest ache, not with happiness but with a kind of disappointment I haven't experienced in a long time. Poppy smiles in return. Yeah, she genuinely loves him as much as he loves her. How can two people who just met share such a deep connection? It took months, maybe even years, before Owen and I forged that kind of bond. Maybe we never really did.

Could I have been wrong all long?

No, of course not.

I stumble as I cross the threshold of the garden door. Luke grasps my elbow to steady me. I shake off his hand, lift my chin, and continue onward, following Luke but with Owen behind me. I avoid glancing back at him. I'm sure I'll get plenty of time to look him in the eye once we reach the sitting room. The thought of it makes my throat go thick.

No, it doesn't. The air must be dry, that's all.

We head through the vestibule and into the hallway, then go straight through the dining room and into the guest wing. I've been sleeping in one of the bedrooms down here, but right now, we walk into the sitting room. A sofa and some chairs populate the room while the hearth stands empty since it's too warm today for a fire. A grandfather clock in the corner counts the minutes and hours.

"Sit wherever you like," Luke says. "Then I'll share your final results, Naomi."

I settle onto the sofa.

Owen takes one of the high-back chairs positioned near the tall windows.

Luke remains standing. "Your physiological reactions to kissing Owen were what you might expect. They show you are genuinely attracted to him and have genuine romantic feelings for him. But unfortunately, Owen doesn't share those feelings."

I can't look at Owen or Luke, so I stare down at the floor.

"You guys need to have a real, serious conversation. And I know someone who can help you with that." Luke walks onto the threshold of the sitting-room door and pops his head out. "Jack! You're up next."

Who is Jack? There are way too many people here for me to remember their names and associate their faces with those names.

Luke walks out the door and shuts it behind him.

A moment later, another man enters the room. He's wearing a kilt and a black T-shirt, not to mention big black boots. The kilt has a pretty pattern of blue and green plaid with narrow orange stripes. The man approaches me first, probably because I'm sitting closest to the door. When Owen starts to rise from his chair, the man waves for him to sit back down.

"Stay there," he says, and I note what sounds like a Scottish accent. "I'm Jack MacTaggart, and I am a trained psychotherapist. Luke thought I should give you two an impromptu, and unofficial, therapy session."

"Oh, perfect." I lean back against the sofa and cross my ankles on the coffee table. "You go give Owen some therapy, and I'll watch. He's the one who's in denial, after all."

"Is he? We'll see about that." Jack stretches his arm out to point toward the chair across from where Owen sits. "Sit there, Naomi."

"Why? I don't need anybody to root around in my head."

"Aye, you do. Shall I call in a couple of my mates to carry you over there? Derek and Rory offered to do it."

I fold my hands over my belly. "Guess you're too wimpy to carry me yourself."

His brows hike up. His lips curl up too. Then he marches over here and scoops me up in his arms, carrying me to the vacant chair by the windows, where he unceremoniously drops me onto the seat. "Never accuse a MacTaggart of being unmanly."

Jack squeezes past us and perches his ass on the wide windowsill. The guy does have hot muscles and a gorgeous face—but he also wears a wedding ring. Even I don't seduce married men.

Owen glances at the closed door like he's contemplating making an escape. Then he gives up and slumps in his chair.

"I specialize in couples therapy," Jack says. "So you can rest assured I know what I'm doing. Naomi, let's begin with you."

"No thanks. Owen should go first."

Jack shakes his head. "I control the flow of the session, not you. So tell me, why did you divorce Owen if you're still in love with him?"

"Very sneaky. I noticed that you said 'if' I love him. You're implying that I don't really feel that way anymore."

"How do you feel about Owen?"

I cross my legs and swing one foot in the air.

Jack gives me a typical therapist look, the kind that's probably meant to make me feel at ease and encourage me to open up. But that expression only annoys me more. I drum my fingers on the chair's arms and avoid looking at either man by gazing out the windows.

"Open up and share, Naomi," Jack says in a tone that reminds me of a parent talking to a child. "You'll feel better once you do that."

"I have nothing to share."

"Let's try this a different way. I'm going to ask you a question, and you will respond immediately without thinking about your answer. I'll count down from five, then ask."

"Yeah, whatever."

"Five, four, three, two, one. Do you love Owen?"

"I thought I did, but now I'm not sure." Why on earth did I play his game? It's stupid.

Owen is staring at me wide-eyed. "You begged me to take you back. But you weren't sure you actually wanted that?"

"I—Ugh. This is a moronic little game."

Jack steeples his fingers under his chin. "Let the words flow, Naomi. It's called stream of consciousness. Say whatever comes to mind."

What the hell. I can't dig myself in any deeper. "I guess I convinced myself I must still love Owen, but now I'm not sure I ever really loved him in the first place."

My ex-husband squints at me. "Why did you really want me back?"

I tuck my legs under me and clutch my hands on my lap. "I married you because I thought I could mold you into the perfect man. When you told me about your career, I wasn't thrilled, but I tried to roll with it. But then, um, people started asking me what you did for a living. My friends, my family, they all kept pushing for an answer. I couldn't tell them. It was too humiliating."

"Is that why you started denigrating my job?"

"Yes." I stare down at my hands, unwilling to look him in the eye. "I tried to wheedle you into quitting your writing career. Now I wish I had never done that."

"But you don't actually want me back."

"Well, um…" I force myself look at him. "Maybe I do still have feelings for you, but I had a more immediate need that's the main reason I tracked you down."

"And what is it?"

The old self-preservation instinct kicks in, and I've never been good at combating that. "It's none of your business. Go back to your Flower Girl and fawn all over her."

Owen starts to speak, but Jack intervenes. "I think I should speak to Naomi alone."

"Yeah, sure." Owen stands up. "Maybe you can convince her to stop acting like a raging bitch."

My ex-husband walks out the door.

Jack lodges one ankle on the other knee. "All right, now it's time you told the truth. Why and how did you track Owen down?"

"How is easy. He made the mistake of mentioning on social media that he was going on vacation to London. After that, it was simply a matter of calling every hotel until I found him."

"Now to the question of why."

I've lost everything, so I might as well confess. "The truth is…"

Chapter Twenty-Nine

Owen

WHATEVER NAOMI'S PROBLEM IS, A PSYCHOLOGIST seems like the right person to figure it out and advise her. But she's not my wife anymore, which means I have no reason to worry about Naomi. Jack will take care of her. I need to find Poppy. After all the craziness today, the woman I love needs to know how I feel. I've known subconsciously that Poppy has come to mean more to me than seems rational after knowing her for such a short time. I don't care. I'm going to tell her.

Once I reach the vestibule, I bump into Damian Petrescu, the self-proclaimed gypsy who's part of the Au Naturel contingent.

"Hey, Owen, I was looking for you. We've got a surprise waiting outside for you."

"The last time you guys gave me a surprise, it involved my ex-wife kissing me."

"It's different this time. The test is over, and this is strictly to help you get acquainted with everybody. Munro told everybody that you don't have any friends other than him." Damian claps a hand on my shoulder. "We're here to rectify the situation."

That damn Scot. He blabbed to a horde of nosy people that I don't have any friends? Oh, I'll get my revenge on him somehow, some way.

"Is this a kidnapping situation?" I ask. "Or can I say no?"

"You're free to make your escape. But I promise this time the surprise won't be as weird as what Luke did."

"That makes me feel so much better."

He slings an arm around my shoulders. "I'm a gypsy, which means I can tell your fortune. My Ludar lidar is never wrong."

"Your what now?"

Damian grins. "My Ludar lidar. You see, lidar is similar to radar except it uses lasers instead of microwaves. What I mean is that I have an intuition about you and Poppy—and Naomi too."

"Oh, great. I hope your intuition doesn't involve my ex-wife stalking me for the rest of my life."

"Relax. Jack is taking care of that problem, so let me and the rest of the gang distract and entertain you in the meantime."

"Do I have a choice?"

With his arm around my shoulders, he urges me to turn around and face the door that leads outside. "A choice? Sure. As long as your choice is to join us out on the green for some fun and games."

"Okay. Might as well see what 'sundry insanity' you people have cooked up this time."

I follow Damian through the courtyard and the garden to the wooden door that opens onto the big lawn behind the castle. A crowd has gathered out here, but it's a slightly smaller group than earlier. I guess not everybody could hang out here all day. They probably needed to get back to their jobs. I spot a familiar head of dark hair and rush past Damian to find Poppy.

When she sees me, she throws herself at me and smacks kisses all over my face. "Have you and Naomi made peace?"

"Not sure. Jack needs to have a private session with her. But I think her desire to stalk and harass me has kind of petered out."

"I'm so glad to hear that. Did anyone tell you about the day's events?"

"No. I was hoping the true love test was it."

She grasps my hands, threading her fingers with mine. "Do you want to stay here and take part in the upcoming events?"

I think she's really asking if I want to stay here with her, and the time has come to fess up. "Of course I want to stay. Wherever you are is where I want to be. I love you, Poppy."

Her smile could light up all of the UK. "I love you too, Owen. I don't care if it's barmy because we haven't known each other for long."

"I don't care about that either. Besides, we can take our time getting to know each other even better and figuring out what we want. There's no rush."

"But you're meant to go home soon."

"Don't worry about that yet." I tug her closer and bend my head so I can look into her eyes. "Let's find out what craziness these people have planned for the rest of today and talk about the everything else later."

"That's a sound plan."

I love that Poppy stays calm even when we're discussing whether we can ever really work as a couple. Maybe I live in Wyoming, but I can do my job anywhere. Poppy's shop is in London, so she can't easily pick up and move. I wouldn't want her to, anyway. Goodburn's Literary Treasures is an amazing place, and she's worked hard to keep it going. My best friend lives in Scotland. The only people I care about who live in America are my parents.

"My parents need to know about my writing career," I tell Poppy. "But I don't want to tell them over the phone."

"If you need to fly home to tell them the news, I'll go with you."

"That would mean shutting down your shop. I doubt that Kendall guy can work there indefinitely."

A large hand clamps down on my shoulder from behind. "Dinnae worry about that, Owen."

I glance over my shoulder at Munro. "Do you know something I don't?"

He grunts. "I always do. But you'll find out what I meant this time when the surprise arrives."

"I thought whatever you guys have cooked up out here on the green was the surprise."

"No, laddie." Munro leans in to whisper to me, "The Brits have something else in mind for today. They insist on inducting you into their cult."

I grab Poppy's hand. "Come on, we need to flee before they make us eat bubble and squeak, then shove blood sausage down our throats."

Poppy grins. "I happen to love both of those foods."

"I might need to rethink this relationship."

Munro grabs my shirt collar. "Do I need to drag ye over there?"

"Over where?"

"Follow me."

He marches through the crowd, and everyone steps out of his way. They probably know the grumpiest MacTaggart doesn't suffer complaints. Poppy and I tag along behind him. Soon, the crowd disperses, and we find ourselves on an open area of the green where Dominic and a couple of other guys whose names I can't remember are drawing chalk lines in freshly mowed grass. They seem to be arguing about where to put those lines.

Munro stops near Dominic, but the Brit ignores him. So, the Scot hollers, "*Bi sàmhach! Èist rium.*"

The Brits freeze and swivel their heads toward Munro.

Dominic scrunches his brows. "What are shouting about? It sounds like nonsense."

"No, it's Scots Gaelic."

"And what did those words mean?"

"I told you and your mates to be quiet and listen to me."

Dominic shakes his head. "Why didn't you just say that to begin with?"

"Where's the fun in speaking English when I can confuse you with Gaelic?"

"Fair point."

Munro studies the chalk lines on the grass. "What are you laddies doing? This looks like something a drunken sailor would draw."

I come up beside Munro and try to sort out what these chalk lines drawn in the freshly cut grass are supposed to represent. They seem to go out in all directions, and none of it makes any sense. "I don't get it either. Maybe the Brits caught a brain fever and it's messing with their heads."

"Aye, that would explain it."

Dominic twists his mouth into a sardonic expression. "Are you two done harassing us? Because I would like to explain the sport to Owen before the match begins."

"What sport?" I ask. "Nobody told me about anything like that."

"I'm telling you now." He spreads an arm toward the chalk lines. "This is our pitch, though it should really be composed of clay. Rory didn't want us desecrating his hallowed lawn. But we'll make do."

"You haven't explained what the hell you're talking about."

"Cricket, mate. We are going to play cricket."

Poppy aims a hard stare at her cousin. "What are you plotting now, Dom? You can't chase Owen away."

"Not trying to. But since he has become involved with one of our own, we decided Owen should be initiated into the sacred sport of cricket."

"If you injure him—"

"You know I would never do that. Not intentionally."

Poppy sighs and nods. "I know, Dom. But cricket can be a rough sport, and Owen has never played the game before."

"We'll take good care of him. And this is all for fun, not a professional match." Dominic waves for me to follow him. "Come on, it's time for a crash course is England's grand old sport."

What the hell is cricket? As I follow Dominic onto the chalked up area of the lawn, I still can't figure out I'm getting myself into this time. Dominic and his friends might be playing a dirty trick on me. Throw the new guy into a game he has no experience with and knock him around until he's cross-eyed and staggering like a drunkard. But I don't really think they'll do that. Poppy would probably slug Dominic if he or his friends tried anything like that.

Dominic halts at one end of the rectangular area laid out by the chalk lines. "This is our pitch, though it's not regulation."

"Okay. What's a pitch for?"

"It serves a similar purpose to a baseball diamond in that it's the area in which most of the game occurs. There are no bases in cricket, however. The pitch is normally made of clay, but as I mentioned earlier, we were forbidden from creating a solid surface for this match."

"Rory MacTaggart loves his lawn, hey?"

"Oh, yes. He does." Dominic leans toward me and whispers, "He's rather uptight. Only his wife knows how to talk him into doing things he doesn't want to do."

"Is Rory playing in this match?"

"Yes, he is." Dominic covers his mouth with one hand this time when he whispers, "We should be very worried about that. You should see Rory play shinty. He's a demon at that Scottish sport."

Well, at least I've heard of shinty. Still have no idea what's involved in that game, though Munro once tried to explain it to me. I'm not a sports guy.

I wave to Poppy, and she blows me a kiss long distance. I pretend to catch it while Dominic bows his head and pretends to be embarrassed by my display. I have it on good authority—from Munro, of course—that the Scots and Brits get mushy about their lasses too. Naturally, the Wild Man claims he never, ever acts that way.

Yeah, right. He's such a liar. During our road trip yesterday, Munro displayed plenty of unmanly romantic behavior toward his wife.

Since cricket has eleven players, Dominic gathers more of his British buddies whose names I sort of remember. The three Dixon brothers—Chance, Dane, and Reese—will participate. So will the three MacTaggart brothers aka Lachlan, Rory, and Aidan. I thought Rory was opposed to sports taking place on his giant lawn, but Munro assures me that Rory is only against putting a clay strip on the green and driving wickets into the ground. He's fine with sports in general.

The Hunter twins, Richard and Nick, also join the team. Bennett Montague fills out our lineup, and I learned yesterday that he used to be the crown prince of someplace called Mithoria, until he gave it up to stay in England with all his friends and the woman he married, Samantha. Ben works for Nick Hunter at his day spa in a village called Cockshire. I swear I did not make up that name. It's really what somebody decided to call the town way back when.

We also need a few more guys to pretend to be the opposing team, though we don't need a full eleven men on the other side. Now that we're ready, it's time for the experts to teach me how to play cricket.

Dominic throws a long, flat object at me. When I catch it, I realize it's made of wood and has a handle.

"That's your bat," he says. "First, we're going to teach you how to handle your weapon and bat the ball when it's bowled to you."

"Weapon? I thought this was a British sport. That means it's low-key and very polite, right?"

He chuckles. "You're about to learn just how wrong you are."

Chapter Thirty

Poppy

I CAN'T WATCH THIS. CRICKET IS A POWER SPORT, NOT ONE OF those games elderly people play at nursing homes. I know Dominic is only trying to get under Owen's skin, but I can't help feeling as if I've let the man I love walk into the Roman Colosseum back in its heyday, and a lion will rip him to shreds. That's ridiculous, though. None of these men will treat Owen that way, especially when they know he has never played cricket before.

The other women on the premises have dashed off to collect chairs so we can all watch the match in comfort. They return with more than chairs, though. They also bring umbrellas, cool boxes full of drinks, and picnic blankets for anyone who wants to sit on the ground. I can't believe how quickly they assembled all of this, but then, they've probably been planning the cricket match for days.

Yes, I've learned that the American Wives Club is more than a name. It's a way of life for these ladies.

Chelsea and Rika have saved a chair for me, and the moment I sit down, they both lean toward me. They speak in hushed voices.

"The boys have taken Owen into the fold," Chelsea says. "You know what that means, Poppy."

"No, I don't."

Rika gets a sneaky look on her face. "It means you're a provisional member of the American Wives Club."

"What if I don't want to join your club?"

"It's inevitable. The more time you spend with us, the more you'll want to be a full-fledged member and help out with the meddling."

"But Owen and I are only dating."

Chelsea smiles. "That's why you're a provisional member."

"That's right," Rika agrees. "But we all know you'll qualify for regular membership very soon. The British Branch needs you."

"Why do you lot need me?"

"Let's talk about that later. Right now, we need to cheer for our guys."

Out on the pitch, Dominic and Hugh are engaged in conversation. It's clearly not a casual discussion but something more serious—in this case, a discussion about the cricket match. It seems like Hugh, along with Derek, will take on the role of the opposing team and serve as bowler and umpire. But first, they need to teach Owen a bit about the sport.

I've never played cricket, but I learned about it thanks to having Dominic as a cousin. He used to be one of the top cricketers in the world, and his team came within a hair's breadth of winning the World Cup. But I believe his greatest achievement in sports was when he and a team of retired cricketers played against the current best of the best in a charity match a few months ago. The retirees won, thanks in large part to Dom's determination and skill. Owen has just as much determination, but he lacks the skill. I believe he can learn quickly, at least well enough to participate in a casual match.

Dominic and Hugh are waving for Owen to approach them. Then the three men begin a brief discussion that ends with Dom taking the bat away from Owen briefly so he can demonstrate its proper use. The training has begun.

I watch with rapt focus as Dom and Hugh show Owen how to hold the bat and what the correct stance is for batting. Do they honestly want him to be the batsman? That seems like too much for someone who hadn't set foot on a pitch until today.

Dominic glances around the green, then shouts, "Where are the wickets? We can't play without those."

Chance Dixon trots over to Dom and whispers to him. My cousin screws up his face in disgust, then says something I can't hear. Chance hunches his shoulders and spreads his arms while shaking his head.

Dominic covers his face with his hands. Then he straightens and shouts, "Who has the makeshift wickets? We need them now. Rory MacTaggart won't let us hammer actual wickets into the ground."

"It's my lawn, ye *cacan*," someone shouts from elsewhere on the green. I assume that's Rory. "Play by my rules or don't play at all."

"Yes, all right."

Chance rushes off to retrieve the "makeshift wickets," and I'm left wondering what on earth they will use to fill in for wickets. If they aren't allowed to sink them into the ground, won't the ruddy things fall over? Well, this is a friendly match, so perhaps it doesn't matter. When Chance returns with the needed items, Dominic and Hugh both stare at what their mate has brought.

It's a pile of wooden dowels.

Dominic pokes them with the toe of his shoe. "These won't withstand a strike from a ball. They have nothing to hold them in place. And what about the bails? Are we meant to cut them down to size with a pocket knife?"

I can't hear what Chance tells him, but it causes Dom to tip his head back and grimace. He throw his arms up and lets them drop down again, a sure sign he has given up. I watch as Chance and Hugh attempt to set up the makeshift wickets, but they keep falling down.

"The match is off," Dominic announces.

Owen glances at me, then shouts, "The match is not off. I want to learn the game. Surely somebody can come up with a solution to the wickets issue."

I swear a light bulb literally pops on in my head. As I race to the pitch, everyone gawps at me. A few people loudly ask what the bloody hell I'm doing. That would be the Brits and Scots. The Americans just smile and laugh as if they think this is a great show. Any moment, they might bring out the popcorn.

Dominic, Hugh, and Owen all stare at me with wide eyes when I halt in front of them.

"I have a solution," I say. "It does not involve dowels."

Hugh raises his brows. "Are you going to serve as our human wicket?"

"No. I suggest you pretend there are wickets."

Dominic's jaw drops. "What? How the bloody hell would that work?"

"It's simple. Draw chalk lines where the wickets would be and tell the bowler and batsman to aim for the areas between those lines. The umpire will determine where the ball landed in relation to the invisible wickets."

"You've gone insane, Poppy. Haven't you? Dating an American has driven you so barmy that there's no turning back."

"Do you want to play a match today or not?"

His shoulders flag. "Yes, all right, we'll try it your way."

The umpire, Hugh, grins. "This is bloody fantastic. Imaginary wickets. Let's have invisible balls too, eh? And if we played in the nude, that would make this the best fucking match in the history of the sport."

For a few seconds, I assume he's joking. Until he says…

"Taps off, as the Scots would say. Let's play nude cricket with invisible wickets!"

And he is absolutely serious about that. I've known Hugh long enough to realize that. Well, he did tell me the story of what happened when the husbands of the American Wives Club kidnapped him to Scotland and he wound up playing nude shinty here on this very lawn.

While Dom gapes at Hugh and Owen seems amused by that, the sound of a car horn blaring causes everyone to freeze. That sound had originated from the other side of the castle compound.

Eve and Val Silva, the proprietors of a nudist resort in Oregon, leap out of their chairs and run for the garden door.

"Where are they off to?" I ask.

Hugh smirks. "I believe the Heirani Motu contingent has arrived."

"The what contingent? Have you invited someone else? I thought all the guests were here already."

"All but two. Their flight from Fiji was diverted to Hawaii and delayed there because of a hurricane."

"Who are these people? Australians?"

Hugh chuckles. "No, Poppy, they are not Australian. You'll meet them as soon as Eve and Val usher them onto the green."

Dominic, Hugh, Owen, and I watch the garden door for any signs of the newcomers. The door had been left open in anticipation of their arrival.

"What's going on?" Reese Dixon shouts. "Are we playing cricket or having a staring contest?"

"Haud yer wheesht. You'll know when you know." That was Munro's voice. He had declined to take part in the cricket match because, he claimed, shinty is the only real sport.

"I'll know what, mate? That you're a grizzly bear disguised as a human being?"

"Quiet!" Hugh shouts with so much volume that it echoes off the castle walls. "They're here."

Four people trot out the garden door and across the green, where they halt beside the four of us. Eve and Val have brought a dark-haired couple with them. A flood of whispers ripples through the crowd.

"Listen up," Eve shouts. "Quiet, please."

The crowd goes silent.

Eve gestures toward the newcomers. "We're thrilled to welcome the newest members of the Au Naturel team, who will join us for the rest of this week's festivities. Please give a warm welcome to James and Holly Bythesea. They are the general manager and guest services manager of the newest addition to our network, Au Naturel Naturist Resort South Seas, situated on the gorgeous island of Heirani Motu, just an hour away from Fiji. Give them a big hello!"

Clapping and whooping erupts.

Once the excitement dies down, those of us standing here on the pitch introduce ourselves to James and Holly. I'm pleased to meet a fellow Brit, and his American wife is lovely. After the introductions are over, Dominic asks James if he has ever played cricket.

"No, I have not," James tells him. "I've never played sports of any sort."

"You should give cricket a go. My mate Owen will be learning the game today, so you could easily join and learn all about the great English sport."

"As an Englishman, I suppose I should at least try."

Holly kisses her husband's cheek. "That's the spirit. Don't get shy again just because we're around a bunch of strangers."

"I have never been shy, love. You have the strangest ideas about my behavior."

She leans toward me and whispers, "James and I love to go nude whenever we're not on the job, but I assume that wouldn't be appropriate here."

Why did she ask me that? Eve and Val are the ones who own a nudist resort, including the one where Holly and James work.

Hugh grins. "Just a few moments ago, I suggested turning this into a nude cricket match."

"You were having us on," Dominic says. "Even if you weren't, none of us want to get whacked in the groin by a cricket ball while naked. We need protective pads."

"Not if we use bean bags instead of balls."

"Then it's not cricket."

My life has become so bizarre lately, with my sweet cousin threatening to beat up Owen and Hugh suggesting a nude cricket match, and I suddenly realize just how bizarre it has become. I think I like it. That must be the case because I find myself bursting into a fit of laughter. My eyes begin to water.

Then I realize everyone is staring at me. They've all gone silent too. Only Owen smiles at my laughter.

Dominic eyes me as if he expects I might strip naked and roll about on the grass. "Poppy, what the devil is wrong with you?"

Owen walks over to me, throwing an arm around my waist. "I think I know why she's laughing. It's perfectly natural. I mean, we are standing around talking about whether to play cricket in the nude. Plus, there's all the craziness before that, when you guys ordered us to come to Scotland."

"Yes, that's right," I say. My fit of laughter has finally subsided. "It's absolute insanity."

Holly grins and pats my arm. "I'm right there with you, sweetie. I had never gone nude in public until I met James earlier this year. Going to Heirani Motu changed my life. And I bet meeting Owen has changed yours."

"Yes, it has." And I have a feeling he will go on changing my life in many ways that I haven't even thought of yet. If I can fall for a man I've known for such a short time and find myself in Scotland, discussing whether or not my mates should play cricket without their clothes on, then who knows what might happen next. "Maybe we should go to that island someday, Owen."

He stares at me for a moment. Then his mouth slides into a slow grin. "Yeah, maybe we should."

Chapter Thirty-One

DID I JUST SPEAK THOSE WORDS? MAYBE WE SHOULD GO to a nudist island sometime? No, I would never say anything like that. But I did. And I meant it. Until the last few months, my life had been monotonous and colorless, except for the times when I visited Munro at his cabin. His stories made life more interesting, but then I would go home to my little house in Yestermont and wonder why nothing like that ever happened to me.

Whitewater rafting? Treasure hunting? I'd never been adventurous enough to try anything like that. I don't need to do extreme things to find fulfillment, though. Sometimes all it takes is a smile from a beautiful woman to turn a man's life upside down in the best way.

Poppy seems a touch surprised by my declaration, but Dominic gapes at her like she announced she's been living a double life as a serial killer. Hugh is still grinning. Holly and James have wandered off with Eve and Val to mingle with the crowd. No one else heard what we had been talking about since the crowd has remained at the periphery of the makeshift cricket ground. Yeah, Dominic told me that's what it's called. The pitch is the part in the middle, but the whole playing field is a cricket ground.

A grassy field always looks like ground to me.

"So, are we still playing cricket today?" I ask. "Or have you guys changed your minds because the nudists arrived?"

Dominic tries to look tough by squinting, but he can't quite pull that off. He seemed plenty tough back in the bookshop, but I guess he prefers not to do that as a rule. "You aren't getting out of it that easily, Owen. We will play cricket today. Anyone man attempts to leave the green will be tied to a caber so one of the Scots can toss him straight into the river."

"You aren't as good at sounding nasty today. Why is that?"

He makes the goofiest attempt at a Munro-like glower, even baring his teeth. "I am always nasty. I'm a bloody rotten wanker."

"Gee, I thought I was the wanker. Or did you call me a prat? Might've been a twat." I chuckle. "Damn, you Brits have the cutest words that are supposed to be insults. I have trouble being terrified when you call me a twat."

"If you knew what the word meant, you wouldn't think it's cute." His lips twist upward like he's trying not to smile even though he wants to do it. "I'm terrible at threatening blokes. It's not in my nature."

"Well, if it's any consolation, you scared the crap out of me that day in the bookshop."

"No, I didn't. You were clearly not afraid at all." Dominic offers his hand to me. "Shall we call it a truce?"

"Absolutely." I shake his hand. "I'm game for a round of cricket if you still want to do that."

He slaps my arm. "Let's play."

I glance over my shoulder at Poppy and give her the thumbs-up sign. She smiles and returns the gesture.

Dominic cups his hands around his mouth and hollers, "Listen up, everyone! The match is on. It will be taps off for all players. That means shirtless, Hugh, not nude. A man who's best mates with a Scot should know that."

Yeah, I'd wondered about that earlier when Hugh claimed "taps off" meant buck naked. I'm friends with a Scot too, after all.

"Sorry," Hugh says. He doesn't need to shout since he's standing right next to Dominic. "I got a bit overzealous. Of course I know 'taps off' means removing our shirts. But I might have…hoped to trick some of the Americans into stripping."

"Why would you do that?"

Hugh shrugs and smirks. "To make Owen squirm."

"I am not squirming," I say. "Never have, never will. Anything you guys want to throw at me, I can handle it."

Now it's time for me to learn cricket.

Dominic serves as my teacher, showing me how to bat the cricket way. Our imaginary wickets work surprisingly well. All it takes is a good imagination to make it work. My crash course also includes bowling and catching, as well as a primer on the rules. If I hit the ball, I run. It seems pretty straightforward. I doubt I'll ever be as good at striking as Dominic is, but I've learned enough that I'm now ready to take part in a match.

"Please return to your seats," Dominic hollers. "The match is about to begin. Taps off, gents! Match rules."

Once all the spectators have sat down, and we players have all shed our shirts, Dominic tells us to go to our assigned positions. We're skipping the coin toss that decides which team will bat first, since we only have one team with Derek and Hugh as umpire and bowler. I'm in the outfield, ready to catch the ball if it flies in my direction. Dominic will bat first.

He steps up to the imaginary wicket and thumps his bat on the ground. As he raises it, preparing for the bowl, he winks at me. No idea what that means. Now Dominic waits for Hugh to bowl.

Lord Sommerleigh hurls the ball.

Dominic swings and strikes the ball so hard that it sails far across the outfield. He and his teammate, Reese Dixon, run back and forth along the pitch to get as many points as possible by doing that. When the ball's trajectory begins to turn downward, the two batsmen stop running.

Everyone cheers.

Though we aren't keeping score because this is just for fun, if this had been a real match, we would've racked up a ton of points.

Dominic waves for me to approach the pitch.

I jog over there. "What's up, coach?"

"Call me skipper. I'm the team captain, after all."

"Skipper?" I do my best to squelch a chuckle but don't succeed fully. "Are you taking us to Gilligan's Island?"

"No, you cheeky sod." He tosses me the bat. "It's your turn to be batsman."

I'm not sure whether I should be excited or scared. Dominic wants me to be batsman, which means I need to hit the ball before it smacks me in the face. Or in the balls. During my crash course today, Derek informed me that the gang really should have brought some protective pads to make sure our nuts don't get whacked by the cricket ball.

I have no protective gear. None whatsoever. Not even a hat.

When I take the bat, Dominic winks and walks away, slapping me on the back. The wicketkeeper, Richard Hunter, shows me where to stand. I'm still not one hundred percent clear on what a wicketkeeper does, but I guess it doesn't matter right now. I need to focus on hitting the red ball.

"Go, Owen!"

Poppy's voice makes me swerve my gaze toward her, though I don't move my head. I've stayed in position for batting despite the fact that the woman I love shouted to me.

Hugh throws the ball, sending it flying toward me at what seems like supersonic speed. I barely have time to think, much less calculate my trajectory, so I just go for it, waiting until the ball sails closer before I swing my bat. The crack of the bat hitting the ball echoes off the castle walls. The red orb doesn't exactly soar across the field. It sort of plops onto the grass about thirty feet away. At least the fielders were too far away to grab it, so I didn't lose any points.

I think that's how it works, anyway.

Cheers erupt.

What the heck? I didn't score the winning run or whatever. Since I didn't try to run toward the other end of the pitch, I'm not out. Is that what Dominic said? Not sure I remember all of his speech. But I still don't get why everyone cheered.

I glance back at Richard, the wicketkeeper. "What's up with the spectators? I didn't do anything. Did I?"

"You managed not to get out. But I think they're cheering because you gave it a go and did very well for a first-timer with minimal training."

"Oh. That's nice."

Dominic trots up to us. "Why don't you return to the outfield, Owen? Maybe you can catch the ball this time."

I hurry out to my assigned spot and wait for Dominic to swing his bat. Naturally, he sends the ball flying to high and so far that nobody has the chance to catch it. Dominic and Hugh switch places, which makes Lord Sommerleigh the batsman now. He misses on his first try, but he nails the second one. The ball sails straight toward me. I watch it coming closer and closer and closer. Knees bent, I wait for a chance to snag that red ball. Here it comes. Just a little further.

Bending my knees deeply, I launch myself into the air with my hand open and ready.

The ball smacks into my palm.

Holy shit, that hurt. I lose my balance and fall backward onto the grass, but at least I still have the ball in my hand.

Ben Montague offers me a hand in getting up. "Good job, mate. If this had been a real match, you would've saved your team and led them to victory."

"Uh, thanks. I don't really know what I'm doing, though, so it was an accident I caught the ball."

"Rubbish. You learned quickly."

The rest of my teammates rush over to swarm me. They shout and slap my back or my arm. Dominic even puts his cricket cap on my head.

"You've earned it," he says, though he needs to shout to be heard over the din despite being right beside me. "You're one of us now, Owen."

Have I just joined the cricket cult?

My teammates fall silent and back away from me. Why? Because Poppy is hurrying toward me.

She leaps into my arms and kisses me. "Congratulations, Owen. You've passed the cricket test."

"I didn't know there was a test. I thought we were having a good time."

"You were. But I know these blokes, and they wanted to test your mettle."

"I see. What grade did I get?"

Dominic comes up beside us. "You earned more than a passing grade. You proved to me that I can trust you with my cousin. Poppy is like a sister to me, and I couldn't let just any American sweep her off her feet. Most of what I did was to test you, and you came through with flying colors."

"Thanks, Dominic."

"Call me Dom. That's what my mates call me."

He has accepted me. I know his approval means a lot to Poppy, though she would never say that out loud, so I'm glad I could give her what she wanted. Her happiness means everything to me.

Dom slings an arm around my shoulders. "Now we move on to the next test of your mettle. How much do you love my cousin?"

"More than anything in the universe." Maybe that was overkill, but it's how I feel.

"Glad to hear it. Because our next sporting event will not be as gentlemanly as cricket."

"Spit it out, Dom. What humiliation do I have to endure next?"

He smirks. "I should let your best mate explain. Munro, get your arse over here."

Munro saunters out of the crowd and straight to us. "It's time, then, aye?"

"Yes, it is." Dominic wags his eyebrows at me. "Have fun, Owen. I will not be participating in the next match."

He walks away.

I fold my arms over my chest. "Okay, Wild Man, tell me what the heck I have to do now to prove I deserve to be with Poppy. Dominic said it's another sport, but that was all he told me."

Munro leans closer, and he gets that glint in his eyes that always means he's shifting into Wild Man mode. "We are going to play shinty, the MacTaggart way."

"What is shinty? I've heard you mention it, but you never explained."

"That's because I was living in America where shinty is not a popular sport. Why would I haver about it to you?"

"Okay. But what's the MacTaggart way of playing that game?"

"It's not a game. Our version of shinty is war."

Chapter Thirty-One

Owen

DID I JUST SPEAK THOSE WORDS? MAYBE WE SHOULD GO to a nudist island sometime? No, I would never say anything like that. But I did. And I meant it. Until the last few months, my life had been monotonous and colorless, except for the times when I visited Munro at his cabin. His stories made life more interesting, but then I would go home to my little house in Yestermont and wonder why nothing like that ever happened to me.

Whitewater rafting? Treasure hunting? I'd never been adventurous enough to try anything like that. I don't need to do extreme things to find fulfillment, though. Sometimes all it takes is a smile from a beautiful woman to turn a man's life upside down in the best way.

Poppy seems a touch surprised by my declaration, but Dominic gapes at her like she announced she's been living a double life as a serial killer. Hugh is still grinning. Holly and James have wandered off with Eve and Val to mingle with the crowd. No one else heard what we had been talking about since the crowd has remained at the periphery of the makeshift cricket ground. Yeah, Dominic told me that's what it's called. The pitch is the part in the middle, but the whole playing field is a cricket ground.

A grassy field always looks like ground to me.

"So, are we still playing cricket today?" I ask. "Or have you guys changed your minds because the nudists arrived?"

Dominic tries to look tough by squinting, but he can't quite pull that off. He seemed plenty tough back in the bookshop, but I guess he prefers not to do that as a rule. "You aren't getting out of it that easily, Owen. We will play cricket today. Anyone man attempts to leave the green will be tied to a caber so one of the Scots can toss him straight into the river."

"You aren't as good at sounding nasty today. Why is that?"

He makes the goofiest attempt at a Munro-like glower, even baring his teeth. "I am always nasty. I'm a bloody rotten wanker."

"Gee, I thought I was the wanker. Or did you call me a prat? Might've been a twat." I chuckle. "Damn, you Brits have the cutest words that are supposed to be insults. I have trouble being terrified when you call me a twat."

"If you knew what the word meant, you wouldn't think it's cute." His lips twist upward like he's trying not to smile even though he wants to do it. "I'm terrible at threatening blokes. It's not in my nature."

"Well, if it's any consolation, you scared the crap out of me that day in the bookshop."

"No, I didn't. You were clearly not afraid at all." Dominic offers his hand to me. "Shall we call it a truce?"

"Absolutely." I shake his hand. "I'm game for a round of cricket if you still want to do that."

He slaps my arm. "Let's play."

I glance over my shoulder at Poppy and give her the thumbs-up sign. She smiles and returns the gesture.

Dominic cups his hands around his mouth and hollers, "Listen up, everyone! The match is on. It will be taps off for all players. That means shirtless, Hugh, not nude. A man who's best mates with a Scot should know that."

Yeah, I'd wondered about that earlier when Hugh claimed "taps off" meant buck naked. I'm friends with a Scot too, after all.

"Sorry," Hugh says. He doesn't need to shout since he's standing right next to Dominic. "I got a bit overzealous. Of course I know 'taps off' means removing our shirts. But I might have…hoped to trick some of the Americans into stripping."

"Why would you do that?"

Hugh shrugs and smirks. "To make Owen squirm."

"I am not squirming," I say. "Never have, never will. Anything you guys want to throw at me, I can handle it."

Now it's time for me to learn cricket.

Dominic serves as my teacher, showing me how to bat the cricket way. Our imaginary wickets work surprisingly well. All it takes is a good imagination to make it work. My crash course also includes bowling and catching, as well as a primer on the rules. If I hit the ball, I run. It seems pretty straightforward. I doubt I'll ever be as good at striking as Dominic is, but I've learned enough that I'm now ready to take part in a match.

"Please return to your seats," Dominic hollers. "The match is about to begin. Taps off, gents! Match rules."

Once all the spectators have sat down, and we players have all shed our shirts, Dominic tells us to go to our assigned positions. We're skipping the coin toss that decides which team will bat first, since we only have one team with Derek and Hugh as umpire and bowler. I'm in the outfield, ready to catch the ball if it flies in my direction. Dominic will bat first.

He steps up to the imaginary wicket and thumps his bat on the ground. As he raises it, preparing for the bowl, he winks at me. No idea what that means. Now Dominic waits for Hugh to bowl.

Lord Sommerleigh hurls the ball.

Dominic swings and strikes the ball so hard that it sails far across the outfield. He and his teammate, Reese Dixon, run back and forth along the pitch to get as many points as possible by doing that. When the ball's trajectory begins to turn downward, the two batsmen stop running.

Everyone cheers.

Though we aren't keeping score because this is just for fun, if this had been a real match, we would've racked up a ton of points.

Dominic waves for me to approach the pitch.

I jog over there. "What's up, coach?"

"Call me skipper. I'm the team captain, after all."

"Skipper?" I do my best to squelch a chuckle but don't succeed fully. "Are you taking us to Gilligan's Island?"

"No, you cheeky sod." He tosses me the bat. "It's your turn to be batsman."

I'm not sure whether I should be excited or scared. Dominic wants me to be batsman, which means I need to hit the ball before it smacks me in the face. Or in the balls. During my crash course today, Derek informed me that the gang really should have brought some protective pads to make sure our nuts don't get whacked by the cricket ball.

I have no protective gear. None whatsoever. Not even a hat.

When I take the bat, Dominic winks and walks away, slapping me on the back. The wicketkeeper, Richard Hunter, shows me where to stand. I'm still not one hundred percent clear on what a wicketkeeper does, but I guess it doesn't matter right now. I need to focus on hitting the red ball.

"Go, Owen!"

Poppy's voice makes me swerve my gaze toward her, though I don't move my head. I've stayed in position for batting despite the fact that the woman I love shouted to me.

Hugh throws the ball, sending it flying toward me at what seems like supersonic speed. I barely have time to think, much less calculate my trajectory, so I just go for it, waiting until the ball sails closer before I swing my bat. The crack of the bat hitting the ball echoes off the castle walls. The red orb doesn't exactly soar across the field. It sort of plops onto the grass about thirty feet away. At least the fielders were too far away to grab it, so I didn't lose any points.

I think that's how it works, anyway.

Cheers erupt.

What the heck? I didn't score the winning run or whatever. Since I didn't try to run toward the other end of the pitch, I'm not out. Is that what Dominic said? Not sure I remember all of his speech. But I still don't get why everyone cheered.

I glance back at Richard, the wicketkeeper. "What's up with the spectators? I didn't do anything. Did I?"

"You managed not to get out. But I think they're cheering because you gave it a go and did very well for a first-timer with minimal training."

"Oh. That's nice."

Dominic trots up to us. "Why don't you return to the outfield, Owen? Maybe you can catch the ball this time."

I hurry out to my assigned spot and wait for Dominic to swing his bat. Naturally, he sends the ball flying to high and so far that nobody has the chance to catch it. Dominic and Hugh switch places, which makes Lord Sommerleigh the batsman now. He misses on his first try, but he nails the second one. The ball sails straight toward me. I watch it coming closer and closer and closer. Knees bent, I wait for a chance to snag that red ball. Here it comes. Just a little further.

Bending my knees deeply, I launch myself into the air with my hand open and ready.

The ball smacks into my palm.

Holy shit, that hurt. I lose my balance and fall backward onto the grass, but at least I still have the ball in my hand.

Ben Montague offers me a hand in getting up. "Good job, mate. If this had been a real match, you would've saved your team and led them to victory."

"Uh, thanks. I don't really know what I'm doing, though, so it was an accident I caught the ball."

"Rubbish. You learned quickly."

The rest of my teammates rush over to swarm me. They shout and slap my back or my arm. Dominic even puts his cricket cap on my head.

"You've earned it," he says, though he needs to shout to be heard over the din despite being right beside me. "You're one of us now, Owen."

Have I just joined the cricket cult?

My teammates fall silent and back away from me. Why? Because Poppy is hurrying toward me.

She leaps into my arms and kisses me. "Congratulations, Owen. You've passed the cricket test."

"I didn't know there was a test. I thought we were having a good time."

"You were. But I know these blokes, and they wanted to test your mettle."

"I see. What grade did I get?"

Dominic comes up beside us. "You earned more than a passing grade. You proved to me that I can trust you with my cousin. Poppy is like a sister to me, and I couldn't let just any American sweep her off her feet. Most of what I did was to test you, and you came through with flying colors."

"Thanks, Dominic."

"Call me Dom. That's what my mates call me."

He has accepted me. I know his approval means a lot to Poppy, though she would never say that out loud, so I'm glad I could give her what she wanted. Her happiness means everything to me.

Dom slings an arm around my shoulders. "Now we move on to the next test of your mettle. How much do you love my cousin?"

"More than anything in the universe." Maybe that was overkill, but it's how I feel.

"Glad to hear it. Because our next sporting event will not be as gentlemanly as cricket."

"Spit it out, Dom. What humiliation do I have to endure next?"

He smirks. "I should let your best mate explain. Munro, get your arse over here."

Munro saunters out of the crowd and straight to us. "It's time, then, aye?"

"Yes, it is." Dominic wags his eyebrows at me. "Have fun, Owen. I will not be participating in the next match."

He walks away.

I fold my arms over my chest. "Okay, Wild Man, tell me what the heck I have to do now to prove I deserve to be with Poppy. Dominic said it's another sport, but that was all he told me."

Munro leans closer, and he gets that glint in his eyes that always means he's shifting into Wild Man mode. "We are going to play shinty, the MacTaggart way."

"What is shinty? I've heard you mention it, but you never explained."

"That's because I was living in America where shinty is not a popular sport. Why would I haver about it to you?"

"Okay. But what's the MacTaggart way of playing that game?"

"It's not a game. Our version of shinty is war."

Chapter Thirty-Two

Poppy

UNRO WANTS YOU TO DO WHAT?" I ASK, SHAKING MY head slightly as I stare at Owen and try to figure out what he's suggesting. I'm proud of Owen for playing cricket with Dominic and his mates, but I do not like the phrasing Munro used to describe shinty. "Honestly, Owen, I don't know what shinty is. But if it involves war, I'm against you joining Munro in that sport."

"He doesn't mean literal war." Owen rubs his jaw. "At least, I don't think he means it that way."

"If you want to play shinty, then you should. But you asked my opinion, and I don't have enough information to decide."

"Will it worry you if I play?"

"Probably. But Munro might feel slighted if you don't do it, and I never want to come between you two. Besides, you let Dominic harass you and never complained about it. I owe you something in return."

Owen gives me a quick kiss. "You're the best, Poppy."

"Have fun with the Scots."

"There are Brits and other Americans playing too."

"I hope your side wins, whichever team that is."

He trots out onto the green, where the makeshift cricket ground has been transformed into a shinty pitch by simply removing the chalk lines and setting up a goal net at each end of the playing field. Soon, the two teams begin to take their positions. As the best friend of a Scot, Owen will play on the Scottish team against the Brits. The three other American men choose their teams based on their affiliations—Gavin Douglas and Luke Turner, whose wives are MacTaggarts, will play for the Scots, while Derek Hahn will go to the British side since he married a Brit.

Ashley MacTaggart, wife of Errol, sits beside me as we watch the men breaking into teams to discuss strategy before the game. She tells me that shinty is essentially a merging of hockey and lacrosse. The men hold hockey-like sticks that have a curved end. But instead of knocking a puck around on the pitch, they will move a ball around and try to keep it away from the opposing team.

"How many shinty matches have you watched?" I ask Ashley. "Do the MacTaggarts often play the game?"

"No, not often. It's a special occasion when they grab their *camain*. That's the plural of *caman*, the type of stick the players use to move the ball around."

"I see. Do the other players all have experience with shinty?"

"They all have at least a rudimentary understanding of the game. But rules are kind of, um, verboten in the MacTaggart version."

"Verboten? Having no rules does not sound like a safe thing to do."

"Nobody has ever gotten seriously hurt. And purposely injuring another player is not allowed. Hugh intentionally knocked Callum down back when those two were fighting over Kate. He whacked Callum's knee. But Hugh quickly regretted behaving that way."

I'm not sure I care to watch Owen being knocked about on the field. But he wants to play, and I understand why. Everyone here today is either British or Scottish or married to someone of those nationalities. Owen must feel as if he doesn't belong in either world. But he does belong, and he'll realize that sooner or later.

My gaze wanders to the pitch, where both teams have finished their huddles and now saunter onto the field. "Are they really going to play shinty in the nude?"

"We'll find out in a minute."

I lean forward in my chair, squinting to see the one person on the pitch who I do not recognize. Oh, but I do recognize him now, though I don't remember his name. "Is that the bloke who helped duct-tape Owen to a chair earlier?"

"Yep. That's Domhnall Sterling." Ashley slants toward me and whispers, "He's kind of infamous in the MacTaggart world. Domhnall tried to steal Jessica O'Connor from Grey Dixon a few years ago, but he lost that battle. While he was trying to make trouble, he met Fiona, the sister of Lachlan, Rory, and Aidan."

"Are he and Fiona a couple?"

"Off and on. They seemed okay for quite a while, but lately, they argue a lot and she keeps threatening to dump him."

I study Domhnall, craning my neck to try to see him better. But I give up and slump in my chair. "Are you lot going to give Domhnall and Fiona the American Wives Club treatment?"

"Possibly. But right now, we're focused on you and Owen."

"We're doing smashingly. No need to meddle with us."

Ashley seems mildly surprised. "Have you forgotten about Naomi? She's still on the premises, though we didn't let her participate in the games."

Oh, bugger. I forgot about that bloody woman. "Where is she?"

"In the house, getting therapized by Jack."

"Therapized?" I say with a laugh. "I've never seen that word in the dictionary."

"Autumn invented the term. She's married to Jack."

"I see. Well, I hope Jack can help Naomi realize she can't push me away from Owen."

"Oh, I think she already knows that."

My attention shifts to the shinty pitch. Domhnall Sterling and Chance Dixon stand in the middle with Dominic between them. A flip of the coin determines which team will start the game, and this time, the Scots win that honor.

"Our team captains are Chance Dixon for the British team and Domhnall Sterling for the Scots," Dominic announces via megaphone. "Before the game can begin, however, we have one more bit of business. These gents won't play taps off. They will go nude. Players, you must now strip!"

I squeeze my eyes shut.

"What's wrong, Poppy?" Ashley asks.

"Can't look at my cousin when he's naked."

"But Dominic won't go nude. He's the umpire or whatever they call it in shinty."

"Oh." I open my eyes and grin. "Then I *can* watch."

"Enjoy the man candy, sweetie."

The men have already removed their clothes and now take up their positions on the pitch. Domhnall will start the ball rolling, quite literally. But first, Dominic throws the ball high into the air. When it hits the ground, Domhnall begins to push it about in order to keep the opposing players from taking it away. He passes it to several Mac-Taggarts along the way until Errol Murdoch gets control of it and scores the first goal.

"Scots one," Dom shouts. "Brits nil. Come on, chaps, you can do better than that. You're making the British team look like schoolboys."

"Aren't ye going to congratulate the Scots on making the first goal?" Munro asks. "Or are ye favoring the other side?"

"I'm impartial. But I reserve the right to comment on the way the match is going." Dom claps. "Good show, you kilt-less wonders."

The match starts up again. Owen seems to have no idea how to insert himself into the match and help his teammates. Munro asks for a time out, which Dominic grants. Domhnall and Rory huddle with Owen, presumably to give him tips about how to play the game.

"Does shinty have a lot of rules?" I ask. "If so, it might take Owen quite a while to find his footing."

"Rules?" Ashley says with a laugh. "MacTaggart shinty doesn't really have those. Technically, they do. But in reality...not so much."

No rules? That does not sound safe. But I suppose I simply need to trust that the men on the pitch will not let Owen get pounded into the grass.

As the match resumes, I have trouble following the action. The players move swiftly, and since most of the movements are at ground level, I can't see much. Cheers from the Scots in the crowd suggest that the team is doing very well. When Munro drives the ball toward Owen, I rise half out of my chair in an attempt to see what's going on out there. Owen is now shepherding the ball, trying to keep it way from the Brits. I think they might be going easy on him since they know he's a beginner.

Ben Montague steals the ball and heads for the opposite end of the pitch.

I drop back onto my seat. "Owen lost the ball. I hope he isn't demoralized by that."

Natalie has just sat down on the other side of my chair. "He'll be fine, Poppy. Not only is he friends with the grumpiest Scot in the MacTaggart clan, but he also knows how to handle any kind of situation—even a cabin siege."

"That's true. I know he's a strong, resilient man. But I keep worrying that he'll get injured."

"Oh, look!" Ashley says. "Owen got the ball again."

It seems as if several MacTaggarts have formed a sort of defensive wall around Owen to help him reach the goal net. They use their *camain* to drive back the Brits, swinging the sticks this way and that without actually hitting anyone. When the Scots open up a pathway, Owen slams his *caman* into the ball and sends it reeling toward the goal net.

Cheers explode from the crowd.

Owen leaps up and down, pumping his fists in the air. Munro wraps his arms around Owen's legs and lifts him off the ground.

"Good show," Dominic declares, using that megaphone once again. "Congratulations on your first goal in the hallowed sport of MacTaggart shinty."

Owen yells and spreads his arms.

But soon, it's time for the match to resume.

Not much of interest happens for most of the match. Well, not much of interest to me. I keep an eye on the game while chatting to Ashley and Natalie about anything and everything. We laugh, we admire the naked men out on the pitch, and we talk about everything except Naomi Hansen.

Near the end of the match, we become more interested in what's going on out there on the pitch. Domhnall Sterling has taken control of the ball, and despite the opposing team valiantly struggling to take it back, he keeps pushing forward, closer and closer to the goal net.

Rick and Nick Hunter try to steal the ball. But they fail. So, the Brits decide to swarm Domhnall in the hopes he won't be able to reach the net and score a goal.

"Do you think they'll succeed?" I ask my new mates. "Could they stop the Scots from winning?"

Ashley bites the inside of her lip while staring at the match. "Maybe. What do you think, Natalie?"

"No way. The Scots will win. Domhnall is one wickedly determined man, and with all those insane muscles, he could kick the ball so hard it would break the net."

"We're about to learn who's right. Look, Domhnall is preparing to do something."

I sit forward in my chair, transfixed by the battle going on out there. Domhnall passes the ball to Owen who passes it to Lachlan who sends it back to Domhnall, the only Scot who is close enough to make the goal. Domhnall had surged ahead of the Brits while his teammates passed the ball around. Now, Domhnall has the ball again. He barrels toward the goal net wearing a fierce expression and swings his *caman* so hard that I can hear the crack as it strikes the ball.

And the ball flies past the goalie, straight into the net.

"The match is over!" Dominic shouts via megaphone. "The Scots team has won!"

Natalie, Ashley, and I leap out of our chairs to jump up and down while clapping and screaming.

The men leave the pitch and scatter, heading for their respective loved ones. Natalie rushes to meet Munro halfway to where we had been sitting, while Errol dashes over here so fast that Ashley has no chance to meet him even one quarter of the way. He sweeps her up in his arms and kisses her passionately. Munro and Natalie are doing the same.

Where is Owen? I've lost track of him. The kerfuffle created by the match's conclusion has become impossible to sort out.

Someone taps my shoulder from behind.

I whirl around. "Owen!"

"We won. Time to celebrate." He pulls me over the chair and into his arms, kissing me so passionately that it literally takes my breath away. When he finally gives up my lips, he grins. "How should we celebrate?"

"Do you even need to ask? We celebrate by shagging."

His lips curl into a steamy smile, and he carries me away.

Chapter Thirty-Four

Poppy

THE DAY AFTER OWEN TOLD HIS PARENTS THE TRUTH, WE ALL gather on the green at Dùndubhan for the wedding of Natalie and Munro. They might have already been married for months, but now they will have a real ceremony with all their family and mates here to witness it. Owen serves as best man with Errol and Magnus as groomsmen. Natalie has Ashley as her matron of honor with me and Piper as bridesmaids. Apparently, married women in the bridal party can still be called maids. I had no idea.

Natalie looks stunning in her lacy strapless dress that has a high slit to show off her lovely legs with every step she takes. She has her long hair flowing over her shoulders, and she can't stop smiling. I've never seen a more beautiful bride.

I get a bit choked up when Munro and Natalie recite their vows, then kiss. Munro pulls his wife close and dips her backward.

The crowd cheers. Whoops echo off the castle walls.

As the happy couple jogs away from the altar, Natalie shouts for all the unmarried women to gather at the end of the aisle. She's about to toss the bouquet. The bride halts at the end of the rows of chairs, glances over her shoulder to wink, and throws the bouquet.

It lands at my feet.

"Pick it up, Owen!" Errol shouts. "Dinnae let anyone steal your lass's thunder."

Owen rushes toward me, stumbling into a few chairs along the way, and snatches up the bouquet. He holds it out to me. "This is yours by rights."

Everyone is watching us and waiting expectantly for me to take the bouquet. What else can I do? I accept it. Maybe I do experience a flutter in my tummy when Owen hands me the bunch of pink peonies. I lift them to my face and inhale their sweet scent as I smile at Owen. He smiles back, and it's the most endearing expression I've ever seen.

Naomi attended the wedding, but she did not join in the bouquet toss. Jack had recommended that she be invited to the wedding and the ceilidh as part of her recovery from being a sodding arse, and we agreed. She has behaved in a much more normal manner of late, though she has the good sense to steer clear of me and Owen.

A few days before the wedding, Munro finally told everyone that he's a book editor, and no one minded at all.

The reception is a ceilidh, of course, complete with bagpipes and traditional Scottish dances like the Gay Gordons and the Highland Schottische. The MacTaggarts are more than happy to teach us those dances. Neither I nor Owen has ever tried them before. It turns out to be the most fun I've ever had, and even our parents join in the revelry. We drink champagne but also single-malt whisky distilled here in the Highlands.

Once the bride and groom have retired to their wedding-night quarters in the castle, Owen and I go to our room. And I've decided it's time to get some answers from him.

I wait until we're both lying in bed, cuddled up while facing each other. "Why did you think that British romance author might recognize you? I remember how relieved you were when you realized she wasn't actually at the conference, only her books were."

"Oh, that," he says with a nervous little laugh. "I met Audrey Corbyn at a publishing conference in Miami. This was after the first time Naomi dumped me but before the second time. Audrey and I hit it off, and, well, I kind of…spent the weekend with her. In her suite. Then we went our separate ways."

"I see. That's nothing to be ashamed of. I still don't understand why you worried about seeing her again."

"Didn't want you to meet my former weekend lover. I wasn't sure what you might think of me if you found out I had a fling."

I brush my fingers through his hair. "Owen, I would never judge you for what you did back then. It's in the past."

He flips onto his back and wipes a hand across his forehead. "Whew. That's a weight off my chest."

"Not as weighty as your pen name secret."

"Yeah, I'm so glad everybody knows the truth now."

In the morning, we bump into Naomi at breakfast. It's an enormous buffet set up in the great hall. As Owen and I explore the food options, we see his ex-wife a bit further down the row of tables and have a whispered discussion of whether we should ignore her. But we agree that would be childish. It's time to find out how much Naomi has really changed.

Owen leads the way as we approach his ex-wife. "Good morning, Naomi."

She gawps at us. "You're speaking to me? I didn't expect that."

"Jack swears you're making great progress emotionally, though you still have a lot of work to do."

"He's right about that. I don't know how to deal with things that are outside my wheelhouse, or how to handle rejection. I need to do more work for sure." She sets down the plate she'd been holding and faces us. "I'm sorry for everything I did. I was desperate, emotionally and financially, but that was no excuse."

"You already apologized," I say. "And we accepted your apology."

"I'm going home to America later today. Rory MacTaggart is letting me fly on his private jet."

"What will you do now?"

She wraps her arms around herself. "Chance Dixon lives in New Hampshire, and he offered to help me start a yoga studio there if I want. I'll be staying at Munro's cabin in Wyoming until I figure out what to do next. Everyone here has been incredibly kind, especially considering the way I behaved. I won't fuck up this opportunity at redemption."

Owen glances at me, and I nod because I can tell what he means to do.

"We wish you well," he says. Then he hugs his ex-wife. "Good luck, Naomi. Despite everything, I'm glad I met you—because that led me to the love of my life, Poppy Goodburn."

Owen Metzger is the love of my life, of that I'm certain.

After breakfast, we go out into the courtyard to say goodbye to Natalie and Munro who are off to enjoy the honeymoon they never had. James and Holly Bythesea offered them a free two-week stay at their nudist resort on the island of Heirani Motu, and to my astonishment, they accepted the offer. Owen wasn't at all surprised.

"When Munro and Natalie met, he was buck naked in the woods. Of course I'm not surprised they'd visit a nudist resort." Owen leans closer to whisper in my ear, "I hear it's an anything-goes kind of place."

Anything goes? That sounds like a raunchy resort.

Maybe Owen and I should go there one day.

In the afternoon, everyone goes out onto the green where Highland games are taking place. The chairs that had been set up for the cricket and shinty matches are still there, so we all watch the events in comfort. Neither my parents nor Owen's have ever seen Highland games before. I haven't either, and Owen tells me this is also his first time.

Errol Murdoch just hurled a hammer, sending it far across the green.

Since both our parents know about Owen's career as a romance writer, I don't need to speak softly. "Owen, I finally had the chance to read those chapters from your work-in-progress."

"*Love in the Bookshop*?"

"Yes. It's wonderful. But it does seem oddly familiar to me." I tap my chin as if I'm thinking hard. He knows I'm teasing him. "A British bookshop proprietor and a romance novelist. They both love books, but the writer has a secret identity. Where have I heard that before?"

He tickles me under my chin, which always makes me laugh. "It's not exactly like our story. I mean, I made the bookshop owner a man and the writer a woman."

"And she writes gritty murder mysteries."

"Well, I didn't want the story to be too close to our relationship."

I push my fingers into his hair and draw him closer. Our lips graze each other. "The naughty bits are my favorite parts."

"Mine too." He kisses my palm. "I've decided I am going to reveal my true identity to the world. I doubt I'll lose any fans, especially when I share our real-life story with them. Not everything. Just the sweet parts. Are you okay with that?"

"Absolutely. But I think the book needs a new title. I've thought of one, if you'd like to hear it."

"Tell me."

"How about *A Novel Secret*?"

"That's perfect." Owen leans back in his chair. "I know you've been calling Kendall every day."

"Not *every* day. I skipped Wednesday." I sink lower in my chair, suddenly feeling awkward. "I can't help it. That bookshop is my baby, and I feel like a wayward parent, abandoning my shop for so long."

"We're going back to London tomorrow. You'll be able to pester poor Kendall in person."

I force myself to stop worrying about the shop and focus on the games going on in front of us. Domhnall Sterling just tossed a caber so far across the green that I can't imagine it was less than fifty feet. Lachlan declares Domhnall the winner of the caber toss, and everyone cheers.

Everyone except Fiona.

Over the past few days, I've heard about Domhnall and Fiona's rocky relationship. I hope they can work out their differences. I've chatted to Domhnall twice this week, briefly, and he seems like a lovely man despite what I've heard about the way he tried to steal Jessica O'Connor away from Grey Dixon. Jessica and Grey are married now and expecting a baby. Will Domhnall and Fiona find their happy ending too? I hope so.

The next morning, we fly back to London in a MacTaggart jet. My parents as well as Owen's mum and dad join us this time, as do a number of other people. Dominic and Chelsea, Diana and Derek, and Hugh and Avery all ride on the jet. We have a sort of party onboard, laughing and playing card games. By the time we reach London, however, all I can think about is my bookshop. Owen and I say goodbye to our mates, and he hails a taxi. Soon, we're walking into the shop.

But I freeze on the threshold, my mouth hanging open.

A dozen people are milling about, picking up books to thumb through them or skimming the titles of books on the shelves. As soon as Owen and I move away from the door, three more customers wander inside.

Owen lays a hand on my cheek. "Poppy, are you okay? You look pale."

"I'm stunned, that's all. My bookshop is full of customers." I swallow against a lump in my throat. "It thrived while I was gone. Kendall is better at running my shop than I am."

"No, he isn't. Kendall is wicked smart and very knowledgeable about books, but this crowd isn't his doing."

"Then how did this happen?"

Owen winces and scratches his cheek, a sign I know well. He feels guilty about something. "Please don't be upset. I wanted to help you, and I didn't think my audiobook idea would work fast enough. So, I, uh…called in the cavalry."

"Did you hire more employees for me?"

"No. I contacted Audrey Corbyn and told her there's an indie bookshop in London that needs a boost. She's a big proponent of indie authors and bookstores, though she's traditionally published. When I mentioned that the shop owner also happens to be the love of my life, she jumped at the chance to lend a hand."

I gawp at him, feeling so flummoxed that I can't cobble together a coherent thought, much less words.

Owen clasps both of my hands. "Audrey called her agent and her publicist, then sent out an email blast to her fans. She's a *New York Times* bestselling author, after all, and has a massive following online."

"Bloody hell, Owen." I gawp at him even more—with my jaw falling to my chest, I think. "You did all of this for me?"

"If I can't help the woman I love, what good am I? Couples should support each other, and you've done that for me. It's my turn to support you."

"Ma'am!" someone shouts. "Miss Goodburn, ma'am!"

Owen and I both glance in the direction from which that shout had originated and see Kendall standing behind the sales counter, waving his arms wildly. His hair seems disheveled, and he has a pile of books on the counter. One of the books tumbles onto the floor.

We hurry over there.

"Kendall, my goodness," I say. "Are you all right?"

"No, ma'am, I'm not. Forgive me for saying so."

"What's wrong?"

He glances around the shop, and his features crimp. "I don't have the temperament for running a bookshop. People keep coming in and wanting to buy things. It hasn't stopped since we opened this morning."

Owen looks at me just as I look at him. And we both nod.

I rush behind the counter and shoo Kendall away. "Sit down and rest, love. You're overworked. Owen and I can handle the bookshop today."

Kendall slumps onto a chair and blows hair away from his eyes. "Bugger me, Miss Goodburn. I have no idea how you do this every day. Maybe I please go home to Sommerleigh?"

"Yes, of course. Owen, why don't you call Hugh and ask him to send a car for Kendall?"

"Sure thing."

Within fifteen minutes, a sleek four-door Mercedes has arrived to pick up an exhausted Kendall. But as he shuffles across the shop toward the door, he suddenly halts. A woman has just entered the shop. A lovely woman with freckles and ginger hair. She stumbles and bumps into Kendall, who gazes at her with an expression I recognize because I've experienced it myself.

Kendall is smitten.

The woman smiles at him, then continues into the shop. He turns to watch her, and his lips curl into an appreciative smile. And the woman keeps glancing back at him.

Owen comes up beside me. "I think I see the next targets of the American Wives Club. What do you think?"

"I think I'd better join that club."

Kendall returns in *One Hot Bash* (Hot Brits, Book Ten), the first-ever Halloween story in the series.

**Domhnall Sterling returns in
Unstoppable in a Kilt (Hot Scots, Book Fourteen).**

**Curious about James and Holly Bythesea?
Experience their story in
Natural Obsession (Au Naturel Nights, Book One).**

Love the
Hot Brits
&
Hot Scots
series?

Visit
AnnaDurand.com

to subscribe to her newsletter
for updates on forthcoming books in these series
&
to receive free gifts for signing up!

ANNA DURAND IS A BESTSELLING, MULTI-AWARD-WINNING author of contemporary and paranormal romance. Her books have earned bestseller status on every major retailer and wonderful reviews from readers around the world. But that's the boring spiel. Here are the really cool things you want to know about Anna!

Born on Lackland Air Force Base in Texas, Anna grew up moving here, there, and everywhere thanks to her dad's job as an instructor pilot. She's lived in Texas (twice), Mississippi, California (twice), Michigan (twice), and Alaska—and now Ohio.

As for her writing, Anna has always made up stories in her head, but she didn't write them down until her teen years. Those first awful books went into the trash can a few years later, though she learned a lot from those stories. Eventually, she would pen her first romance novel, the paranormal romance *Willpower*, and she's never looked back since.

Want even more details about Anna? Get access to her extended bio when you subscribe to her newsletter and download the free bonus ebook, *Hot Scots Confidential*. You'll also get hot deleted scenes, character interviews, fun facts, and more! Plus you'll receive the short story *Tempted by a Kiss* as well as multiple bonus chapters available in ebook and audiobook formats.

Visit AnnaDurand.com to sign up.

9 781958 144206